SAVING BOONE

Legend of a Kiowa Son

By

Monette Bebow-Reinhard

Cover by

Adam Reinhard

D1737635

UnravelingTheMyth.com

Formerly published as "Saving Boone: Legend of the Half-White Son" by All Things That Matter Press (2017), rights reverted and herein further edited.

Dedication

To the "Half-Breeds" of history whose character I tried to capture; to the Kiowa, whose culture I tried not to mess with; and to my family, who taught me how important it is to belong. Learning from history means to never forget history.

CHAPTER ONE

The Wishing Rock

Kansas 1857

Lynelle Tyler wiped sweat from her face as she worked her garden. The sudden sound of galloping hooves froze her there in the dirt, fingers clawing soil. "No! Please!" Breath held, she didn't move until the sound of hooves faded off again. The Missouri Regulators, most likely. They passed by regularly and never bothered her. They wanted Kansas to enter the Union as a slave state, though most living here were in favor of staying a free state.

Yet whenever she heard horses, the thought of her Kiowa husband coming for her son Boone had her crying with fear.

She loved Kae-Gon. But she feared allowing Boone to live in his world. She could not erase this love embedded in her heart since before Boone was born in December 1844. But she could not allow Boone to live in a culture her father predicted was doomed.

Kae-Gon told her once that he must take Boone before he turned 13, only two months from now. She would die first.

Boone knelt behind his mama in his potato garden and saw her wipe at her tears. She looked so small and vulnerable in her garden world. Boone knew she cried for his father. She told him the story once of how her father, General William Tyler, attacked Kae-gon's village to get her back. "Let my father move in with us," Boone asked many times.

"He cannot leave his people," she responded just as often.

Boone knew the story of how his parents met. In a river, swimming. "He was so gentle. He knew some English and I knew some signing. He came to see me every day, and finally, I left my home for him. I lived in his village, and we married in their ceremony. One day my father came to get me … oh, all those beautiful people he killed. All my fault!" She told him that story nearly every month -- as though a fairy tale that needed retelling. "You must always stay white," she told him, with her eye on the horizon. "The way of life for his people will be destroyed. Promise me, Boonie."

Boone promised never to go with his father. His mother needed him. But he knew Kae-gon wanted to teach his son to be a man.

When he saw she was about done, he grabbed his bag and ran into the house with his small sack of potatoes. He had sprawled out on the dirt floor, picked up his etching stick, and appeared busy drawing pictures when she came in. His tousled black hair was still coated with the sand and sweat from the morning's chore, potatoes stashed near the cellar door.

"Where's my vagabond mama been this time?" He took to calling her vagabond because she often wandered off for hours at a time. There were many words he loved and used from his Shakespeare readings. *You are a vagabond and no true traveler.*

She smiled at her lanky son deep in concentration, one foot kicking up small dry dust clouds behind him. "Boone Tyler, did you check your garden yet?" Boone looked like his father except for the freckles on his small nose and flecks of green in his brown eyes. The whites called him a "half-breed," and she feared he would grow unable to live in either world. But she often reminded him that the world will treat him according to his own behavior.

"Look, Mama, the horse is running free as the wind. And I drew me over here, so that it runs to me."

"The garden, Boone. After dinner I will listen to the newest Greek fable you learned, and then you can pick the Shakespeare story for us to act out." Lynelle had sent him to that Leavenworth school for a few years, but when they forced him to sit in the corner against the wall so that no one would worry about being scalped, she pulled from school. She taught him herself -- math, reading, and all the great literature she could find. She even taught him the art of dramatics as they read Shakespeare aloud.

"It is a shame my twin brother died. You would not always need to entertain me."

Lynelle grabbed him, yanked him to his feet, and threw him outside. Without a word. He got to his feet and brushed off, not surprised by her sudden moods.

He peeked in the window.

She was on her knees, staring down at the dirt floor, her hands pulling at her hair. "Booonnnieeeee!" He ran back in and sat by her, and she held him with trembling arms. "How did you know? No, no, don't answer that. Answer that you love me. That you love our home. Tell me, Boonie!"

"I love you, Mama. I will tell you about Heracles, who killed the monstrous lion that threatened the village." He felt her nod against his chest as she pulled him tight again.

"I have a hard time keeping that stone fireplace lit, and our eating table wobbles."

Boone knew, because she told him once, that his twin brother had died at birth. Why couldn't she talk about him?

She sniffled and wiped her nose on her sleeve. "Boone, why are you sitting here? I told you, git. Harvest your garden."

"I already picked all my potatoes for today." He pointed toward the corner.

"Don't fool me. Those are yesterday's potatoes. Now do as I say! You will tell your story of Heracles at supper." She got up to stir the beans.

"You won't eat without me, will you? Your baking smells good today."

"Oh, and what day doesn't it?" The small shack had filled with the smell of Boston brown bread, cornmeal and rye steamed in molasses. "If you don't get out there, those potatoes will pack their bags and leave."

"Oh, Mama, that's such a tall one." Boone looked down at what he drew -- a kind of half-circle with an odd design inside. "I don't think they are ready today. But I will look. And one day, you'll see that I'm old enough to do my work without being told."

He jumped up and ran out before she could rap his head with her sticky wooden spoon.

*

Boone walked back to his potato garden, but his thoughts were on the design he'd just created in the dirt, like a brand on that horse he drew running free in the wind. He didn't know what that drawing was, a kind of crescent moon with an arrow by it. Even if his mama swept up his dirt, as she kept trying to do to keep the dirt floor clean, he would not forget his symbols. He would run free someday, too, on his own horse.

"Watch da path, your feet, Tadpole."

"Oh!" Boone almost ran into Jack -- Big Grizzly, he was called. Jack lived in a shack up on the hill. He moved from the Dakotas when a tribe of Lakota had grown too familiar for his own comfort. "Sorry!" Boone backed away as though repelled by something foul.

Jack had on his plain buckskin coat, not the fringed one that Boone admired. He kept his ball and powder six-shooter tucked in the pants that he kept roped tight, and the tail of his fox hat bobbed as he laughed at the boy. "Hey, Tadpole, no hurry, earth still be here, another day yet."

"Gotta find me some potatoes now!" Boone ran from Jack as though he had twenty things to do. Big Grizzly Jack frightened him, but Boone didn't understand why.

He felt Jack's eyes on him as he dug into the earth for a spud or two he might have missed. Jack seemed like a friend, and somehow not.

*

Lynelle walked out and stood beside Big Grizzly as the boy bent over his garden.

"He's of ripenin' age, Lynelle."

"I know. I worry what will happen to him if there's war like they keep talking. To protect slavery," she said as though the words tasted dirty.

6

"You have more war in your heart. Talk on him his papa." An old French fur trapper, Jack hung onto his bad English like a lifeline to the Old World.

"Oh, I already told him everything." She wrapped her arms around herself and rubbed hard. "He's not going to find any more potatoes today."

"Time to treat him like man he is become."

"No! He can't grow up. Ever. Come on, have some coffee with me."

That first day they met, a year ago, he had been out trapping, suspecting he could catch a family of muskrats down near the river. He came upon her crying over an empty bucket.

"I caught no fish. My line got away from me." She had that habit of wiping her face with dirty hands, causing streaks that looked like war paint. "We'll just have to make more bread."

Jack reached into his pocket. "Here."

Her hand trembled as she reached out. "What is this?"

"Smoke it myself. Raccoon meat."

Lynelle nodded and tucked it in her apron pocket.

"It ain't much. Traps tomorrow might fill. Meet you here?"

"Oh, no! I couldn't!" She ran from him at that first meeting, leaving Jack scratching his beard.

Later that same day she found Big Grizzly and Boone standing in the river, though not close, watching each other's fishing lines. Boone listened as Jack told him about the fine art of catching those nibblers. She learned later that Boone had been too terrified of him to move. Now Boone could catch fish with his bare hands but still didn't cotton to Big Grizzly much. She hoped he would once the size difference lessened. His father was so much taller than any white man she knew and Boone fast approached that stature.

Jack grunted a happy thanks for the coffee offer and they went inside.

"You ever have children, Big Grizzly?" She got the water pot on the fire and took out a shiny knife to start chopping vegetables.

"Seen plenty half-breed. Not have my own but marry plenty Indian woman too." He used the term half-breed with respect. "When I teach you boy to trap last week he give me gift." Jack slapped a rock down on her table. "He calls it wish rock and say he wish for you to let him meet his papa."

Lynelle grabbed the table for support. "No."

"You love dis Indian papa. Your boy should love him, too."

"Why did he give the rock to you?"

"He say not good rock. Wish not come true."

Lynelle picked up the simple piece of granite with what looked like an etched 's'. "Some wishes aren't meant to come true."

"Kiowa are not—."

"I don't want Boone to die!" Lynelle looked back over her shoulder to make sure Jack hadn't disappeared before dumping her carrots in the steaming pot. Jack put one leg up and easy over the other and, with his nose in the air, appreciably smelled the bread. She poured him the coffee and added sugar. "Would you like to stay on? For supper?" She thought about having Jack over more often, maybe suggest he use some lye in his wash and perhaps give himself a shave. She picked out a few potatoes to chop.

He grunted. "Tell me about why you fear Kae-gon."

"He found me two years after Boone's birth. Said he would come for Boone when the boy was 12. Came again a few more times, just so I wouldn't forget. Boone will be 13 in the snows of December." She whipped the knife into the potatoes, unable to meet Jack's eyes.

"Not bad he meets his Papa. Give boy's papa a listen."

Lynelle slammed the knife down. "He said *take*!" She paused to catch her breath. "Boone's only chance is in the white world. Oh, Jack, you can see that, can't you?"

"Sound like you listen to white folk too much." Jack sipped at the dark liquid. "I believe tribes will keep own land. Your son can talk Indian to whites. He can heal both worlds—."

"My son is no savior!" Lynelle covered her eyes for a second and looked at Jack with fierce determination. "I will protect my son. With my life I will."

He patted her hand. "Dis is good, your feelings. Dey yours, so good. But boy must know. Protect him, but he must know what you protect."

"Jack, do you think there will be war? Out east?"

"War is already here until they settle this thing." Only the week before a few of the Regulators tried to string him up for calling them "slavers." But Jack beat two of them senseless before the rest ran off. "You not worry. I let no one hurt you. Or the boy."

CHAPTER TWO

The General

Boone stood near the door of the squat little shack and flicked at clumps of dirt hanging on his knees and elbows, unable to look at Jack when he came out.

"Got some good potatoes?" Jack stayed back, respectful of the boy's space.

Boone held one out, and then two. "For you."

"Day's good ones. I tank you." Jack pocketed them and followed as Boone headed for the river to wash up. "Your mama not sure how to tell you about life. You must learn to ask."

Boone splashed water on his arms, the chill of autumn making his hairs raise. "What Mama and I talk about is none of your bloody affair." Arms wet and still half muddy he jumped to his feet and started up the hill with his empty sack.

Jack grabbed his arm. The big man's face was the grizzly that chased him in his nightmares. "You getting to be a man. You have right to know your papa."

Boone jerked his arm free. "Why do you care, anyway?"

Jack only shrugged and walked back to his mule to drink water from his jug.

Boone ran back up the hill. "Mama!" He ran into the shack. "What you got to tell me?"

Lynelle was on her hands and knees, digging in the dirt floor. She looked up, hair half covering her wild eyes as she patted the dirt. "Oh, Boonie."

"You gonna grow something in here for me to weed now?"

"Come here and sit on the floor beside me." She patted down the dirt long after it needed patting. With a gentle hand she traced the dirt on his face. "Your father used to rub dirt on my face so the whites would not take me away."

Boone sat next to her. "Does Papa hate us? Is that why he won't live with us?"

"I promise you, your father does not hate us." Lynelle wiped the tears from her face and with the same hand wiped the dirt on Boone's face, creating streaks on his cheeks. "Your father is the son of a Kiowa leader, keepers of the medicine. Boone, as much as I loved your father, I wasn't strong enough to live with him."

"What did you bury in the floor, Mama?" He didn't like secrets. Mama once said secrets, like badgers, can bite.

"Boone, I will sleep outside tonight, and tomorrow we'll make a new bed for you."

"Why?"

She gave him a quick hug. "Tell me why you don't like Big Grizzly."

"There's something bad about him. Something quiet and dark."

"Your mama needs a man in her life."

"Not him. Papa."

"Oh, Boone."

"Tell me why Papa won't live here."

She kissed his head and stood. "If you were a girl, your father would have left you alone. You remember when I told you about the Cherokee? About how they had a great home back east and learned to adapt to white civilization, and yet were still forced to leave? Indians don't understand how whites own the land. We see it … I mean, the Kiowa see it as providing the resources needed to survive. No one should be allowed ownership over survival." She stood and threw wood on the fire still burning strong. "Boone, how can I explain how I feel? The Kiowa … can't hold off a whole country wanting their land. If you live with the Indians, you will die with them. And your father will never leave his people."

"But I can help them talk to whites. Even Jack says so."

She shook her head. "Do you remember the story of Jesus on the cross?" She checked her bread cooking on the stove. "You are not a savior. Don't ever get that complex."

"Did you love my Pa?"

"I did, Boone. But I had to choose." She threw her arms around him. "Promise you'll stay in the white world and be safe. Promise me, Boone!"

"I'd never leave you, Mama."

She looked out the window, suddenly startled. "Shhhhh!" Lynelle pointed at the bed in corner. "Hide. I hear a noise." Years of training made Boone respond without question. He hid under the buffalo skin while she ran outside.

Sun Hero was his favorite Indian story … hide until the time to come out and shine. But how to know when to be a hero? Boone wondered as he fell asleep hiding.

*

"Mama, I had a new dream last night." Boone had found a round piece of rubber that he worried between his palms as Lynelle finished cooking the oatmeal with maple syrup, his favorite breakfast. Boone thought that's all she ever did -- try to find a way to keep him fed.

"What this time? Fire monsters that fly and eat the rolling fire horses? I wish you would learn to start a fire as well as you dream it."

"At first I was alone and screaming because I was cold. But then so many warm hands surrounded me and as they clapped, the air around me warmed, and I floated on a cloud. The cloud turned dark and stormy but I wasn't afraid because you held me up, and Papa held you up, and even though the ground began to tremble we weren't afraid."

Lynelle stood frozen as she stared outside. "Boone! Get to your feet!"

"No, Mama. My dream said to be a man and protect you."

"I said get to your feet! Go out the window by the bed, go out the window and run." She pulled him away from the table and pushed him to the bed. "Run like you never ran before and don't look back, do you hear? Don't look back!"

Boone pushed the tarp aside but hesitated. "I want to stay."

Lynelle gave him a shove and he rolled out the window onto the hard ground below. At first he couldn't get up because the air had poofed out of him. He heard the sounds of many horses and the shouts of men, words he could not make out. He crept up along the house and peeked into the window.

Five Indians had come inside and faced his mama but she stood them off, yelling at them in return, her knife clutched tight in her hand. The tallest had a hand on her arm and seemed to be trying to gentle her. Boone ducked back down, thinking. Mama still loved Kae-gon. If he left them alone, maybe she'd find a way. *Why rebuke you him that loves you so?*

He turned and ran, down through the fields and up another hill to Big Grizzly's house but couldn't bring himself to go inside. Instead he ducked inside the small shed where Jack's mule lodged in bad weather. He huddled himself tight, not dressed to be outdoors. If only his grandfather had never interfered.

He remembered the move across the Mississippi when he was two ... the big waters -- the big river, his mama called it ... wider than any river young Boone had ever seen. He clung to his mama's leg in fear. His grandfather, General Tyler, barked orders at the three men who followed them everywhere. Boone hated those men because they tried to get between him and his mama. The men got out their axes to fell some trees for a raft, but then they saw a keel-boat headed across the river toward them.

Boone kept saying, "No water, no water!" so General Tyler picked him up and threw him into the river. Lynelle screamed but a soldier covered her mouth as Boone thrashed around. He managed to dog paddle back to shore. Not very far, really, before Boone found land under his feet again.

The General laughed and pointed, a hand holding back one of the men who wanted to go in after the boy. "Told ya. Part animal."

Lynelle ran to Boone when he got to shore, careful not to sound frightened. By the time she stripped him down he was laughing. "See me, Mama, see me?"

Lynelle found an oversized shirt for him to wear until his clothes dried. "You'll be a great swimmer someday, Boone." Boone nearly went back into the river on her encouragement but she held him back, laughing and crying at the same time.

The keel-boat got close enough for the boatman to call out, "Engagee?"

The General grumbled. "Shoot, it's a Frenchie. Anyone know any?"

"I know a little," Philip, his tall soldier, stepped forward, and using French said, "Across the river. You take us."

Boone and Lynelle emptied the wagon that would be left behind, to be used by someone who crossed from the other side.

"Oh. Oui. Cost you," Frenchie nodded as Philip interpreted.

"Huh, I understood that much," said the General. "What's your price?"

"One horse."

"One horse!" The General turned and waved at his adjutant. "Give him that rangy mule." He turned back. "Ask him if he wants it in the keel-boat."

Turned out he didn't. Frenchie gave a wave of his own and two Indians ran out. They grabbed the offered mule and ran off.

"You are good company!" Frenchie shouted in English. He waved them on board but not all their goods would fit. They tied some to the horses that would be pulled along behind to swim over. Halfway over Frenchie decided to demonstrate the sturdiness of the boat by making it sway while talking nonstop in French. When he got a little too close to Lynelle she gave him a shove and he tumbled backward with the swaying, right into the river.

While the men struggled to get him back on board, Boone and Lynelle clung to the side.

"Mama, am I a good swimmer now?"

"Not yet, Boone. But don't worry, you won't drown. You'll be a great man someday."

Once across they all leaped out, pulled their horses up to shore and ran up the hill without a look back, leaving the extra goods on the boat. Up, up a hill, they stumbled on rocks and caught shoes in the shrubbery, better at first than being on the water but soon Boone thought he would go crazy from being tired, cold and always wet, first from river, then from rain. They found no wagons this side of the river, which meant just to keep running and sometimes share a horse, but they finally found the fort and the general got them all more horses to ride.

But Grandpa didn't want this fort. Boone remembered how the wagon trail they got on sometimes disappeared, like a hole had opened up and swallowed it. "Will it swallow me?"

"No, Boone, not you. You are meant for better things."

The trees slapped him like he said a bad word and every few minutes he thought he heard the hoot of an Indian.

"Owl, Boone," Lynelle reminded him. "Would you like to hear a story, Boonie?"

"Yes, tell me why you're so afraid."

"Oh, let's save that for after I'm gone."

Boone didn't want Jack's help. He didn't want Jack telling them she would feel better if she had a man. Boone would remind Big Grizzly that she has her son -- that her son was a man.

That day would be tomorrow. For now, he curled up under the standing hay, to wait for his mama to come and get him.

CHAPTER THREE
The Kill

Boone pushed the door open and peeked inside. "Mama?" Their bed had been thrown aside, buffalo skin lying in a heap on the floor. "Mama?" Her knife was stuck in the table. He grabbed hold of the handle and wrenched it free. The blade was covered with blood.

He heard a thump outside and ran back to the door.

Big Grizzly Jack stood outside the shack. "You come with me now."

"I can't find my mama. The Indians were here yesterday, and --."

Jack pushed his way inside and scanned the room, his heavy brows narrowed as he focused on the buffalo skin on the floor. Boone noticed the skin covered something that had darkened in one spot. The tips of three fingers protruded from the buffalo skin.

"Mama!" Boone ran to her side and fell to his knees. He picked up the corner of the skin and saw his mother's face, eyes open and empty, mouth slightly sagging. Tears rolled down his cheeks, hot and wet, spilling onto his dead mama as though to wash her life back.

"Sorry, son." Jack stood over him, a heavily breathing grizzly. "So sorry."

Boone's hand trembled as he patted her hair. "I should have protected her! I would have gone with him to protect her."

Jack bent over Boone, hand on his shoulder. "Come back with me."

Boone saw that she had started digging in the dirt, the same spot she had patted closed only a day ago. He dug where her fingers had started a hole and found a small solid object. He held the rock up for Jack to see. "I gave you this. Why was it buried?"

"Her wish, boy -- could not live without you."

"I would have protected her! I would have told him no, I won't go!" He flung the rock at the overturned bed and grabbed the knife off the table. "Now, when I meet my father, I will kill him." Boone slipped the skin off her face again so she could watch him. "You were wrong. Living with the Indians is better than this." He threw the knife to the floor and picked up the small wood chair lying on its side. "Better than not living at all!" He slammed the chair to the floor, splitting it into quarters. "You looked for months to find a shack where the door faced east! You wanted to be like them! Why couldn't you live with them?" He flung her cooking pot against a far wall. "Now you're dead!" He dug his hands into a pile of broken glass. He flung the handful of smashed goods to the ground. When he saw his hands bloodied he burst into fresh hot tears and flung himself to the floor next to her. He grabbed the skin that covered her, baring her corpse to the air. She had sewed ribbons on as fringes and they used it together to snuggle tight, to keep warm at night. He pressed his wet face into it to smell her death. "I cannot live in the white world without you."

His mama looked blankly up at the ceiling, answers on silenced lips.

Boone rocked and sobbed, hugging his knees, before he collapsed next to her. As Jack watched, he seemed to pass out.

Jack picked him up.

Boone stirred weakly and muttered, "don't" but offered no other resistance. "I will kill my father," he muttered against Jack's leathered chest.

*

Boone dreamed of a time when he was three and saw the Kiowa for the first time. They sat on their horses and Mama hid Boone behind her. Boone thought they looked grand. He tried to stand beside her but she pushed him into the house. After a few minutes Mama came in and threw the latch on the door. She crouched down and pulled him close. "Don't go near them again, Boone. When I tell you to run, you must react instantly." She held him at arm's length, making him cry. "I'm sorry if I scare you, but I mean instantly. Do you understand?"

The memory turned into a dream where he did not run. He stood with Mama, telling the Kiowa to leave. One of them threw a knife at Boone. Boone ducked, and the knife went right into his mother's chest.

Boone awoke hard, gasping. His mother died protecting him. She should have known he would have preferred to die with her. Now he was alone and didn't know what to do. How could he keep his promise to live white without her in his world? When he woke the second time he heard a humming, like the buzz of bees, and his eyes flew open. The skin that covered him filled him with the sweet smell of Mama's home, but she was not here.

He peeked out from under the skin.

Jack sat at the table, his back to Boone. His cabin was filled with peculiar things, like that shelf with all kinds of jars of stuff. Some kind of lumpy mud -- perhaps for wounds? His mama preferred to get mud fresh from the river. Two bundles of hair hung in another cupboard. A string of claws that could have come from a bear next to it. In the corner near Boone stood a mangy dog. Boone put a hand down for the dog to sniff until he realized the dog was old, moth-eaten and stuffed.

Jack ate out of that pottery bowl with his fingers. He picked up a tin cup and used his long finger to wipe out some of the goo clinging to the side. "Larder for da barter," he said with a chuckle.

Boone thought Jack spoke odd English, but maybe not even that much when he was alone. Inside he seemed older and dirtier, too. Jack lumbered over to the door and peered outside. "Getcha anything today." He looked over his shoulder at Boone, but Boone feigned sleep so Jack went outside.

Boone wrapped the skin around him, with a ribbon wrapped around one finger, and sat up. He needed to go outside bad, too. He walked over to the table and found remnants of what Jack had slurped down. He didn't like the smell. Next to his meal lay a large rolled-up parchment paper. The paper revealed some kind of map, full of long scratchings and odd words, and in a few places were drawings like mountains or squiggles for water.

The paper rolled up again as Boone reached over to the brim of a brown hat. Jack wore an old plum slouch hat. He tried on the brown brimmed hat -- perfect fit for the boy, too small for a mountain man. Boone decided Jack wanted him to have the hat so he left it on his head. He wrapped the skin tight and secure around him, ribbons for finger holds. He put his ear against the rough wood door but could not hear Jack.

Mama was gone and Boone never even learned to sleep without her. He slipped down against the door in tears, pounding against the wood until he realized how loud he sounded and shushed himself with a hiccup. He pulled himself up like the man he wanted to be and stepped outside into the early morning chill, with a view of the sun peeking through the trees over the river below. Jack had picked a nice spot to build his shack, and Boone thought maybe he could live here. Of course all the dead carcasses would be buried and the smell cleaned out.

Boone had finished his morning toilet when Jack's mule let out a long bray and made him jump. He had not seen the critter tied to a fence post. Boone scratched its nose. "Nice fella. Don't be so loud. I don't want Jack to hear."

"Hear what, little sort? Dat you sneak down, not let me see?"

"I don't know what to do, Big Grizzly. I can't stay here."

Jack took Boone's arm and led him back inside. "I teach you be a man."

Boone sat at Jack's table as the big man put some food together for him to eat, only slightly more edible-smelling than what Boone saw him eat. He forced down the rough dried meat with a pulpy liquid like well-beaten bird eggs but watched Jack out of the corner of his eye. "Mr. Jack? Will you take me back to see Mama? Can we give her a good ceremony?"

And then he smelled the smoke in the air. "No!"

CHAPTER FOUR
The Escape

After the house finished burning and ashes cooled, Boone and Jack retrieved what was left of Lynelle and buried her. Jack sang as they did, but Boone's voice was gone. He had screamed at Jack all the while the shack burned. "It is tradition for many," was all Jack would say, over and over. "Hush, and listen for her spirit," he said as they bundled the bones that were left. Boone listened.

He could hear her voice in his head as she read to him the death scene from Romeo and Juliet. He pictured his father's blood on his hands. Boone drifted in memory of the last time Kae-gon came to talk to Lynelle. Kae-gon told her that if she did not let the boy go to the tribe willingly, he would take Boone during the boy's 13th year. And she would not be able to stop him. Well, this time she did.

At that time, Lynelle ran back into the house, slammed the door and threw the latch. "Why is there so much pain?" She sobbed against the door and sank to her knees. Crouched near her, Boone saw hate come out of her like a snake and crawl around on her skin. She grabbed his arm and pulled him outside. Boone went because he trusted her. He thought maybe she changed her mind and wanted him to go with his father. But their horses were gone and his mama still pulled him.

Boone thought Mama played a new kind of game, as they went farther into the woods than he had ever gone before. When she stopped she turned him to face a tree. "Close your eyes and count to 12, Boone. To 12, you hear me? I don't want you to move until then."

When Boone finished counting he looked around. He was alone in the woods. "Mama?" He sat on the ground and picked a mushroom off the nearby stump. "It's okay, Mama. I know you wish I had never been born, like my twin brother." As he ate the mushroom, tears rolled down Boone's cheeks, but he began to listen to that odd little voice inside him, who he came to believe was his brother Sam. *Don't worry. All will be taken care of by nature and your own instincts.*

After a day without food or water, Boone began to feel as though he soared. He did not feel real anymore. He had entered another world, one of his own choosing, one where he controlled his destiny. He saw herds of horses and he roped them all. He talked to Indians and whites in one language they all understood, a language that they could feel, rather than hear -- a language cool and refreshing for all of them. He saw himself soar with the eagles, the land below on fire. He saw that he could save the land with water--.

He felt his mother shake him awake. She put a jug of water to his mouth. "I'm so sorry, Boone, oh, I am so sorry. I never ever want to hurt you. Please." She pulled him, wet-faced, into her bosom. "I love you more than your father, more than I've ever loved anyone. Please forgive me."

"I'm an eagle."

She held him out at arm's length. "Boone, do you realize what will happen to you if you go to your father? Do you understand what waits for you if you leave the white world?"

"But Mama, I've left the white world already. I don't look like you."

She cried louder as she pressed Boone against her chest. He promised, over and over, just so she would stop hurting.

Boone nodded at the crude cross he'd made to mark her grave. "I will stay white. And I will kill him for you, Mama." He followed Jack back to his shack without a look backward.

The rest of the first day Jack told stories of trapping, of crossing blazing deserts and eating the horses that died, of being swept downstream in raging rivers, and of fighting settlers. Indians didn't always want to fight them, but couldn't make them understand.

The second morning Boone pushed his carrot and egg mash around on his plate.

"Boy! We do not waste!"

"Sorry, Big Grizzly." Boone picked up a forkful, stared at the food and put the fork down.

"Missing mama is not good sport." Jack stood, clad in leggings, his heavy hairy chest and gut sagging. "Dally come lately, dance with me, girl," he sang. He stomped the ground and whirled around. "Come boy, we dance, you eat. Moon go up lightly, dance with me, girl."

Boone watched wide-eyed as Jack stomped in circles about the room. When he ran out of words Jack grabbed Boone's arms and picked him up off the chair. He swung the boy about with a wild Indian scream. By the time he let Boone back down on the floor the boy danced and whooped as loud as Jack himself.

In no time Boone found himself eating his food with a hungry grin, as Big Grizzly sat at the table panting happily beside him.

*

On the fourth morning Boone recited some of Mama's favorite Shakespeare as he washed up in the river, his cleaned clothes on the shore to dry. "Oh, swear not by the moon." He wiped tears away but felt comforted. "The inconstant moon? That monthly changes in her circled orb?" He wouldn't forget her, ever. Her own moods had been as changeable as the moon, so he would see her face there, every night. He hoped to stay white by keeping her Shakespeare in his head.

"Mama, did Jack ever tell you the story about how Big Grizzly got the bear claws? He said no one believed the story because the only witnesses were a couple of elk." He talked as easily as though she sat next to him. "But Jack spit on his hand and slapped the spit to his heart. A bear was catching fish and tossing them on shore, and Jack was hungry. He crept up to the shore and picked up a couple fish, forgetting in his hunger that the bear had a great nose for smelling. The bear chased him and was gaining but Jack leaped on the back of an elk, and with his butchering knife slashed the elk's throat. The bear was distracted by this fresh kill, which gave Jack enough time to retrieve his buffalo rifle. He shot the bear in the left eye, dead center. And then he held the claws up, Mama, the claws he cut off that bear!" He believed that the claws aided Jack in living such a long time in the wilderness.

Jack made Boone his own medicine bag, with one claw and his wish rock. But Boone didn't feel like running anymore. He wanted to stay close to her spirit.

He rinsed out his brown hat and tossed it up on shore with his clothes. He swam like a fish in his naked skin. He dove under deep and counted to see how long he could hold his breath. One hundred, and then he broke through the surface of the water into the autumn wind turned cold against wet skin. He shook the water off his hair and wiped his eyes clean as he looked for his clothes.

He ducked back down in the water again. Five men on horses watched him. One, the tallest, with large headdress, alighted. This was the man he saw through the window, the one who must have killed his mother. His father!

He came up again in the middle of water grasses, hoping they couldn't see him. But they could. He froze there, staring at them staring back, shivering.

"Hold!" Behind them, Big Grizzly ran down the hill. "Not yet! I not told--."

Boone swam to the other side of the river. He reached the shallow end and started to run, picking his feet up high as he raced to hide in the underbrush. His father had come for him. His father killed his mama. And Big Grizzly Jack was their friend. He ran hot and hard but felt the Kiowa close behind. Boone darted up the hill and over rocks as though the wind pushed him, his mind as frozen with thought as his naked skin.

Behind him came the horses pounding, pounding -- all five were after him. Boone veered off through thick underbrush. Branches tore his skin but he did not slow. His mama died to keep him safe in the white world.

Ahead was the cave he often hid in when Mama was in one of her crazy frightened moods. He dove inside as horses pounded and shook the ground above him. Boone closed his eyes, breath hot and hard, as tears spilled out.

He was truly alone now, naked to the world.

*

When nightfall came Boone had his arms around his knees, trying to get warm. He heard footsteps above him and shrank back from the grizzly face of Jack peering into his rabbit hole.

"You dere?"

Boone tucked himself tight and held his breath. *One, two, three…*

"I know you be, boy." Jack dangled Boone's buffalo skin down in front of the hole. Boone ripped the skin away from Jack and wrapped himself up like a cocoon. Jack placed a neat pile of his clothes, that hat, medicine bag and his mama's knife next to the hole. "I still 'low you belong with your papa, boy. Dem not kill your mama. You come, you talk, you see."

"Go away."

"You go talk to your ma. Sit by her bones. She tell you, if you listen close." Jack walked away, his steps heavy and slow.

But Boone was running with Sam now, the only voice he could trust.

CHAPTER FIVE
The Slave

Trees. Trees. Trees. So many trees in front of him that Boone couldn't find a path. He had long before lost all familiar terrain. His only need now was to go south and find the fort where his grandfather lived. His mother had stopped talking about the general but he was still family, so Boone thought he would at least want to know about his daughter.

Through bog, through bush, through brake, through brier. Sometime a horse I'll be, sometime a hound, a hog, a headless bear, sometime a fire. And neigh, and bark, and grunt, and roar, and burn. Like horse, hound, hog, bear, fire, at every turn. Shakespeare kept him sane, closed off Sam's sometimes disturbing voice, helped him to remember, as his mama said, the common humanity that followed the centuries. Sometimes he pretended to be Jason hunting for the Golden Fleece, that which only the brave could find. He was almost 13. Time to be brave. His mama wouldn't let him be brave and now she was gone.

For the first couple nights on the run Boone avoided strangers. They would make him a slave, Mama told him. He didn't know who "they" were. After a few days of running, when hunger set in and the nights got colder, he realized he should have listened more to her lessons on survival skills. He could track water sources, start a fire and knew the difference between poisonous and edible plants -- but discovered he wasn't very good at starting a fire. The first day he found some eggs and wanted them cooked. So he found a stick but without his mother's trick of a gunpowder laden rag, he had to use a bird's nest as kindling. He almost got the spark but got excited and the stick flew out of his hands. So he ate the eggs raw.

To find water, he observed what an animal looked like. A bird called Dirt Dauber had an empty mouth when it headed toward water. A muskrat had a wet snout coming away. But he had a hard time finding an animal at all and instead looked for ways out of the woods to run through open prairie. In the open prairie along a tree line, he found a creek that went south, so for a time followed that and caught some small fish. He could tell the directions, at least when clouds broke away. He came to appreciate the rain, though, and kept a cup-like piece of bark handy. But his skins and clothes were scratched and ripped because he had to forge his own path along the way when the woods became thick again.

On his third night a wolf trapped him. He kept his knife tight in his hand, but the animal had more right to life, he decided. He dropped his hand to his side as the animal circled him. As the wolf took growling nips out of his skin Boone dropped the knife to the ground. The wolf knocked him backward and Boone screamed in fear and rage. "Mama!"

The animal jumped off him and ran, as though Mama had shot at it.

After a week Boone's clothes started to shred and hang on him. He had gotten meat off four babies from a bunny's nest and cried the whole time he ate them, even though he got the fire going good for the first time. Eggs became impossible to find until he happened on a barn with chickens. He took extra to have later but they all broke. After that he only took what he could force himself to eat right away. He found a farmer's field this late October but most edibles had already been salvaged.

In the second week he swam with his clothes on for speed and security. He also tumbled down two hills, stopped by trees both times, cried himself to sleep every cold night huddled under the buffalo skin under rocky buttes or nestled on deer moss, and avoided signs of humans anywhere. He didn't know who to trust. His mama used to have to bolt the door to keep out the vagabond tramps, varmints with guns who looked for slave owners, or who looked to kill slave owners. Boone once heard Mama say, "What someone does, or lets have done to him, is no one else's business." That meant Boone was responsible only to himself.

He ran south, always with the morning sun on his left shoulder, and the evening sun on his right, and kept himself covered with the buffalo so his skin wouldn't burn. His mama told him years ago that Grandpa was at the Arkansas fort. So Boone made sure he kept running south, because that's where Arkansas was.

Boone didn't know he had gotten into Arkansas until he ran into an old man on a mule and made him the first one to trust. He asked proper, too -- first say his name and ask for one in return.

Harrison smiled with handsome vigor during the introduction. Before Boone could ask the direction to the fort, the old man had a rope around his neck.

"No, please, mister," but the words strangled in his throat.

"Caddo Indian? Some of them is kinda light colored like you. No? Well, don't matter. I need me a slave."

Boone fell to his knees as the rope tightened. He fought to breathe.

Harrison tied Boone's hands on a lead rope to the saddle and allowed more slack to the rope still around his neck. "A dead slave don't do much work. Come on, let's ride." Harrison got the mangy animal into a reluctant trot, forcing Boone to run behind to keep up.

When Boone tripped and fell, the mule dragged him along and the rope nearly choked him to death before Harrison noticed. He tugged at the rope to get Boone to stand. Boone couldn't move his hands up to wipe the bloodied dirt and sticks from his face enough to open his eyes.

The old man got off the mule and squatted by him. "You gonna live, little feller?"

"Please. Let me go."

"Go? Boy your age? Where were you headed, anyhow?" Harrison's voice had softened some but he made no move to take the ropes off.

"I gotta find my grandpa. Mama just died. My father killed her." Boone sobbed into the dirt, feeling the moment he'd just found her body and even worse for the loss of freedom.

Harrison took the rope off Boone's neck and rubbed at the bruise there. With a hanky he wiped the boy's face and grabbed his chin to study him. "Ah, half-breed. You got nothing to fear from me. I'm gonna take care of you."

Boone gave his tied hands a tug and pulled the rope from Harrison's hand. "I wanna find Grandpa."

Harrison yanked the boy to his feet. "And I need me a farm hand. Never owned a slave before. You'll do as good as any." He brushed the boy off. "I'm too old for my chores."

"If you were a good boss, people would want to work for you."

"You're injun, ain't you? I offer you a life, boy. A place where you're taken care of. There's nothing wrong with that kind of world."

Harrison handed the boy a piece of jerky. As Boone chewed, he wondered if he could be a slave for food and a warm place to sleep. He lost the muster of anger because the food tasted good. "Mama says I'm white."

"I kin tell a half breed. You know, boy, if one half of you were to cancel out the other, that would make you nothing."

Boone only nodded, mouth full of jerky.

Harrison laughed. "Well, both halves of you are my slave now, and if you try to get away, I'm gonna have to shoot you."

Boone swallowed hard and accepted the water. "Why would someone want that choice? Work or be shot?"

"Smart one, eh? Well, you gotta eat, don't ya? You gotta do something for a living. What's wrong with doing it for me?"

"Because I didn't choose it. I have dreams. I'm gonna be someone. Then fate o'er rules … in the sense
of --."

"Grow a little first."

"I'm nearly 13, and I want to gentle and raise horses."

"Spoken like a true Indian."

"Don't whites raise horses?"

Harrison laughed. Boone came to hate that raspy sound. "You got book learning?"

Harrison waited but Boone was too tired to answer. "Okay, tell you what, you work for me, just a few years. You learn how to break horses for me."

"I gotta find my grandpa. At the fort."

"All you know is he's at some fort? Well, there's Fort Smith. I can send word over there. You got his name?"

"Tyler." After a pause Boone added, "General." Grandpa hated Indians. Mama told him the story about why she had to leave Kae-gon, already pregnant with Boone. Because of a massacre when he came to get her. He heard her nightmares one night and made her tell him. The love, the hate, the blood, the screaming … He hated the story then, but now, because his mother died to keep Boone safe, he had to find General Tyler. Maybe his grandpa will kill his father now. Or Boone will have to live with this hate until he became a man. Until he became … the general.

Or become Indian, Sam whispered inside him.

Harrison sucked his lips in the silence. "Can't say as I heard of him. Stay with me, boy. Get some proper food in ya. Why, pretty soon you'll be calling *me* Grandpa."

Boone lost the energy to argue, like a snake that had slunk back down into a hole. "I *am* hungry."

Harrison helped him up onto the mule. "Don't get used to this fancy treatment. I just don't want you falling and getting broke behind my mule. Hyah!"

*

Boone lasted three days with Harrison -- long days of work and long nights spent tied up in bed at night, crying with pain, sadness, exhaustion. During the day he got maybe an hour to play with the greener horses and spent the rest of the day hoeing. Hoe hoe hoe until his hands were split and bled to get the rows ready to plant the winter wheat. But he ate some of the best-tasting food ever, which he didn't think possible because his mama cooked good food. But she never let him go hungry for very long, either, so easing the hunger made food taste so much better.

Boone laid store for his running by tucking food that could be portable into a canvas bag that he stole from the shed. The clothes Harrison gave him were plenty too big for him, so when he escaped the bag will be easy to hide.

On the third day Boone felt ready. He had the food bag hidden under the bed where he slept. He got on one of the greener horses and grabbed the mare's mane to see how long he could ride. All of five count. When he went flying, he tucked and tumbled, and then sat up and held his right arm and shoulder, crying in pain.

The mangy mule looked up and went back to eating weeds on the side of the corral. The old black man who shelled peas on the house porch at first went back to shelling but finally dragged his weary tail over to the corral. "You ailing, boy? Want me to get the massa?"

"Please. Help me up. My shoulder. Hurts."

The old slave wrapped his arms around the boy and helped him to his feet.

Boone leaned against him, sobbing and moaning -- but not too much.

Harrison came out of the house, picking the lunch from his teeth. "Had to go and mount 'er, eh?"

Boone looked at the ground, doubled over in pain.

"You know, you're more trouble than you're worth. I could use some shooting practice."

No one moved. Boone felt the old black man's heart beat an erratic tempo against his arm as he tightened his grip to hold the boy up. Boone struggled not to breathe the man's lye soap as he gasped in pain.

He didn't know why because no words were spoken, but the old man helped Boone inside the house and laid him down. Sure enough, Harrison tied the ropes around his feet again. Then he did the next thing Boone expected. Tied only his good arm to the bed post.

"I suspect we'll let that sore shoulder heal some. I gotta go to town for the chickens. You get the rest of the day off." Harrison pointed a bony finger in Boone's face. "But you be ready to go to work tomorrow. That'll be soon enough for target practice, if'n not."

Boone heard Harrison ride off. He couldn't hear the old slave anywhere but felt little threat from that old man. As he used his untied hand to free the rest of him, Boone wished he could bring him along. He grabbed the bag with the dried beef, peas and onions and a small bag of salt from under the bed and crept outside.

The old slave shelled peas, paying him no attention, and the greener horse pranced and pawed the ground as though daring Boone to give him another try. Boone saw the barn door open and the mule's tail swishing. He crept over to the barn with an eye on the back of the old slave, who never turned because there was no noise to turn to.

The dark barn smelled of dried hay the mule had loosened enough to reach. Boone patted its nose. "Shhh, remember me? Let's go for a ride."

A voice boomed out. "He won't come for you. He will for that mule."

Boone froze. He peeked out the door but the slave hadn't moved. He looked back at the mule, tucked his pack back under his shirt and ran off.

CHAPTER SIX

The Outlaws

Running again. Boone still had Big Grizzly's hat and Mama's knife and buffalo skin, and he had a new shirt and shoes. The food he stole wouldn't last long, and he missed having someone to care what happened to him. He thought as he ran that he might have been better off with Harrison. Maybe Harrison needing him healthy for work was charm enough to live by.

But then Boone remembered the pain and sleeplessness of being tied in bed at night and forced to work all day. *They have tied me to a stake. I cannot fly!* He wasn't used to force. "Can I chop for two hours every morning when it's cool, Mama?" She usually agreed, unless she was in that mood again. Having his own stake in his life, that's what he wanted.

Sixteen days without Mama became twenty-one, when he found the river and let his tears flow. In December he would be 13 -- a man, Mama would say. He missed her so bad and cried just about every day, but each day his tears felt a little drier.

Sam was usually a quiet voice inside him, but sometimes shouted things Boone did not understand. He remembered the first time he asked his mama about his twin brother. Lynelle had been startled. "Why do you think you had a twin brother?"

"I dream about him. I thought maybe he was my guardian fairy. But then he told me."

She tried not to look frightened, but failed to Boone's eyes. "What did he tell you?"

"That he would protect me and keep me safe."

His mother's arms trembled around him. "I never told you, Boone. Your twin brother was stillborn. I never told you."

"Twas his ghost, madam." He wanted to make her laugh, like she often did when he quoted Shakespeare.

"Boone, tell me how you know! Have you been with your father?"

"But how would Father know, if you left him before I was born?"

Now that he was alone, Boone began hearing Sam more and more, as though he now had permission to exist. Sam told him things. *He was with her when we were born.* Maybe Sam was the one who could feel their mama's thoughts, all those times when Boone sensed her pain and fear, and stopped asking questions.

Mama told him nothing lived without breath, so Boone became conscious of his breath as he ran, often feeling like he left his breath over that last hill, or down in that valley -- like now, breath so hot and painful after another climb up another treacherous height.

"Sam? Is Mama with you? Is she happy?" He listened for an answer, feeling sure, like Hamlet, he could converse with a ghost.

Not a sound, save the wind in the trees. Or were there ghosts in the wind? He began to feel wind as the breath of so many ghosts. But nothing lived without breath. So that meant Sam was alive, but in a different way.

His path, one even Sam couldn't help with, was to find his way to his grandfather as his last best hope to be cared for. He will tell the general that Lynelle was dead and that a Kiowa killed her so that he would …

Civilization or extinction. Boone woke to those harsh words of his grandfather's that 33rd morning of being alone. "The white race *alone* has received the divine command to subdue and replenish the earth. Keep him white, Lynelle, or lose him." Did General Tyler say that after he had massacred people at her Kiowa village? *Out damned spot, out, I say.* Mama said her father never felt guilty.

At the river to wash the night dirt off his skin, Boone scrubbed hard to get at the white skin beneath his darker surface. His skin got lighter in the winter and he thought maybe if he scrubbed hard enough he could get the rest of the Indian off. While he scrubbed he saw some fish in a school swimming lazily. He leaped in after them and came up coughing and laughing with one in each hand. He ended their gasps with his knife. "I know how you feel. I'm sorry."

Making a fire got easier every time he spun the stick. He wished he had taken more matchsticks from Harrison, but the days on the run kept moving by, more than he could ever count. Boone couldn't let this fire go out until after tomorrow's ceremony.

He napped after eating his fish. By the time he heard the horses they were too close for him to hide. He jumped up and greeted them steadily, with the trust of a boy whose mama was nearby. But he pulled the buffalo skin up around his shoulders, as though to hide.

One already had a gun drawn. "Told you smoke meant fire."

"Didn't know it was an Injun with smoke signals."

"Think we should be scared?"

"Of him? Looks like he's gonna cry for his mammy."

One of the men leaned over for a closer look at the boy. "Got us a half-breed here. Your mother get raped by an Injun, boy?"

"My Pa will be back any minute."

"Could be an Indian woman tried to get herself a white husband."

Boone wanted to tell them about his mother, a fine French woman born and raised in New Orleans whose only mistake was to love a Kiowa and now she was dead. He analyzed them as they alighted, two nearly as short as he was but all three had muscle and could take down his scrawny frame even without those guns.

"Think he's got Indian friends watching us?" The short one with the red hair and a missing tooth, eye to eye with Boone, gave him a shove backward. "You got someone out there with a bead on us, huh?"

Boone fell, his legs tangled in the buffalo skin. One arm landed in the fire until he jerked it back out. But he had the knife in his hand again. He also landed with the renewed desire to clean his teeth like his mama taught him, with ground up birch bark she got in trade from the Anishnaabeg. Odd thing for him to think but he wasn't very good at controlling his thoughts lately.

The three men laughed over him, and the tall one with a red kerchief aim his musket rifle at Boone. "We better kill 'em. Likely go running back to the tribe, tell 'em where we are." Only one of the three held the musket. The other two left theirs with their horses.

With his hat still tight on his head, Boone untangled himself and got to his knees.

The one tried to shoot at him but the musket misfired. "Shoot, keep an eye on 'em." They seemed like half-breeds themselves, from down near the Mexico border, some of the new Texans with nothing better to do than wander the countryside.

"Come on," another muttered as he cleaned his musket. "We ain't got all day here."

Boone remained crouched on all fours and wrapped a ribbon around his thumb. Feeling a boot to his behind Boone gave a sudden blood-curdling yell that came from nowhere he could remember. Out came the knife as he whirled and jammed it through the man's foot. As the man screeched and howled above him, the musket dropped into Boone's hand. He pulled the knife free and leaped into the underbrush, buffalo skin flying like a flag in the wind, and disappeared.

The other two grabbed their rifles and fired into the ghostly wind he left behind.

CHAPTER SEVEN
Gramma

Boone raised his hand to get attention but the door slammed shut again, and his finger caught a sliver from the door frame. He was slumped down on his knees, cold and wet from the rain of the night before, with nothing to eat since the fish of two days ago. At least the bleeding from the musket fire he caught in his rear had stopped, but not the pain.

How many days had he survived alone now? He kept track on the stick he carried but that and most of his other goods were lost behind him. Those riders got in a lucky shot as he ran, but he found little time to sit after that anyway. He made his campfire on the night of Hallow's Eve, though, and did the dance his mama taught him to bring in the good and keep out the bad spirits. He flung himself across the fire to singe off the evil that had found him in the year since the last fire ceremony. He didn't do the ritual quite right, though, and caught a flame on his big toe to match the throbbing burn on his arm and the stinging in his behind. But the ceremony left him feeling sane. Mama said ritual gives us more control over what happens around us.

Then last night came close to ending him. He didn't see who they were but kept going when he heard the horses. They shot at him, figuring him for game of some kind. Boone made light footprints in the snow that they'd tracked, but he veered into brush to evade them. One shot just missed his head.

He feared this homestead belonged to another fur trapper like that traitor Old Grizzly until he saw, by the dim glow of moonlight, the petticoat that hung in the tree. Whoever lived here, after answering his shy knock, must have thought him an oversized muskrat the way he was wrapped in his buffalo skin, come to claim a foot for its dinner, and slammed the door.

Boone tried to sit up and look less like a river monster. *What's the use*, his Sam-voice thought, *they're gonna reject us anyway*. He prayed every day to have the wind at his back, the sun on his head, and the river at his left hand. He didn't have Harrison's shoes on anymore because his feet hurt less this way, once he got used to the sharp sticks and stones. The air was colder, rain more often turned to snow, and now he was froze near to death.

"To be or not to be," Boone muttered as he pounded on the door again. He repeated this even louder as the door opened again.

The old woman heard this time and squatted down by him. "Eh, what's that?"

Boone shivered as he muttered, unable to look up. "To be or not!"

"Oh, my baby precious, look at you. First time I thought my old ears were a'goin'. You really are a little boy, aren't you?"

"I'm…" Boone sneezed. "… almost 13." And he passed out.

*

When he woke, Boone was stretched out on his side in front of the fire on top of his buffalo skin with a heavy wool blanket over him. Still he shivered but the smell of meat and vegetable stew gradually warmed him. The old woman sat hunched in a chair next to him, and as he woke she leaned over him.

"Say, you're Indian."

"No. White." He pulled a hand out from under the blanket and pointed in the direction of the smell. "I will teach Indians how to live in the white world." He felt bandages on his rear.

"Is that so?" With garlic breath she peered close at his face, and her gnarly fingers ran patchwork through wild hair. "Half Indian, anyway." She cackled. "Not that I mind. A child is precious in any color. Just make sure you don't grow like an Indian. Gotta stay tame to live in this world."

"Mama says … being an Indian would kill me. But she was white and she's dead."

She grunted. "Sad. You can call me Gramma. How are you feeling now?"

37

He pointed at the pot again. "Hungry."

"That's good." She got a bowl and spoon and dished him up some stew. "Sad, losing your mama. Wicked world, you know."

As she busied herself with cleaning, and as he ate, Boone studied her. She had been big at one time, big-boned, big breasts that sagged, shoulders drooped, hair fine and tied back in braids and a bun, but with hairs loose about her unequally lined face. The way she stirred the stew and cackled when she laughed made Boone think she might throw him in next. His mama read him stories about witches who ate children. She called these stories fairy tales and myths, and said all myths had a kernel of truth. Boone figured Mama just wanted him to stay close to home. Well, this wasn't a candy house -- that much he could tell right off. He held up his empty bowl for more.

"No, young'un, that's all for now. Your stomach might not take to being too full." She watched him drink his water. "What do I call you?"

"Boone. Boone Tyler."

"Good. And Boone." She sat with a grunt. "If I got your story clear, you're running away. From what?"

"My mama was killed by my father's people. Then our shack was burned to the ground so that I would go with my father. But I want to find my grandfather. He hates the Kiowa. He'll help me kill my father."

"Oh." She sat and rocked but Boone felt like sleeping again and stretched out. "Well, if I'm gonna feed you again, I'm gonna need some more game. I got some broth and onions cooking over here. You stir while I'm gone, you hear?"

"No! Don't go."

"Eh? What's that you say?"

"There's something out there." Boone realized in the warmth of her little house how tired he was. "Something bad."

"What do you mean, child?" She stood and grabbed a knife from her table. "Who would try to hurt a little one like you?"

"Monsters. In the woods." Maybe, in all this time, he got to be such good friends with the forests and underbrush that they protected him. He wondered if he could turn into a tree and suck all his food out of the ground. That would be a good life.

She put the knife back down and bent over Boone. "Tell me about how your mama was killed."

Boone closed his eyes as he laid his head on the buffalo skin. He smelled the old lady's hand as she sat near him and fingered the skin's ribbons unraveling into threads. He thought he might fall asleep before he found the words to explain. "She protected me."

"From what, child?" When Boone didn't answer she picked him up off the floor, dusted him off and led him to the cook stove. "Stir. I'll go hunt rabbit. You can sleep later."

Boone picked up the wooden spoon protruding from the pot. The stew she served him was almost gone and he could never eat up all her food without her permission. He never had a gramma before and didn't know what they were like. Maybe when women get old they become like the Great Mother, the one who controlled the clouds, the rains, and the rumbles of the earth. She had a smell to her of dust, decay and long ago.

And of garlic. His tummy grumbled again but he just stirring.

*

Boone stretched toward the fire after Gramma woke him up. The crackling fire felt good to his fingers, as sore and cold as if he had been chafing wheat on a particularly windy day. She sent him to sleep after she returned, and the rabbit she'd killed now cooked in the soup. The smell made his mouth ache. For distraction he stretched his fingers and curled them again. He felt old and stiff as a tree.

After they ate the soup she told him she didn't like conversation during the meal because soup always fell out of her mouth, making him laugh long and hard.

Be wary. Boone shook Sam away.

"General Tyler. Fort Smith." He hoped that would satisfy her but he could tell by the back of her neck where she washed pans that she wanted more. He used to drive his mother crazy when he read her body parts.

"Honey, them at that fort hate Indians. You're Indian."

"He's my grandpa."

"Did he kill your pa?"

"No! Mama and him lived in the Kiowa world until Grandpa took her back."

"Ha! Tell me about them together. Your parents. I want to know about 'em together."

"Why?"

"Why? Look at you. Look at the world! Fighting, killing, hatred. But you're love. You're made of love ... unless'n he raped her."

"No!" Boone wasn't sure what that meant, but it sounded like the opposite of love. "They loved each other, and she married him at his village."

"See? That's who you are. You must go out and tell them."

"Tell who?"

"Everyone!" She cackled again. "Start with me."

"Mama said to always know I was created with love. But Grandpa hated her living with the Kiowa and when she refused to leave, he attacked them. She told me once that she felt this horrible guilt, never figuring her father capable of butchering children with the men and women. They had all been sleeping when the army attacked. Grandpa made sure she was taken out first. When Papa found her again, I was three and he wanted her to come back but she refused. That's when he told her he would come for me to make me a man. So he did."

"But why would your father, this Kiowa, kill the woman he loved?"

"She didn't want me to live with Indians. She felt I was safer in the white world. So she resisted him." He started to sob but didn't want to. He didn't want to tell her all those things. But now he couldn't stop crying.

She pulled him up and hugged him hard. "Oh, you have found a place to belong, my little pup. I will keep you with me, and safe, until you feel ready to move on. I promise you. No one will ever hurt you here."

*

Boone's eyes remained closed in sleep but he could smell the bread baking, a smell of long ago and a warm home. "Mama?"

He sat up and saw Gramma fussing over the milk, getting just the right amount into two cups, plus a little in the saucer for Rupert, the beat-up black and white cat she adopted. Milk was a premium anywhere if you didn't own a cow and he wondered if she had one. His mind with thoughts felt as big and bright as the moon. He could try and hide but his mind eventually came out to find him again. Though he cried himself to sleep last night, at least his belly was full, he felt rested and his nose happy with bread smells.

Gramma brought him a freshly sliced hunk of warm bread and the milk. "You'll stay with me?"

He chewed and swallowed, thoughtful. "My grandpa, he needs to know what happened to my mama."

"I'll get word off for you. If what you say is true, he would kill you as soon as look at you. I'm an old woman, but I got a few years left. Enough for you. Stay here."

"I need to see him. I could come back after."

"Well, you shouldn't go alone. Head south, take the Arkansas River to the Poteau. Get yourself a raft to move faster. But I gotta tell you, boy, I think your grandpa is dead. I want you to think of this as home."

"Thank you. I want to, too." He smiled at the thought of staying. "Maybe sending them a message would be good. Make him come here, if'n he wants. I'd be great help to you."

She cackled merrily. "That you would!" At the sound of horses in the yard Gramma turned to the window. "Finish your breakfast. I'll see to whoever's out there. You stay here."

Boone grabbed his buffalo skin and stood, instantly alarmed with the memory of his mother's last words. "I won't let them hurt you."

Gramma smiled and kissed his cheek. "I know that, Boone." She walked outside.

Boone ran to the window. Those were not Indians. They were those three outlaws -- they found him! He clamped a hand over his mouth. She was too smart to take chances. He had his knife and could throw several of hers, if needed.

He watched them get off their horses. He sought a good window to throw knives at them if they made any threatening move toward Gramma.

One of the shorter ones, the red-head, hugged her. And she hugged him back. *But those were bad men. Why would Gramma hug them?*

His mama was good and now she was dead. What did that make him? Bad or good? Indian or white? Gramma told the three men to wait outside and she would get them food. When she got inside she couldn't find Boone, because he had already slipped out the back.

Boone ran on. He only had the time to grab his buffalo blanket, her bread, and an extra knife. He couldn't stay with Gramma. She was going to turn bad on him, too, like Sam said.

Oh brave young prince! Thy famous grandfather doth live again in thee! Long mayst thou live to bear his image and renew his glories!

He needed to listen to Sam more often.

CHAPTER EIGHT
Buffalo Hunt

Boone hit a stretch of prairie expecting to see this open land because of the way the trees bent and parted, allowing sunlight in. His buffalo skin was still wet from the washing in the Mississippi where he dunked himself and his wearable belongings, before heading sharply west. The buffalo hide dried in slow patches in the crisp November wind. He kept the skin out at arm's length as he ran into prairie sunlight to get warm.

There, unperturbed by his presence, grazed a herd of buffalo. He wrapped his buffalo skin around his shoulders to blend in. If he made a noise, would they stampede? He couldn't see the ground for the thick brown sea of beasts in front of him and believed they would lay a five-mile area of grassland flat in just seconds with him embedded beneath it. Every few seconds one raised a head with a bleat or a bray but otherwise they saw him as a non-threat.

The loud thud in his chest gave room to hunger. Vast prairie hunger. He had just a couple of knives and he couldn't bring himself to use them on a small and weak calf. But he couldn't walk away from this much food, either. *Now the hungry lion roars, and the wolf behowls the moon.* Boone listened to his Shakespeare stomach mixing with the low monotone bellows as a cow limped out into the open, away from the herd. Could he take that weakened one down and not alarm the herd? She appeared to be sacrificing herself to him.

He waited. Depart in patience, his mama told him, and he would beat a hungry bull to dinner. He couldn't remember what Greek story that was from. She limped farther from the herd, almost as though she sensed her need to be culled from the healthy runners.

Can you do this? Can you not?

Boone ran to her right shoulder, intending to force her farther away from the herd. Instead she moved back toward the others, trapping him between her and the herd. With no time to spare, Boone leaped and straddled his legs around her shoulders and jammed the knives down into her neck where he hoped her biggest blood veins were. He used the handles of the knives as choke holds and pushed in as he held onto the beast that jumped and ran to dislodge the pain and unfamiliar weight on her back.

Boone gritted his teeth so they didn't rattle inside his mouth. "Die, just die!" He got ready to leap off but wanted her to stagger first. He thought he could feel the blades touch inside her throat and even though the blood streamed over his hands, she ran on and on through the herd.

Before Boone could figure out an alternate plan, he heard a low roll of bison brays and soon the whole herd around him jumped and began to run in response to her panic. Boone leaned down to the massive woolly head to ride her out to the death. But her sudden jump whacked its bony brains against the boy's nose so hard that daylight faded. At the same moment the beast came to a sudden stop. Boone sailed over her head and hit the ground. He cowered, arms over his head, waiting for the sea of hooves to finish this maddened run over and around him -- waiting for his life to be over, finally.

Boone thought he had passed out but somewhere he heard the sound of hooves fading into final silence. Numerous hooves scrapped his skin but somehow missed killing or even fracturing him. He pulled himself up, glad he wasn't any taller because that would have been more muscle and bone to hurt. As his eyes cleared and his mind grew less foggy, he saw a lump of brown a couple hundred yards away. His cow. She snorted and bled, tried but couldn't get up again. Finally died.

Forgetting his pain but feeling anguish in causing hers, he ran to her side, pulled out a knife from her neck and jammed it into her heart, just to be sure. As the blood oozed out, he lowered his lips to drink.

*

Boone kept away from people for weeks at a time, ducking into the woods or tall brush, covering himself with snow to avoid being seen. With the theft of some clothes and his two buffalo blankets he managed to stay warm on his trek south to the fort. The buffalo meat didn't last as long as he hoped because the sun was supposed to dry it, but instead turned the meat rancid. He hadn't paid enough attention when Mama smoked meat. Maybe he needed to slice the meat thinner or wait for less humid air. He made some spears and practiced on small game but caught more with his hands and a knife. He loved to fish with his bare hands but the cold water allowed little more than a quick hand-bath. His first two attempts to make a travois failed when both fell apart during use, but he got the two long poles to hang together after stealing some rope from a ranch. He came to call this makeshift carryall his home.

He found a creek to follow but when that headed south he left it alone and headed west on a trail that appeared traveled enough to lead to a fort. Boone saw one slave building a fence, sharing hammer and nail with his white boss. He saw another tied to a tree, getting whipped for some infraction. So many different attitudes in this white world.

Boone stole a horse from one farm but didn't get far before the horse bolted back to the barn again. He leaped off and dashed through the wheat field before anyone spotted him. He did his thieving at night but lately, with the light crust of snow, being invisible was as hard as staying fed. One thing for sure. If he ever got that horse ranch that he and Sam dreamed about, he'd need to learn how to handle horses.

His mama never had horses. She said they would just be stolen.

Boone wished every winter day to be a bear. A bear slept with his fat in the winter. Big Grizzly told him once that he would never kill a hibernating bear. When Boone asked why, Grizzly laughed. "It's de challenge, you see? Never eat easy meat. Bad for stomach!"

Boone figured he would make a good bear. His feet felt like oversized paws and he could catch fish as good as any big four-footer. He hadn't found boots to fit his feet but managed to make a near substitute from that buffalo he'd killed. He found a big old coat, way too big, but warm and easier to wear than buffalo skin, which he wrapped around him at night. He felt bad about his thieving and took only what he had to. The coat ... a pair of shoes that he saved for when his fur shoes fell off and change of clothes so he always had something dry to wear. He felt bad thieving from farms, but Sam didn't need to remind him to do what he needed to survive.

"Another reason to be a bear, Sam. They never feel guilty. Or wet." Stealing meant nothing to Sam. Boone wished to be a mind without a body, too.

On this well-traveled road he tried to groom himself up, but his hair was now longer and wild. He wondered if the Indians from the South were forced on this road, the road to Fort Smith, to his grandfather, on their way to Indian Territory. Maybe his grandfather was with the ones who forced them. Boone wondered if he might see one of those who dropped along the way, maybe as a spirit or a lost skeleton.

A couple of times he found an Indian village. He could never be sure who they were, and never stopped to ask. He was afraid to steal from them, afraid they were Kiowa. Once Boone stayed to watch as they formed a snake-like procession and weaved in and out of the lodges, carrying some smoking sticks. Maybe they blessed the lodges to have more babies. Mama told him about a ceremony like that.

Boone had to talk to people now. He had to learn to trust again. He couldn't remember how long since he had seen General Tyler, and perhaps the old man won't believe who he was.

February turned warm and mellow. His 13th birthday came and went without note, and now he had to make himself the man he wanted to be. At the river he slicked his unruly hair back with water and washed his face and hands well.

When he heard the click of the rifle he whirled around, knife out.

"Oh, stay your hand, George. He's just a boy."

"Looks like a mean one, though."

"What do you expect? He's Injun. They all look like that."

46

Three army soldiers sat on horses in front of Boone. Boone wondered if bad things always came in threes. "I'm looking for my grandfather. A general. At the fort."

"Huh?" The blonde-haired one laughed with his companions. "An injun like you?" He peered at Boone so close Boone tasted his last smoke. He ran a hand through Boone's carefully wetted hair and turned his face to see his profile.

"I'll be doggoned. Not Injun, half-breed. Who's your grandfather?"

"General Tyler." Boone stood and wrapped his buffalo skin around him.

"Boy, there ain't no general like that here. You come to the wrong place."

"Can I just talk to someone who might know him?"

*

They brought him to what they called a colonel. He asked about General Tyler and when this puzzled the colonel Boone told him Tyler was his grandfather. The man told him the old general had died, and would never have claimed someone like him as kin anyway.

Boone clammed up after this but no one would let him just walk away. Boone didn't know where to go anymore. They took him to town, set him down in the town square and told him to wait. They set him amidst forlorn black children.

Boone no longer had a path to follow. He found a stick and started to draw into the dirt. The motions were free and natural, as though his grandfather's death and loss of hope broke some part loose inside him.

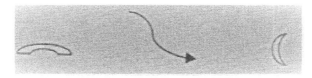

Where he will go now became his mantra and the symbols come out of that mantra. But these symbols answered no questions for him. Going over the mountain and around the trees. No, that wasn't a tree. Over the hill and around a … city. C is for … Chicago.

His mama had a sister in Chicago.

Behind him soldiers stopped all the wagons coming through the fort's small town. Boone didn't commiserate with the black children who shied away from those adults who got near them. He didn't look up as one particular man in one particular wagon stopped and cast a keen eye on him.

Because the symbols had captivated his mind, Boone didn't realize what was happening until the man had a rope around his neck.

CHAPTER NINE
The Captive

Boone paid little attention to the route the man traveled on. At least he was in a wagon this time. As the symbols became a part of him, Sam told him things from his childhood that Boone had forgotten. Like the times his mother spanked him and then sang him to sleep while crying with him. How his mother sometimes disappeared for days and he didn't know where, leaving him to scrounge for food. "Go away, Sam. Mama was good. I don't want to remember the bad." Were the symbols what his life would now be without her? The arrow could be running away, and maybe running around something. Or through something.

Roberts glanced back every now and then at the boy who sat in his wagon bed but Boone paid him no mind. The rope wasn't tight around his neck this time, the wagon clean enough, and a better meal than he could scrounge on his own waited for him ahead somewhere. Boone planned to stay with this new master long enough to figure out where to go next. Hill -- arrow -- to Chicago? Mama's sister. Tyler … Samantha! That was her name! He named his dead twin brother after her.

But whether she would even care about him, Boone didn't have a clue.

*

Bill Roberts took Boone southward to his homestead on the Oklahoma/Arkansas border. Boone worked in the fields all day, weeding and keeping the critters out, with spring coming on strong. He had to treat the field, too, to be ready for spring planting. They had all manner of miscommunication, but Boone found he could read Roberts' body language, like he did his mother's, and learned when to avoid that anger. But not always. Every time Boone did his chores wrong, he got a board lashing. Every time he got up late, Roberts got out the whip.

Then came the day Boone made it clear he didn't understand Roberts' Cajun accent. Roberts told Boone three times where to find the shovel and reached for the board when Boone shrieked out, "I don't know what a shivel is!"

No board lashings after that. Roberts and Boone talked until both knew the other understood. When Roberts saw the symbols Boone had taken to etching on barn walls with charcoal, he asked Boone about them but gave the boy no scolding. Boone had only shrugged, not sure what to tell him.

One day he told Boone he had to ride into town and thought maybe this time he wouldn't need to lock the boy up. Neighbor Dick Samuels rode into the yard as he was ready to leave. Samuels offered to pick up the feed Roberts needed, and they got into another heated debate over the merits and detriments of the Kansas-Nebraska Act.

Boone found it funny that Roberts had his own "Sam" to argue with. He didn't himself have any opinion about President Pierce, but Roberts sure yelled over him "letting the country get ruint." But running a Republican for president was sure to ruin the country even more, Roberts reminded him. Boone remembered his mama complaining about politics -- that the country had been set up by the military under Washington to fail. That the country would have to do something about slavery someday, like Jefferson wanted.

Boone wandered into the open because he wanted to tell them that, and the two men turned to yell at him. Samuels kept his mean look as he rode off.

Roberts grabbed Boone's arm. "You eavesdropping, boy?" He picked up the lashing board that leaned against the porch. "You got no business anywhere but where you're told."

"Huh?"

"Get back to work."

Boone ran off. But he wasn't afraid of Roberts anymore. Roberts just yelled like that to look good to Samuels, like Boone often agreed with what Sam said just to shut him up. *Yes, yes, I'll talk to Kae-gon first, before I kill him.* Boone really planned to sneak up behind him and slit his throat.

One day in the early spring of 1859, after Boone turned 14, Roberts did something Boone didn't expect. He asked Boone to help him break horses. He said he threw his back out that morning, and besides, they had enough hay cut for a while.

Boone stayed on the first horse all of ten seconds.

"Not bad, boy. Get on him again. Show him you're boss." Bill wore a rare smile as he watched Boone mount again.

Though Boone sprained a foot, he got right back on the horse. After the third toss, he figured out how to fall, and didn't go back to the wrong way again.

*

More and more, as Boone proved his worth in every aspect of horse breaking and care, Bill brought Boone inside the house to eat, where they sat silent across from each other. Bill lived without any frills or frivolity, although an occasional bit of lace and one sketched drawing demonstrated there had once been a woman in his life. Most things inside were what he needed to eat, sleep, and work with outside.

One late summer day, Boone didn't go right out after eating. He finished his milk, wiped his mouth, and asked, "Why are you alone?"

Bill sat with his thin-nosed gaze fixed on his half-eaten chocolate cake. He made each forkful of the rare treat a slow and deliberate endeavor. "Why are you?"

"My mama was killed."

"By who?"

"Indians."

Bill sat back, his tongue playing with his teeth. "But you are Indian, too."

"Mama was white. She told me to run."

"Foolish world." Bill picked up his coffee and held the cup to his lips, as though waiting for it to cool. "Indians took her."

He didn't seem willing to talk but Boone plunged ahead. "So you never wanted to get married again? Do you hate all Indians now? Because they killed your wife?"

Bill took a gulp of coffee and held the liquid a moment before swallowing. He followed with a big gulp of milk. "No, I don't hate Indians. I suspect my wife fired the first shot. She didn't want to come west. I was off in the field. Found her in the yard with a hatchet in her chest." He got up and pumped some water, drank noisily and turned back. "Don't you ever drink whiskey! It'll make you crazy!" Bill stabbed at the air around Boone with his words, then leaned back against the cabinet. "Don't like much about this world. But youth has the power to change it where they can." Bill waited but Boone stared at the floor. "Well, we all have, I reckon. I've been watching you close. You got some kind of gift, some kind of power. Something special thing inside you."

"I don't got anything special." Boone didn't want to tell him about how Sam could see things coming before Boone. "But I know I gotta kill him."

"Who, your father? He rape your mama?"

"No! They loved each other."

"That should make you feel kindly toward him."

Boone squeezed his hands tight. "Before I was born there was war and she left him. My father killed her, because she wouldn't give me to him."

This hit Bill Roberts like a fist. "You saw him do this? You can't be mistaken?"

Boone could barely breathe. "I didn't see, but I know."

"I thought I knew, too. But I only saw her dead. Would your mother approve of your plan? To kill him? Maybe she'd rather you live with him."

Boone focused on unclenching his fists. "She made me promise to stay white."

"Keeping a promise to the dead who can't change their mind." Bill stood and pumped water into the bowl for the day's dirty dishes, and added some hot from the pot always simmering on the stove. He started washing, and Boone joined him to dry. "Why don't you use the spare room? To sleep at night, I mean."

"Why?"

"To keep you safe. Just in case." Bill turned back to the boy who stood with the cleaned plate dripping soap on the floor. "I can help you and you can help me." He tilted his head back, eyes closed. "I mean, if I help you, that helps me."

Boone dried the dish he held. "Mama wanted me white. I want what she wants."

Bill grinned. "I saw your carvings in my barn posts."

Boone felt his face go red. "I ran out of charcoal."

"Are they yours or imitative?"

"Imitative?"

"I've been to New Mexico and I've seen what many haven't. Ancient drawings. Studied 'em for a while. Think I can help you interpret them, if you want." Boone's puzzled look made Bill chuckle. "Rock art, boy. Etches on rock by ancient people. Maybe of dreams or--."

"Yes! I got mine in a dream." As though the river burst through thawed ice Boone told Bill everything -- the dream, the way he felt he had to draw, the soldiers, why he ran from Big Grizzly, why he felt so sure he needed to kill his father, about his grandfather's massacre of Kiowa to get his mama back.

Bill cleaned his face with his handkerchief during Boone's tales, several times. He had to clear his throat when Boone was done before he could talk again. He told Boone about the life he planned with Laura, how she had been pregnant and lost the baby both times. And how he's lived alone since her death because he can't bear being attached anymore. "Boone, you might not understand this, but you got too much Indian in you to ever be white."

"Only half."

"But it's the half most white folks will see. I do believe there's a special place in this world for people like you." Bill got up and walked to the window to look out. He gripped the window frame hard and sighed. He turned back. "Can you stay with me, Boone? Stay and be my son?"

"You want a son who wants to kill his father?"

Bill looked out the window again. "Thy mother's son! Like enough, and thy father's shadow." He continued reciting until he realized that Boone was reciting with him. He stopped and let Boone finish the quote alone …

"So the son of the female is the shadow of the male. It is often so indeed, but much of the father's substance." Boone looked down, suddenly shy.

Bill grinned. "You are a learn'ed boy!"

"We didn't like Henry IV much but Mama quoted that one part often." *Even if you want to stay here, you can't.* "Do you know what my symbols mean? I can't figure them out."

Bill got a piece of aged paper and a pencil. "Draw it." Boone did. "Okay, look at this.

Could be a frown. Or a rainbow. Too simple, though. Symbols are never that simple. Look at the last one.

Do you think that's supposed to be a moon?"

"Yeah, I thought that, too. Or mom's sister."

Bill studied him a moment. "Did you come up with anything for this first one?"

"I thought of a sunset. I always liked 'em."

"Sunset." Bill nodded. "Good symbolism, sun falls below the horizon with the radiance of color above. How about this, when you add this arrow -- moon comes out after sunset."

"So the arrow means comes out?"

"Well, arrows are for shooting. They come out of a bow. Sunset shoots the moon?"

"No. They're not violent."

"Okay. Look at the way the arrow is positioned. What if we move it, like so? Does this make a difference?" He drew the arrow with straight edges instead of the curvy one.

54

"Yes!" Boone erased the bad arrow and drew the right one with a sigh.

"Okay." Bill stared until his eyebrow went up. "Around. Or under. As in shooting an arrow to go around a target. Under. Sunset goes under the moon."

Boone closed his eyes. "Boone goes under ground. Into the underworld." He saw himself swim and when he looked up, saw whites attack his father's village. Somewhere in the background he heard a scream.

"And you're the sunset that struggles to come out from behind the moon again. Maybe the moon is symbol for your mother?"

Boone almost said no, but instead he shrugged. "Maybe."

*

Boone hid in the hay when the riders came into the yard. He feared Bill could make some foolish mistake and get himself killed by those Kiowa. Boone didn't look to see if his father was there. He listened but was unable to hear the quiet talk.

Boone wished he would have told Bill right off that he would stay on and wondered if Bill would offer again. He liked his new spare room, where Bill made horse blankets. His mama tried to work one of those looms but she always got frustrated. A small cot placed in the corner with a single blanket and something like a pillow waited for him. But that pillow turned out to be his sack, with his hat, and everything he had while on the run, even his buffalo skin that had covered his mama after she died, and the knives the soldiers took from him. Those soldiers weren't all bad -- they made sure his new owner got his belongings.

Shouts got loud and angry and Boone's heart nearly leaped through his mouth. He wanted to go out there but heard Bill shout that they had no right here and he will shoot the first man who stepped off his horse. The enormous silence that followed cut through Boone's mind like a big ball of fire.

Finally the horses rode off. Boone heard footsteps but didn't move. "You okay, boy?"

Boone crawled out, ignorant of the hay clinging to him. "I was afraid for you."

"I was too, kinda." Bill chuckled and helped Boone up. "Come on, let's go us get some lunch. I got me an appetite."

They ate the bread and gravy with onion, and Bill spoke occasionally of a favorite horse's training. After they were done, he asked Boone about his schooling, and they laughed as they traded more lines from the immortal bard. "You know, I got a copy of Shakespeare plays and I would be honored to give it to you. As a gift. For all your hard work."

Boone's face lit up. All he could do was nod.

Bill leaned back and popped a chaw in his mouth as he changed the mood of the conversation. "They are either your family, or enemies of your family."

Boone hesitated. "Both."

"They didn't ask for you direct. Just wanted to know if I'd seen any of their people."

"I would kill them before I would go with them."

"Oh lad, you are too young to carry hate." Bill studied a cobweb on the ceiling. "My momma died when I was born. My father was too young to care for me, so he gave me to her parents. I never learned to love them, and then they died. I was cut loose early, too, and the bad things … well, I don't think about them. Since Laura died, you're the first one who helped me see the good in life again. The offer still stands, Boone."

"I was happy ... with my mama." His voice trembled. *It's too late for tears.* "All she did was love him."

"I suspect she feared him, too."

Boone fled the house. He threw himself into his old hay bed in the barn, with his mother's voice in his head telling him to run, that he wasn't old enough to be a man. Bill was right. She feared that he would take her son, but she feared him for even more reasons than that. She feared love.

In the back of his tear-swollen mind, Sam told him only truth. *Love made her insane. If only she had told you my name. My Indian name. I was supposed to go with father, but then I died.*

CHAPTER TEN
The Horse Breaker

At Sam's urging to find his father, Boone realized he had to leave. He found Bill wrestling with weeds in the garden where they'd just planted the early corn. They were both startled -- when Bill stood next to him, at how tall Boone had become.

Bill listened to what Boone had to say. "Yup. I understand. I won't try and stop you. Come here." Bill gave him possession of a small mare Boone called Robbo, as pay for his service, along with, as he promised, a book of Shakespeare plays and sonnets. "When you gonna leave?"

"Want to make sure all the crops is planted. Boss."

Bill gave Boone a wry and teasing slug on the arm and they hugged. But Boone felt something missing, and he knew Bill felt it, too.

Not many mornings later, Boone led his horse out of the barn before the sun rose. He said quick prayers to the east and the rising sun, and slipped the bridle on but not a saddle, preferring to ride the horse bareback. Boone felt like he had control of his life now. He earned his freedom this time. He was a horse breaker.

He pulled the horse up short outside the barn, closed his eyes and felt the cool morning air on his face. He remembered the day he hid in the barn and let Bill confront the Indians alone. He concentrated until he sensed the direction they headed when they rode off -- west and south. He knew some of that territory, often rode the area when he wasn't hard at work. Flat and open for a while, but shortly to begin a slow climb up into the mountains, into the tall world of pine and rock bigger than Boone's imagination. Land had been hilly in Kansas where he lived with his mother but nothing like what faced him if he went to up into those high hills of western Kansas Territory. He felt if he were to keep riding west, he would reach the very top of the world, where all of life's answers might be found. Perhaps he would even find his mother again, if he had the courage to look for her. Or even the courage to listen.

He looked back at the house. Bill was always up by this time, but they both knew that parting can be such sweet sorrow. Boone lifted his hand at the house and rode off. He could always return someday, like the lost Dane of his dreams.

Boone felt like a very old 14.

He followed the river until he reached a spot where they could cross safely. But Robbo would not take the river. He leaned over and patted her neck. "Robbo, without you I cannot go anywhere. This is the shallow bank, you may have to swim but only a little. I will get off in the deep part and help you." He nudged her again, and she neighed with a shake of her head.

Boone sighed and alighted. He patted her nose, and with her reins in his hands walked into the river. The water was cold. He pulled her, and after she got a couple of hooves wet, she followed him. He patted her nose again and when they reached the deep part, they swam together to the other side.

If he made good time he would get to a camping spot just as the half-moon lost its light for the night. He hurried Robbo on, at times getting her into a gallop. She was a good horse, but someday, he would have better. He would have the best.

He wondered how quiet an Indian would be as his throat was being slit.

*

Another dream-filled night bothered him. His mama didn't want him anymore. She kept giving him away but he kept coming back. One time she took him deep into the woods and tied him to a tree, and he turned into a skeleton. He woke in a sweat to Sam's laughter.

Riding on after a light meal on Bill's supplies, Boone stopped, sensing voices ahead, more than the murmur of trees. He backed Robbo up, far enough that he did not hear them, and tied the horse. He didn't want them to hear the sudden whinny Robbo made when left behind.

He snuck sideways to their camp, making no sticks crack under his feet, no leaves rustle. He hid behind large trees and paused often to hold his breath. Could his father have stayed in the area all this time, waiting? Or was he following since Lynelle died?

The Kiowa -- or Comanche or Ute, he wasn't sure -- had settled into a clearing surrounded by cracked dry rock and pine. The pine grew thick, squeezing the life out of immature trees. But the smell was of warmth and sweet haven. Boone studied the five men, his first real chance to see them. At first glance the five men looked alike, with coats and leggings of buffalo, and moccasins but without any ceremonial ornaments. They ate strips of dried meat, although one had caught a raccoon he gutted. Boone winced and looked away. He'd never eat a raccoon.

The long flaps of their moccasins had been individually embellished and Boone saw symbols in the unique bead work. He supposed all Indians had special symbols, but since he was supposed to be white, couldn't figure out why he got symbols. Maybe they belonged to Sam. Two of the men were tall and thin, and one of them could be his father. One was small but thick with flopping muscle, at least where Boone could see muscle because they had their night coats on. And the other two were what Boone called average. They all had long hair, several with hair braids, some with feathers woven in.

Doesn't he look nice? Sam whispered when Boone started at the tallest one.

"Not if he's the one who killed Mama."

One fellow who had fur around his braids made some adjustments to the ropes of the travois. Another had what looked like ground beans that he tended. Boone listened but knew few Indian words. One talked loudly and gestured as the others laughed or grunted while otherwise eating. One remained quiet as he studied and contemplated his surroundings, as though not sure they were safe. A third, full of repetitive gestures as he laughed, ate quicker than the rest, and the fourth, with a kind and generous face, seemed in agreement with everyone's words.

The fifth one held Boone's attention. He was the tallest, with a large scar on his right arm, as though a bear had taken a chunk out of him. His hair was tied back, with feathers. He too enjoyed the stories, though not quite as openly as the rest. At times he settled deep in thought.

Boone sank back to the ground to the distant sounds of their gaiety. Did that pleasant looking fellow kill his mother? Had she taken that knife swipe at him? He crept to his horse and rode off, away from a man who could be Kae-gon. He had to be sure before he acted, sure that killing his father was right, and sure that his mother would not ask him to do what shouldn't be done. Perhaps he was Hamlet, after all.

Boone felt his mama may have gone insane after leaving his father. But that didn't change how he felt seeing her dead body. He sat on a rock far from those gathered at the campfire and with his knife cut his hair short again before riding on. As soon as he knew he had the right man, Boone would remember his mama's dead face and kill him.

"Shut up, Sam."

CHAPTER ELEVEN
The Vaqueros

Oklahoma, Spring 1860

When Boone crossed back into Indian Territory he saw more of those natives that were called "civilized" but they ignored him. He was taller now, with more muscle. With Bill's letter of recommendation, he picked up field jobs along the way, spending most of the winter in one barn or another, pitching hay to animals. He turned 15 alone and without ceremony, but no longer went hungry for days at a time.

Aunt Samantha and Illinois were the next part of Boone's plan -- "shooting around the moon," like Bill said. But first he wanted to see if he could find Mama's grave, and see what was left of the house. Maybe find her favorite silver spoon. He owed Bill a lot -- clothes that made travel easier, bedroll for sleeping, and this horse. Boone was too big to cocoon in the buffalo skin but he didn't mind the extra cover on cold nights and wrapped the bedroll around it.

He found Sam's voice welcome when he was lonely. Sam reminded him of his Kiowa half, that two people had created him with love. Sam found memories of times when she went crazy because Boone was born a boy, stricken with grief because her second son didn't survive. Kae-Gon could have been happy with one.

Sometimes when Boone awakened from a nightmare, Mama punished him for frightening her. If he asked for seconds of supper she made him go the whole next day without food to curb his "greed." He didn't want these memories, but Sam was part of his growing need to remember his past so he could face his future, and the need to kill his father.

And oh! How his butt got sore from sitting on a horse all day -- worse even than breaking horses because that hurt only a few minutes after the few seconds of being tossed about. But after a week of steady riding he couldn't sleep at night until after he turned every which way on hard ground to find a comfort zone.

How close Illinois now? Sam asked him as if a litany of countless sheep at night. Boone said that Illinois was as far away as ever because they were going to Kansas first. He wondered if these two halves of him made him run by staying in the same place.

He got hired but never for long. As soon as the crops were processed, or the water buckets carried, or the old crops were removed or wood chopped, they'd cut him loose with food or money or a little of both. He heard one tell his wife that he didn't want the Injun kid's relatives to come looking. Another told him straight out that he didn't like Boone's looks but he needed the water carried and his back was sore. Most never acknowledged his white upbringing, and gave him dumb looks when he quoted Shakespeare.

Along the way Boone tried to sort out why he felt Bill's interpretation of his symbols was wrong. Maybe the crescent wasn't a moon but only looked like a moon. Not a sunset but a sunrise. He couldn't see the first symbol as anything but a sun now. Something going into or coming out of hiding. The thought that the symbols were evil or violent didn't feel right, either. Although Mama did say that the good and evil ways of the Kiowa world weren't the same as in the Christian world. Thunderstorms weren't evil but you had to pray so that their lightning won't start a fire. Nature was never evil but could treat people badly.

Often while riding a boring trail he pulled out the book Bill gave him and read aloud. His mama used to say that the sound of his voice was something normal in an insane world. One Shakespeare quote puzzled him: "Thyself and thy belongings are not thine own so proper as to waste thyself upon thy virtues, they on thee. Heaven doth with us as we with torches do." Mama told him doth meant does. So heaven treats us as property as we treat property? Mama never talked to him much about heaven, and he'd only seen the inside of a church once that he remembered.

But what are virtues? Did this mean our soul? Was that the torch? Or was the torch just our property that gets taken away or used up? Mama said figuring out the words was part of what made Shakespeare fun.

Boone didn't keep track of his long days anymore. Spring was coming again. The winds were still cold at night but the snow melted in places during the day. He no longer had to wrap his buffalo skin around him to sleep at night in the warming winds. Still not as bad here as back in Chicago, his mama used to tell him, where snow drifts could get up to a foot deep because of the harsh beauty of all those lakes. Here, snow was a rare treat except in these higher elevations.

What would Samantha think if he just showed up there? He didn't look much like his mama. He thought to send her a letter when he got to Kansas.

*

Men who looked like Mexicans, wearing big hats, were on the trail ahead. Vaqueros. Since the Mexican War many had become U.S. citizens, while others continued to fight that lost cause. Some raised cattle and sold their longhorn steer wherever they found people hungry enough to pay a high enough price. They traded with whites and with Indians and went back and forth across the border with ease not afforded to whites.

Boone watched this herd of about sixty cows and three riders approach. One seemed to be pure Mexican -- the other two wore big hats but were a mix of some blood, like him. He waved at one and they welcomed him over. He didn't see any sourness in their faces and hoped these men weren't the fighting kind.

Boone let the Mexican speak first and shook his head as the man rattled off a line of Spanish. "Ah, you don't speak the language of former owners of your land?"

One of the half breeds rode closer. "Oh no, maybe you Indian, former owner of former owner's land." He spoke in clear direct English and then spit on the ground in front of Boone.

Boone ignored the gesture. "I wonder if you need help."

"Help? With these beasts?" The man Boone came to know as Raoul chewed and spit. "Hey Victor!" He called to one of the men and rattled off some more Spanish.

Victor rode over to Boone and handed him the reins of four unsaddled horses. The two men laughed as Victor slapped the rear of one of them and the four horses

64

bumped each other, causing them to run -- headed, Boone figured as he ran with them, for the creek and green grass. Boone didn't panic but veered them to a stopping ground and sure enough, and without any of the reins tangled, they stopped and began to graze. This deftness was more due to their experience on rein, but a lesser man might have panicked.

Boone looked back at the herd to see the men moving on and caught the glimpse of a few frowns thrown at him that he didn't give them a show. Victor breathed dust at the tail end and Raoul waved at Boone to catch up with those animals.

Boone thought of himself as a man now.

*

Raoul said that there was little business in driving cows from place to place, but soon there would be. Whites were too foolish or stubborn to eat buffalo, calling it "wild Indian food." How else to get beef from settlement to settlement other than hoofing them? Boone didn't care about the cattle but he did about the horses -- spares they needed to be fresh and ready "in case."

Boone inquired "in case what" at the campfire one night.

Victor guffawed and the three others joined in. "You'll find out!"

But Boone didn't, and when the drive ended at Fort Smith they gave him some meager pay for a job he would have done just for chow. They said he could join them again if he was at loose ends. But Boone decided on a plan. He was going to rebuild Mama's house just the way it was and find himself a girl to do the sewing on his patches and the cooking and whatever else a girl did.

They chuckled at his youthful plan as they rode off.

Boone was on the road to Fort Leavenworth, well-traveled, but finding his mama's grave could be a problem. He had one hand on Robbo's reins and the other on the reins of his pay -- a greener stallion one of the vaqueros had caught. He hoped the additional pay of $5 in gold they gave him would tide him over until he found the house. For now, he would go to where he'd been schooled. Boone was last at Leavenworth in October of 1855. Mr. Collins had him tutor the other children to read. He wondered if old Collie still had that awful habit of holding his nose around the students.

Boone rode over to the part of town where the school was and saw a woman, face hidden by a hat, wearing a heavy black shawl and a gray dress. She had her grip on the arm of a boy who appeared to be crying. She shook him and, though Boone couldn't hear, he thought her words were harsh. He rode in their direction, leaped off and tied his horses up.

"He said you don't pay attention. He says you don't mind. Do you want me to get out the switch again? Is that what you want?"

Boone remembered a boy he tutored made fearful by constant scolding. "He'd listen better if you don't yell."

Startled, the woman looked at Boone. The kid broke away and ran. "I beg your…." Her eyes narrowed at him and she raised her voice. "You filthy Indian, get away from me and mine. Don't you come near me, you hear?!"

Three men ran out of the nearby mercantile as Boone turned to walk away.

"And don't you turn your back on me, neither."

"Mrs. Johansen, are you all right?" One man held her up as though to steady her but she wasn't the slightest bit faint.

The second grabbed Boone's arm. "You a stranger here?" This man was some sort of lawman. "What's your name?"

"Boone Tyler. My mother was Lynelle and I studied with Mr. Collins."

"Never heard of you. We got some Comanches giving us trouble, you Comanche?"

"Whoa, Neil, easy. I know this kid."

Neil the lawman shook Boone, but then turned him over to the third man.

"Knew his ma once. That don't give him no right to upset our lady citizens, though. Why don't you apologize to her, Boone?"

"A mama is supposed to listen, that's all." He turned to walk away.

Neil laid a fist alongside Boone's head and knocked him to the ground. Boone bit at the dust in his mouth but ignored the pain as he leaped on Neil and pushed him off the walk into the street. The man struggled on his back but made no effort to keep the fight going. The third man grabbed Boone's hands to stop his punches and pulled him away, with Mrs. Johansen looking appropriately appalled behind them.

"Boone, I suggest you get out of town before you cause any further trouble."

Boone jerked his arm away and reached for his horses. Several men surrounded him, some obviously drunk.

"You commit a crime in this town, you forfeit your horses."

"What crime?"

"Two people will attest to be aggravated."

"Maybe they had it coming."

"Boone Tyler!"

Boone looked toward the familiar voice. Old Collie himself.

"Boone, where've you been? I heard about your ma. Tried to find you."

Boone remembered the last time he saw the old man. Collie had grabbed for his mama like she was a piece of meat, making her struggle. He leaped on Robbo, ripped the reins away and rode off, before any of them moved. He left the greener horse behind for their due.

*

Boone rode hard out of Leavenworth, headed east but didn't find Mama's grave, which could have been north for all he knew. He didn't get to send Samantha that letter, and couldn't figure out where to go now, so he turned hard south, toward Wichita.

One morning he woke to find Robbo gone. Just like that, vanished without a track. Boone had become a pretty good tracker, too, but this was a rocky area and Robbo didn't have shoes to nick the stone up. Boone followed the rock until he nearly collapsed from dehydration. He had to turn off the trail and head for the closest sign of vegetation.

His pockets held all he had left of civilization and so he returned to that early life of struggle, food from hand to mouth, stealing all he could to get by. He missed his daily dose of old English from Roberts' book. He tried to remember lines when he became desperate to feel human. *Wilt thou be gone? It is not yet near dawn.* But as the weather warmed Sam took over, making Boone look and feel savage.

*

Amidst the rocky buttes and caprock upheavals sat Simple the fur trader with cooked armadillo meat wafting on the breeze. Boone thought the food he smelled belong to Comanche until he saw, from where he sat high above the camp, the unmistakable markings of his horse in a fur trader's camp. In these steep inclines getting to the smell without being heard was the challenge, where the Red River cut deep canyons with its four forks. As he crept close, muscles trembling from the descent of rock walls, Boone listened to the noise of this trader who had the nerve to steal his horse, yet continue to trap in the area.

"Well, Gendear, unless we want to create a market for armadillo hides, I'd say our trapping days are done. What say Gendear and Simple head to Dakota Territory and wrangle us some buffalo hides? I have a hankering to see if Miss Jenny would still look on Simple Larson favorable-like." He heard a tree branch crack behind him and felt for his knife at his side as he checked the grilled state of his dinner. Beside him sat large bottle and a small one. "Sounds like we're getting company."

He heard nothing further and reached for his larger bottle. From his sack he pulled out some bread and wild onion and used his knife to carve both into edible slivers. As he reached over to slice off a hunk of blackened meat after an ample drink from his bottle, an arm went around his neck with a knife to his throat.

"You live? Or you die?"

Simple slipped his knife back to his side as he considered the voice belonging to a young fellow. He turned his head slightly and saw the scrawny Indian boy, long-haired and wild-eyed with the trace of a ragged beard. "What you want to let me live?"

"Just get up and walk. Take nothing."

"All right. Okay." Simple felt the boy's arm loosen and started to get to his knees. He lashed out with his left hand, the one with the knife, to catch the boy in the face, and he would have succeeded, too, had his knife still been in his hand.

Boone had taken the knife and slashed Simple's throat.

As he lay dying the boy grabbed his bread, onion and meat and devoured. Boone ate long after the man's eyes had gone blank and then he grabbed the man's smaller bottle for a long drink. His eyes widened as his throat began to burn and his eyes watered. He threw the bottle to the ground as he staggered away from the dead man, coughing and stumbling. He grabbed for the reins of the horse but instead fell to the ground as the world spun and turned under him, and, as Robbo nuzzled his face, he passed out.

The sun burned his eyelids when Boone finally awoke to find the horse still next to him, the dead man still dead. His head hurt and gut rumbled in wretched need of something Boone could not name. He crept over to the big jug, eyeing the dead man's stare. Boone kicked the smaller bottle around until convinced its contents were empty. He tasted the liquid in the bigger jug with his tongue and took a cautious sip before gulping.

He cupped his hands and fed some water to the horse. "Glad to see me, Robbo?" He gathered all the goods he could use and found a few of his own, including his Shakespeare, its pages now ripped and dirty in spots. He packed up and rode off, in search of his lost humanity.

CHAPTER TWELVE
The Gold Piece

Texas Summer, 1860

In the small shed her family used as hay storage for their one burro, Emily Arendt waited for her new lover. Ever since her father gave up gold panning, her whole family had gone out in many southerly directions every day for work or food or both. But she was considered useless for working.

They would have moved on but her father was loaded with German stubbornness, and they had established friendships with the local tribes, the same ones that kept most other settlers out of the northwestern part of Texas. Emily's mother was a feisty one and relished the challenges of the frontier, throwing herself bodily in front of potential danger without a moment's hesitation. The first time Indians arrived at their homestead Emily thought her pa was gonna be shot and watched as her ma protected him with her body. Pa had collapsed to his knees and pleaded for their lives as the best friends the Indians got. But he spoke in German. They understood Ma's offer of food, and rode off again, laughing.

Her family gave them supplies even to the last in their cupboard. But the Comanche always brought back twofold. They seemed to know when to show up with buffalo meat. Sometimes they came just to watch Emily walk, which made her feel special.

Emily asked her father why he didn't have the normal settler's fear of Indians. He said that every German school boy learned about their Germanic tribal past and could understand the native's desire to keep their old ways in their own country. Pa also told her these natives were also too busy fighting the Tejannas to bother with a few settlers who treated them fairly.

Because of her deformity, all Emily could do was work the garden. But she had dreams of a family of her own someday. So on that particular day she waited in the shed, half dressed, for her suitor to arrive. She knew the boy should ask her parents' permission, but they were in America now, and besides, her father once said there wasn't anyone out here good enough for his daughter. She never asked to be born deformed but the part that made her a woman still worked. Anyway, as her mom liked to say, we deal with what we're given. There's no running away -- not that Emily could run anyway.

She needed to help the family, and this was the best idea she had. Pa didn't deserve his bad luck -- the cattle fever, the traces of gold that disappeared and left him back tired and feverish for money, and just this last summer her ma's garden got eaten up by grasshoppers. Her younger brother Billy was rented out to every rancher in 100 miles so she never saw him anymore. And Stewart lit out for back east long ago. Or somewhere. Every so often he sent money to keep his piece of the homestead.

So hers was just a useless mouth to feed.

But Texas was short of girl folk to marry, too, so even *she* should have some luck finding a fellow. She didn't think she was that bad to look at, otherwise. A month before she found one young fellow adrift in this godforsaken territory that she might consider acceptable to marry. When he asked her if she could be deemed marriageable she said, "Try me."

The door opened and a crack of light fell on her lightly clad and bulky form. The tousled red-head poked his face in. "You in here?"

"Can't you see me?" She swallowed her sudden fear down hard.

"You ahhhh … you expecting me, right?"

"Maybe. Maybe not."

"Oh. Ha!" He stepped in and closed the door but paused to allow his eyes to adjust to the small pinholes of light. "I know a tease when I hear one."

"Do you?"

His pause indicated confusion. He stared at her and looked around for a place to sit as he stepped closer. "Been wanting to get to know ya."

"I know."

"Since you waved at me the other day. Where you from?"

"Colorado. Pa heard of some gold there."

"Not Californee?"

"Never made it that far."

"Before then?"

"Illinois."

"Huh. Lincoln' party's gonna be trouble, you know."

"Sure. My Pa's a Democrat."

"Good. Can't be arguing politics these days without some blood being shed."

"I know. We got out of Kansas right quick. At least here people know where they stand."

"Yeah, hiding from Indians." He sat down beside her and put a warm hand on her knee. "How come you walk funny?"

"Ma says my hip broke when I was born. One leg didn't grow right. Foot neither."

"You handle yourself okay, though, I seen ya."

"I get around."

"I like that." He leaned over and kissed her, pushing Emily back with the force of his eagerness. Their legs got tangled as he tried to kiss her again but in the darkened shed kept missing. He grabbed a breast too hard because he started to tip over and Emily yelled out before she could stop herself.

The shed door opened. Pa stood there, with a young fellow behind him. "Emily, what's this?"

She sat up and brushed hay out of her hair. "Just helping you out, Pa."

"How? By tangling with this loco?" Pa grabbed the boy's shirt and flung him out of the shed. He pointed at her. "We'll talk on this in a minute." He turned to give further eviction notice to the youth who had already taken the hint.

Emily saw the young man, not much more than a boy, who'd come with Pa. He gave her such an intense, penetrating stare, he seemed to peer into her soul. She felt what had been impossible to feel a moment ago. Warmth rushed through her veins as she fought the desire to have every inch of him in her arms. He looked rough and wild but she noticed a pureness to his eyes that attracted her. He carried a poor-looking satchel made of buffalo skin but looked like he owned the world.

"Boone." He nodded at her.

"Emily. You Indian?" She shifted into sunlight.

Boone turned and disappeared. Emily wanted to clamber after him but she had to put her dress back on first.

*

Boone noticed a clean austerity to the Prussian family's cabin. Most cabins he had seen had bare floors and walls, but the wood floor had a big clean rag carpet, and both windows had patches of white lace curtain. He guessed they came from the East and brought a wealth of goods that got eaten by gradual poverty. Henery told him on the ride back that he didn't have a lot of farming experience, and that he learned how to work in this western country the hard way. The one room shack had a table and wood cook stove that made the ceiling grimy with smoke, with hay-filled blankets pushed tight against the wall so they had room to move about. Boone guessed they didn't spend much time here except on bad weather days. Reminded him of home. Crates empty of supplies and a barrel half-filled with water sat in the other corner. Under the lace curtains they had some kind of black fabric that shivered in the wind. A long mountain rifle and powder horns hung on rafters and makeshift shelving kept track of their kettles and dry goods.

Henery filled the remainder of the room with exuberance as he introduced Boone to his wife and daughter, her indiscretion forgotten for the moment. His wife, neither big nor small, seemed hidden by her lack of forcefulness. Boone liked her instantly. Margo accepted her lot and the small smile that sat on her face made her look young, regardless of the hard life she endured.

Boone had helped Emily into the house, at first dismayed at her limp, but then he relaxed into her ease of acceptance. He remained at her side, as though to protect her from her father's wrath. He wondered if she was a whore, the way she threw herself at that young fellow. Bill Roberts had pointed whores out in town once, and said they lived to attract men into their beds.

Henery then got wound up to tell the story of how they met, but Boone figured that once he finished he would notice Boone's half-breed blood and boot him all the way to Mexico. Until then, Boone enjoyed having Emily beside him.

"So I was coming … riding the burro, back to home and I could barely keep my head up because I was so down, all the bad things weighing on my mind and no … and that's when I saw it, like a gift from God!"

Emily looked at her father in surprise.

"Yes, there in the river!" Pa danced around the room, making them duck his flailing arms. Each time he got near the water barrel he scooped up another ladle. He drank and kept talking so they also ducked sprays of water. "Did I tell you I followed the Salt Fork? Yes!"

Margo ducked outside and came back in with a small towel that she tossed over his shoulder the first chance she got. Boone figured she didn't know as much English as her husband, because she only spoke foreign words the few times she talked. His mama said once that it's only when we need to learn that we learn.

"There it was, gold! Glittering in the water, biggest chunk I ever saw. Now Salt Fork runs over some pretty fast and rocky ground, but at this point the land swells up, making it …" he motioned with his fingers for words he didn't know, "so I could see it. And I figured to be careful and I was but when I picked it up. Oh Lordy, gold! I looked around to make sure there weren't no more and POW! I slipped in the river and … well, the rock flew out of my hand and into deeper waters. Gone." He smacked his mouth as he feigned the utter disappointment he felt and paused for another quick gulp.

"But you didn't give up, did you, Pa?" Emily winked at Boone.

"No! I found my landmark by looking at … along the riverbank. Got my rope from the burro and found a big tree. Tied the rope to the tree, and the other half to my waist."

Boone glanced at Margo. She looked ill, but enthralled.

"I jumped … no, I walked carefully into the water, but several times I slipped and fell under. I got to my feet, but then I couldn't … the river was deeper than me!" His exuberance made everyone smile.

"He was in over his head when I found him," said Boone on cue.

"I tried to reach down, several times, but could not find the bottom."

"The rope started to loosen. So I tied it again."

Henery laughed. "I came to the surface, coughing, saw him, yelled he should help!"

"I started to pull on the rope but he fought me."

"That was the wrong kind of help. Find the gold!"

"I see he would not come out. So I--."

"He dove into the water. Swims like a turtle, this one!"

"He comes back into the water, still tied to the rope, to help me. We get tangled up!"

"We almost drowned together." Henery could not stop laughing.

Emily and her ma watched the two of them, puzzled, not getting the humor of the situation. Boone reached into the knapsack that had been tossed careless onto one of the blankets. He pulled out a rock. "I can hold my breath a long time."

"Gold!"

Ma caught her breath, hand to throat, and Emily laughed as loud and exuberant as her pa. She threw her arms around Boone and kissed him.

They stared at each other.

What would she do if she knew you were only 15? A mature 15, Boone reminded Sam.

Pa placed the gold reverently on the table. "Now, Emily, let's talk about you."

CHAPTER THIRTEEN
The Remuda Guard

Boone rode drag behind a hundred stomping steer, breathing their dust. He took the job because he needed the money. He squinted at the setting sun as he pulled his bandanna up over his mouth and nose. Moving cattle wasn't exactly a business -- they didn't get far from Texas into Kansas before they found a settlement or a volunteer army hungry for beef.

He felt lucky to find these vaqueros again, because with the money he made on this drive he planned to ask Emily to marry him. In the month since he'd signed on to be their ranch hand to help them break wild horses to sell, they'd become inseparable.

Her pa gave Boone permission to court her not long after they met, and they didn't even ask his age. All he knew of Emily's age was that she was old enough to know her own mind. Emily told Boone about Pa's special liking for Indians. Pa wanted to know all about Boone's people, so Boone told him all he could but left out the part about his mama being killed by a Kiowa. He was sure Pa wouldn't understand.

He also did odd jobs anywhere he could to help their household income and slept in the barn at night. Boone was getting up his courage to be honest about his parents when, just before he turned 16, someone shot Pa in cowardly fashion off his horse. Boone figured someone wanted that gold rock back. He had tried to warn Pa that someone must have lost it, but Pa always laughed, saying something about "finders owners," and, without fear, told his story to everyone who would listen.

There had been odd things about Pa getting shot off his horse. His jacket had been gone through but nothing taken. Whoever killed Pa felt nothing could be gained and moved on, as far as they could tell. Ma became sadder and lonelier, though, and finally agreed to go back East. Emily's brother Billy rode with Ma as far as Cincinnati, while Emily's older brother Stewart could not be found, even for the funeral.

After Ma and Billy left, Emily sometimes stayed with friends when he went off on the job, rather than being left alone. But she felt her garden needed proper care daily and professed to having no fear of living alone.

She was his midsummer night's dream and he lived every day in fear of losing her.

Robbo reared as one Longhorn steer tossed its head but Boone held on. With eyes still squinted he spurred his horse a little distance back with the remuda, which followed on a rope string system he devised after a stampede. One of his horses had gotten mangled in the ropes they provided and he didn't want to see that happen again.

The dust was thicker in dry grass. Weeks of no rain sent dust swirling as the herd's pace quickened. Boone had studied buffalo grass, where even during drought the ground held together. He figured the grass and buffalo lived so long together that they adapted to each other. He spent lots of time thinking, and kept Sam at bay. Sam appeared most often when Boone was having his murderous thoughts about his father.

Raoul risked their hides to get in two extra miles before nightfall. The delay crossing a swollen river made Raoul even more determined. Steers were temperamental, unused to moving hard, and neared an anxious pace.

Boone wondered over his boss's ability. He seemed drunk too often so he decided this was his last drive. He was gonna take a wife and start his own business breaking and selling horses. He needed to stay closer to her now, with all the raiding and such -- maybe by Indians made anxious north of them but maybe not. There was also all that conjuring about secession with the coming election that had Boone worried.

The cows bleated and the dust was unrelenting -- in his eyes, his nose and mouth even through the bandanna, and worked into his chest until he felt he was drowning … this time feeling he'd never reach that gold. *Pa drifted out of reach and Emily married some red-haired fellow, while he sunk to the bottom of the river….*

"Half-breed! Pick your head up out of the saddle! You're losing two of 'em to the south!"

Boone spurred his horse after the strays, his remuda trailing behind him. He pulled double duty because he was young. Or Indian. Or both. He called these vaqueros names, too. Blackie, who always wore black, and another he called Blue for his disposition. That one was Lacker for the way he sat in the saddle as he rode, and Runt, for Raoul's size and disposition. He couldn't complain about "half-breed," because that's what he was. Except he wasn't an animal bred for pleasure.

He rode hard to push the strays back into line, and at first thought maybe he had pushed too hard. For whatever cause or reason, the cattle began to run.

"Stampede!"

Through thickness of dust and roaring thunder Boone spurred Robbo on, though he couldn't see and he coughed out the ache in his throat. He pulled his bandanna up and his hat flew off. Too many lost beeves meant he might not earn enough this drive. He would fight 100 steers to keep that from happening. Boone ran the remuda into a grazing area and let loose the rope. These men who thought him half a man depended on everyone to do their share. His share was twice as much to prove himself half again as good.

Boone rode hard left of the stampede, and his painted pony matched their strides without encouragement. The milling should turn them right, unless these fool drovers headed them back to the swollen river. Cows bellowed and jumped over each other. Men yelled, whips cracked, loud shouts, guns fired skyward to frighten the cows but still the noise of the stampede drowned out most human sounds. Men's courage over steer's fears, the one to conquer the other -- they must intimidate, not *be* intimidated!

He could smell the river ahead and heard the first of the steers splashing. He prayed to the heavens that they would lose no more than a few dumb animals this night. He tensed his muscles as Robbo dove into the river.

*

Boone got to chow that night in time to scrape the bottom of the pot. The remuda hadn't been where he left them and he had to go further than expected to retrieve them. The tail horse he called Baby had wrapped itself around a small willowy tree, thankfully uninjured because of the give he built into the rope.

As he rode them back he recited the Shakespeare Emily enjoyed the most. "Now, fair Hippolyta, our nuptial hour draws on apace. Four happy days bring in another moon." Boone couldn't see the moon. "But oh, methinks how slow this old moon wanes! She lingers in my desires like a step-dame or a dowager, long withering out a young man's revenues." He knew what revenues meant, needed for his plans to marry.

He and Bill had spent many nights with the bard. Bill was amazed at how well Boone comprehended these seemingly foreign English words. But now, even in the lines he thought he understood, Boone found new meaning. This last line he now figured meant that if you pursued a dream too long, you won't have the money to make anything come true.

The drovers already had their day horses bedded in some prime grazing field, so Boone took the night horses close to the river for scruff grass and water. Every few minutes a cowhand got up from his meal to go after another steer that had broke loose. Boone thought to volunteer for night riding, but he tended horses, not cattle, unless they told him otherwise.

He ate alone, away from the others. After he finished he picked up a stick and drew his symbols in the dirt. "I am beloved of beauteous Emily. Why should not I then prosecute my right?"

"Hey, look, the half-breed talks to himself!"

"Figures himself better company than the likes of us."

"Hell, I ain't gonna bother setting him straight."

They all laughed as Boone turned to them. "I only wait to be asked." He nodded down at his now empty plate. "And food like this needs to be blessed pretty hard to be edible."

This got the snickers he wanted, but Lacker stood, angered. "What's that you're drawing in the dirt?"

Boone looked down. He didn't figure they needed interpretation. Two crosses, one big and one small. He didn't know why. They came out of his hand like Sam's play toy. Two crosses, that's all. One for Mama and one for Sam. Or maybe one for his father, the other for him.

But Lacker, whose real name was Stu, got up and stood over him, wanting a fight.

The rest of the fellows watched, eager for some rough play to help unwind nerves. Boone pretended no response. Raoul told Stu, the drive's troublemaker, to go check the herd.

Blackie came over, half soused with whiskey, and sat next to Boone. "Why you drawing, anyhow? Don't look like words."

"They're not. They're crosses. Like someone will put over your grave someday."

"That a threat?"

Boone looked up at the big man. "I hardly think so. Just a statement."

"Then why you draw them?"

"Don't know. Maybe … I honor what I lost."

"Why you so quiet all the time? Hard to trust someone who don't talk."

"Hard to trust some who do."

Blackie started to laugh. "Well, son of a gun. I 'spect so!" He stood, still laughing, but shushed on hearing a voice behind him at the campfire.

"Raoul Vegas hasn't got the sense for this job," Stu said with a shout at his opponent. Stu seemed young to Boone. He'd stop calling him Lacker if he sat straighter in the saddle and looked interested in something.

"We lost four and no drovers, and that ain't bad," Rolley muttered. Boone called him Blue, but not to his face. His lean but wide open face made the rest of him look fat. But he always seemed sad -- like his best girl just died.

Boone shook his head. "If we lose four every stampede we may as well go into some other business."

All heads jerked up as though connected to a rope suddenly yanked.

"Hey, look, the half-breed's got an opinion." Rolley laughed, uneasy.

Boone set his plate on the ground. "My name is Boone, and my parents are no concern."

Sudden stillness and then a shifting as all but Raoul stood. Stu took a step forward and Rolley reached out to stop him but changed his mind. "What you trying to say, boy?" Stu's expression reminded Boone of the last time Emily got mad in her cornfield.

Boone's fists alternately squeezed and opened, but a smile for Emily creased his face. "Was agreeing with you, Stu."

"Agreeing? Then what was that remark you made, that I oughta mind my own business or find myself flat on my back?"

"Is that what you heard?"

Stu shoved Boone backward off his stump. "I heard you, boy. You told me to shut my yap. Everyone heard you."

Boone stood with the hope that Raoul wouldn't stop them. Just two young pups wanting to chew and scratch to relax. He stood full tall and squared his shoulders. "You're older than me by a full year or more. Wouldn't be a fair fight." Boone meant that the other way, though. He had a good four inches of height on Stu.

Stu had his fist up. "What's that supposed to mean?"

"I think he told you to come on ahead, he's willing!" Rolley yelled.

Stu came swaying at Boone like a steer with horns too big for his head, his arms up and swinging. Boone put his arms up and sidestepped each swing. Stu got in a lucky punch and clipped Boone's shoulder, staggering him, and followed with a good one alongside the head that sent Boone to the ground.

Boone looked up in time to see Stu jump down on top of him and rolled out of the way. He kicked out with a foot to push Stu backward. With a fist tight as stone Boone threw himself on top of Stu and got in a couple of good punches before

Stu got a hand up on Boone's throat. Boone gasped and grabbed Stu's hand but Stu pushed him onto his back and sat on his chest, choking, until Raoul pulled Stu off with a jerk and threw him to the ground.

"Stu, you remember one of the rules on my drive? Don't wreck the other men. I don't give many chances to roosters like you."

Coughing, Boone eased himself to his feet. He never fought anyone before and wondered if there was a better way to learn how to fight.

Raoul turned on him. "I know you was part to blame, Boone. A fun fight is all right, but this one tends to play for keeps. Stu, I told you that I'd pay you the same wages as everyone else, but you had to keep up the pace and not cause trouble. This'll cost ya. Boone, so far ya ain't done much but say two words the whole time. These men prefer their half-breeds that way. You keep to the remuda and nothing more."

"That mean I don't have to help in stampeding?"

Raoul had started to turn away but turned back to Boone with a miserable scowl on his face. "You know well what I mean, boy." He ran a hand through his thick gray and black hair and turned back to the rest. "All right, fun's over. Let's get some sleepin' done. That sun will be back up before we know it."

Boone accepted a biscuit from the cook, who'd taken a liking to him. Rolley sat next to him, but Boone didn't turn. "You know Stu was gonna kill you back there."

Boone shrugged. "Raoul stepped in before I could break him."

"Don't treat this lightly, Boone. I saw his face when you dodged him."

"He still got the best of me. This time."

Rolley stood. "It's a tough world, Boone. Maybe someday…." Rolley stared at the ground. "I don't mind you myself. But don't let me catch you telling anyone. Just stay with the remuda and you'll survive." Rolley felt around inside his head before he continued. "Maybe you should find a different line of work when this is done. I can tell you're not happy here."

"Are you?"

Rolley looked off at the horizon. "You got a story, too. I kin tell."

Boone shrugged. "I got enough saved after this trip." Boone turned his back as though to walk away. He took a swig of water that Rolley offered to wash the biscuit down and told a brief story about his mother, as though the story belonged to some far distant past.

Rolley took out a kerchief and wiped his eyes. "You think you was too young? When I was 13 I was kicked out. My pa had him 18 sons and he kicked us all of us out, one at a time. Couldn't find a use for all of us. Some straggled back, and he put them to work in his fields. But the rest of us found our way, right enough."

Boone stood and glared at Rolley. "You asked." He walked away.

Rolley grunted behind him. "Mighty big log to carry around, for sure."

Boone didn't want sympathy. How could he go back to Emily and ask her to marry him if he couldn't get treated like a man?

CHAPTER FOURTEEN
The Newly Born

Boone crawled out of his bedroll the next morning before the sun touched the horizon, even before the cook roused himself to slap together the biscuits and gravy. Boone had a restless night, dreams filled with starving people and Emily a skeleton in her bed. He awoke feeling old with the taste of skin and blood in his mouth. He didn't like Sam's dreams.

Boone walked over to a tree to relieve himself. He had a clear vision of the cattle, little more than black blobs on the ground below. In the dawn he could count each and every one if he wanted to. He sat with his back against a tree to watch them. Every now and again one got to its feet or raised its head and bellowed. After a moment of concentration, he prayed the way his mother taught him, to the stars and moon in thanks for deliverance from the night, to the east and the sun in hopes for a good day.

Lynelle told him once how proud of him his father would be. How would she feel now? Same as him -- ready to kill Kae-gon for killing her. He felt sure, even if Sam didn't agree.

Boone heard the cook opening boxes as the cows acknowledged the approach of the sun with grunts and swishing tails. Boone got to his feet with the cold ground still in his veins. His canvas jeans chafed at his saddle sores, dismaying him at the thought of the dung poultice treatment. The cook enjoyed treating men's backsides a little too much for his liking.

He walked down to the river where some cows lapped water. He didn't agree with Raoul's desire to bed along the riverbank, although some did. Cows were gonna be plumb hard to move this morning.

He leaned into the river and splashed his face. He thought to let the whiskers grow grungy like the others so maybe they would accept him, but Boone couldn't stand the feel past the second day. The smooth face made his Indian features more marked, but Emily preferred him smooth, too. The first time she puzzled over his smooth face, he told her how Indians removed facial hair, plucking them out one at a time. That's what made a real man, not those darned shavers she made him use. She said plucking made men more like women.

That's what he loved about Emily -- she saw things straight and said them straight. He figured men were jealous of women in *some* things. And he liked being woman-like in some things. Lynelle explained to Boone once that facial hair interfered with shooting bow and arrow.

Behind him the other cowhands rose, grumbled, passed aromatic noise and laughed, and slapped each other on the carbuncles to hear painful yells in return. Boone turned back to the river to wet his hair down when he heard a loud bray and a splash.

He ran over to get a closer look. "Ole Martha has given birth!" he shouted as he ran into the river.

Ole Martha found the only beever who got away without getting his balls cut. The men agreed, though, to let her stay that way, because the herd led easier behind a pregnant cow, and they always welcomed the milk in their diet. But why hadn't someone seen that she stayed on high ground with her time so near?

The little calf, barely able to walk when it was born, was drowning. Boone swam for it. The calf thrashed in the water as the river swept it downstream in the easy flowing current. Its mama brayed in agony over losing her young one, staying safe herself in shallow waters.

Boone caught up to the calf and grabbed a front leg. He hung on and pulled on it to swim back to shore, but the calf kicked him in the eye and he dropped his grip for a terrifying moment. Boone kicked his legs to keep himself moving because he couldn't touch bottom anymore and secured the calf's two legs over his shoulders to keep its head out of the water. The terrified newborn struggled as Boone swam by moving his hips and legs, eel-like. Several times Boone went under and lost his grip on the legs, but as he fought with the scrawny and struggling calf he got to shallow waters again.

As though welded together in the water, Boone and the calf found their feet under them and crawled to shore. The calf bleated and licked Boone's chin but seemed unable to get up. Boone pushed the calf to its side and looked for signs that she was suffering. She bleated pitifully at him but her eyes were bright and she didn't cough up water.

The cowhands had gathered on shore to watch the spectacle. "Hey, Boone, kin I have me the next dance?"

"I reckon Boone wants to start his own herd."

"Ya shouldn't have done that in front of the other cows, Boone. Now they're all gonna want you to bathe 'em!"

Boone got to his feet. "A Friday dunk won't hurt the lot of you." He headed up from the river. The calf bleated and, after a few wobbly falls, followed, and Martha jogged to catch up to them.

"Hey, Boone, your little friend thinks you're Ole Martha!"

Raoul walked over to Boone. "Nice, Boone, but you shouldn't have."

"Why?" Boone felt an answer sink into his gut as he wiped at the blood that trickled into his eye.

"We can't go slow enough for a calf to keep up. You oughta heard us talk. We was gonna put it out of its misery right off."

Boone watched the calf run on wobbly legs to its mother. "I couldn't let a newborn drown." He watched their happy nuzzling. "At least it got to meet its mama."

After Cookie put the salve on the gash above his eye Boone swallowed his breakfast chow. He went back to see Martha alone and mournfully bleating. At chow that evening they didn't name the stew but the smell soured in his nose. He just ate the bread.

Boone couldn't sleep that night, but not because of a calf. He heard a noise off in the brush that he recognized. Over the years of running he became aware of

Indian sounds and managed to stay clear. They weren't the only ones who knew stealth. He even managed to steal from them a time or two.

He got to his knees and threw off his horse blanket as he felt in the dirt for his rifle. His boots were down against a tree, tops tucked tight against scorpions and the morning dew. He feared rousing anyone, so he felt his way in the dark in wool-clad feet.

He checked first that the horses in the remuda were secure and moved off toward the river that reflected meager light from the stars and half moon. Along the shore and up into the grazing pasture, cows were tucked in sleep like so many small mounds. But something moved in the river, like a log but with mind and purpose.

Boone froze at the feel of a rifle barrel at his back.

"Okay, half-breed, what's your business? Remuda don't need no tending."

Stu the suspicious. Stu usually snored heavy and had to sleep away from the others. Boone realized he hadn't heard any snoring that night. "Not the time to be against me, Stu. Something out there."

"What something?" Stu pushed the barrel against Boone's back without waiting for an answer. "Didn't think so. What's the truth, boy?"

"Someone's in the river."

"Then let's go see." Stu pushed him forward a few steps but as quickly as he had appeared at Boone's back he was gone again.

Boone heard a thud and wheeled around. Someone had a hand over Stu's mouth and he struggled weakly against the knife at his throat. His rifle had dropped. The Comanche spoke to Boone but not in English. On pure instinct Boone raised his rifle and fired, hitting the Indian square in the forehead.

He squeezed his eyes shut as the body fell to the ground. *Maybe that was your father.*

Stu grabbed him and shook him. "You coulda hit me, you fool! Don't ever shoot so close to me again!" He turned and went back to the herd, staggering a little.

Boone was glad that the gunfire hadn't started another stampede. He dropped to his knees next to the dead Comanche. He touched the man's buckskin and brushed the hair off his face. He wondered what the Comanche had tried to tell him.

But what was done was done. He chose his side -- this time, in blood.

Boone walked into the herd and roped a runt cow. He pulled the animal back to the dead Indian and laid him across the animal's back. He went off to find that hunting party to offer the steer in exchange for the kill.

*

The day's drive down the canyon gave them little time for casual chatter. Stu bragged up his escape from the Indian without mentioning Boone, and Raoul hustled them out before they could get their coffee down. Boone returned from his fool's errand in time to mount up. He had found a trail but if they were out there, they didn't let him know. He left the cow with the dead body tied to a tree. Rolley acted surprised to see him, and Boone figured Stu told them he ran off with the Indians.

"All right, heads up, let's move 'em!" Raoul pushed Martha out into the lead.

Just as the drovers began to get easy about the drive through the canyon, the wind picked up and heavy gray clouds gathered over their heads.

When Rolley rode up, Boone pulled his kerchief down off his face. Rolley warned them to stay alert should there be thunder and lightning inside those rain clouds.

"Think maybe we ought to find another route to town?" Boone asked. He didn't like the canyon rock ledges that threaten to throw rocks down on the herd at the slightest tremor.

Rolley turned to Boone, his laughing eyes clouded with doubt. "Raoul don't figure on this storm waking anyone up until we're clear through the canyon. He also says that since they're so full of their watering this morning only a heap of noise will get 'em to run."

Boone pulled his kerchief back up as Rolley rode to the front of the herd. At least the ride through the canyon meant some relief from this dust. So would rain. But cows with lightning, thunder and walls of rock seemed like gambling.

The cows began to lag but Boone kept his prodder saddled. He allowed the remuda a longer line behind the cattle because the horses tended to mimic the cattle's leeriness. Boone figured to lag behind, at least until they crossed through the canyon. He could ride up on a moment's notice if he had to.

He was glad no one favored the longer route. He wanted to get back sooner than yesterday. He tried all the long drive not to think about Emily. Until he proposed and she accepted, she was little more than a dream. He hoped the story of saving a calf and that ornery Stu were enough to make her say yes, even if he didn't make enough money. He didn't plan to tell her that they killed the calf and that saving someone's life doesn't make them grateful.

Not telling and lying weren't the same attitude. As he realized this, he felt comforted about her pa dying before knowing the truth about his own pa.

But Boone felt sure he could have herded the remuda with that little calf across his saddle. Emily would have loved it. The colt she'd helped birthe still follows her around the yard.

Lightning flashed and Robbo reared up. The cattle jumped but calmed again. Boone tucked his gun in his saddlebag and reached for his boot but remembered he left his spurs in his saddlebag. On his first drive he saw what happened to a feller who kept metal spurs on in a lightning storm. It wasn't pretty. As he eyed the sky Boone wondered what he might have done with a saddled calf in a stampede.

Just then the thunder rolled up as if shook loose from the ground and the rain fell in a rush, casting a dim gray around them. Boone heard clicking horns ahead of him. The cows wanted nothing more than to head for safety, and get there fast. Boone let the remuda loose and joined the drovers to calm the cattle. He noted by the direction that Raoul wanted to force them into the canyon with all that loose rock so they'd at least stay on the right trail. A bunch of those clicking, hot-headed horned beasts attempted to turn out of the canyon and head back to the river, but the drovers forced them forward again with whips and shouts.

"This is foolish!" Boone shouted. "We gotta mill 'em first, slow 'em!" Boone didn't get as far as the swing riders when he saw more trouble. Rolley had attempted to move cattle away from the canyon trail back into the open to mill, to keep cattle from bunching down the canyon slope. Intent on the cattle, he ran into a low hanging rock that knocked him senseless off his horse. He lay close to being trampled and the other riders didn't see him. Or figured him dead already.

Boone rode to Rolley and jumped off his horse. Holding tight to the frantic Robbo's reins as cows ran a close path around them, he roused Rolley and got him up in the saddle, then jumped up behind him and urged the horse on. Robbo slowed up some with the weight but still they pushed at the cattle to get at least some of them milling away from the trail as others continued through.

The frightened stream of cattle became a more condensed controlled herd as the milling slowed them up enough to enter the canyon in a thinner stream. But something felt wrong. The thunder had stopped but the rain still poured, which also helped the cattle slow up. The wind whipped through the canyon, lifting hat brims so the rain poured into their eyes and mouths.

"Hang on." Boone said to Rolley, who didn't grip tight. "The trail's stalled. Something's blocking the route."

Boone rode over to the trail that cut through rock to the other side, down and on to the end of the drive. He looked behind him to see cattle and drovers followed and continued to push on around him. One waved him forward, scattering rain with his arm, before going back to steering cows again. Boone waved back and wiped his vision clear as he peered around Rolley's shoulder.

He urged the horse to the edge and looked down. What he saw wasn't pretty. "Rolley, I'll have to leave you here. You sit against rock on this side here and you'll be fine."

The trail bent downward through the canyon and was jumbled with trampled cows and a barrage of rock. Some cows were still alive, but bloody, squirming to get up.

Where the trail dipped down Red and Stu worked hard to round up those that could walk into the managed herd. The drive will be another day long, whether or not any of them were in favor. As Boone rode down, he wondered if any others that looked injured could be saved, or would, with a little gentleness, finish the drive. The dead were dragged off the trail and the crippled destroyed before sending more steers down.

Raoul sat off to the side on a rock. The rain let up some, enough for Boone to see that he pressed a bloody hand against his leg where he had taken a nasty stab from a longhorn.

"Boss!" Blackie yelled through the rain. "We gotta move these injured cows, get the rest down here so we can count!"

Raoul looked up, slow, hesitant. "I couldn't help this. I couldn't stop it."

Boone's anger rose up. "Get off your ass, Boss! Or we move 'em without you!"

Raoul looked up at Boone, eyes glazed over in pain deeper than any wound, his hat shoved back on his head, face wet with rain and wrenched with sorrow. Boone jumped off his horse, grabbed him by the vest and yanked him to his feet. When Raoul didn't struggle, Boone clipped him in the jaw. Raoul fell back and caught himself on rock, the wind knocked from his chest. He slid off and landed face up, wedged between boulders. Boone braced himself but Raoul didn't strike back.

He shook his head and and got up. "All right, Blackie, let's get those cows that can move out of here. Boone." Boone glared at Raoul, ready to defend the anger that he began to see wasn't Sam's. "Get back up there and wait for my yell to send the rest on down. Once we clear the cows through the canyon, you go back for the remuda."

Boone felt his anger relax. "Sure, boss."

"Rolley okay?"

"He will be."

"Good." Raoul squinted at the clouds. "We gotta get what cattle we got left to a buyer who can make this drive worth something."

*

Boone was happy as a fed snake as they drove the healthy herd into the holding pen just outside Wichita. He would miss a few of those mangy critters that he'd named for their spunk, but not as many as the last drive. Never again would, after having his calf taken away.

He took his pay without a word. He didn't even look at it to see how poor the pay left him. When he mounted Robbo again, he got the courage to look. Not enough for the horse ranch he wanted to start with Emily. Not near enough to buy gear or stock but enough to plant his feed field. He turned Robbo to take the trail back to North Texas, where he hoped Emily still waited for him. Too long a ride for his impatience, but no other way to get there except as fast as Robbo could go. He was scared and nervous that she hadn't been able to handle herself alone, even with all the people he alerted to keep an eye on her.

After several nights on this southern trail Boone became aware that someone followed him. He kept his gun close but the scoundrel made no other move than to remain behind him, so Boone decided he wasn't worth the worry.

CHAPTER FIFTEEN
The Home Coming

Boone sat on Robbo for what seemed hours outside the small house where he had first fallen in love with Emily. The house looked too dark -- likely abandoned and he would never see her again. A dream after all, and now the nightmare began.

"Boone!"

Her voice still so vivid in his mind. His eyes closed.

"Boone! You're back!"

He wheeled around in the saddle to see Emily coming out of the shed. He jumped down and ran to her. Pleasant to look at, Emily had soft honey hair and wide smile, and being a little on the heavy side made her easy to hold. She threw her arms around him and, overwhelmed with relief, he held her just as tight. They stood, both silent, eyes closed, just holding on.

Until he got a whiff of himself mixed with that sweet smell of her. "I gotta clean up. Had my last rain days ago." *Propose and get her in bed.* Sam's sudden thoughts could be so alarming at times. "Soon enough."

"Soon enough what?" Emily looked up at him with a giggle.

"Ah, I have this inner voice telling me to eat. But I want to wash up --."

"You need to listen to that inner voice. I know what a smelly old cowhand wants the minute he gets home." She pulled him into the house. "Got a fine piece of pork stewing. Made you a fine new bed, too, in the shed. But Boone, I wished you'd change your mind and sleep in the house. There's plenty of room for the two of us. You just make yourself a bunk, like you made one for me. Or sleep with me." She snuggled against him. "You know I want you to."

Boone felt that tension rising up in his muscles. Hard to explain how two people conceived him who thought they were in love but had no kind of love at all to hold them together. Not Romeo & Juliet but the opposite. They wouldn't leave their families for each other.

Hard to say any of that to Emily without the rest -- that once he found his father, Boone had to kill him. "Emily, there's something I gotta ask you first."

Emily grabbed his hand, pulled him to the house and stood him in front of the wash bucket, already dirty from the morning's chores. "Later. With dessert. I made your favorite pudding and it's better fresh."

Boone washed his hands with the soap next to the bucket and jumped inside the house with still wet hands to smell the good cooking smells. "This isn't even mealtime. How did you know I would --."

Emily responded to a rap at the door. Boone couldn't see who she greeted with such surprised favor at first.

"Stewart! Is that you? Where in holy hell have you been?"

Stewart answered so low and soft that Boone couldn't hear. Stewart. Stu. And then he knew. Emily's brother was also Stu from the trail drive, the one he called Lacker. That's why he seemed familiar and why he gave Stu so much unrequited favor, not deserving.

"Yes, I do have a … well, he's not a visitor. Come on in. We're ready to eat and I have enough bread to feed three. Come on in and meet Boone."

Boone turned with dried hands to face his old trail adversary. Stewart stood in the doorway, well aware he had followed Boone here, and stood braced to renew the fight.

"Boone, this is my long-lost brother! I haven't seen you, Stewart, since before Pa died. Come on, let's sit and eat and we'll talk." But she saw both men frozen with stares at each other.

"What's he doing here, Emily?"

"Boone? He's my --."

"Don't say beau or I'll have to kill him. You know that."

Emily took a step away from Stewart toward Boone as she tried to control a sudden anger. "Maybe you never favored Indians the way Pa did and that's why you left. But I won't have you take your irrational attitude out on Boone."

"Irrational! You want your children to look like *him*?"

Boone put a hand on Emily's shoulder and stepped forward. "Why don't you tell her, Stu, how you happen to be alive today?"

"Oh, you want to brag about how you led me into a trap and then saved my skin to make yourself look white?"

"I *led* you? Emily, I was on the trail of a Comanche preparing to steal a cow and he accused me --."

"With every right!"

"With no right!"

Emily put her hands up between them. "Wait a minute. You two *know* each other?"

"I had the misfortune of herding cows to Leavenworth with this miserable half-breed."

"Stewart! I won't stand for you calling him miserable! You don't know him! And if he saved your life…." Emily beat on his chest until he grabbed her hands.

"You sound like Pa, a weak-livered man too scared to stand up for his rights."

"*His* rights? Who had this land first?"

Stu aimed an accusing fist at Boone. "Boone, you better leave before I kill you. I'm building a good rage here."

Boone had closed his eyes in pain as they argued. He squinted at Stu. "I'm not leaving."

"He doesn't have to go anywhere, Stewart. This is *my* house! *My* birthright! You left long ago."

Stu grabbed her arm so hard she stumbled. "I'm the eldest son. Doesn't matter that I left. I sent money all along and brought more to run this farm proper."

Boone pulled her back. "We could use the money, Em."

"Well, you'll have to share the homestead, then, because we're getting married and starting a family and horse ranch, right here."

Boone felt he had been fisted in the gut. "Emily, I wanted to ask you proper."

"I knew you were gonna ask with dessert if this galoot hadn't charged in." She threw her arms around Boone, partly to steady herself. "Stewart, Pa blessed us well before he died. You got no say in this."

"The day I let someone in my family marry a no account --."

Boone charged at Stu and pushed him through the open doorway outside, off the porch, and backward to the ground. Boone gave this fight all he had, but Stu was lean and scrappy, with more anger toward a people he felt ruined his relationship with his father. After blows followed by bloody blows, Boone laughed and lay back in the dirt, as Stu still punched him. Boone only said owwww and laughed with every hit.

Emily ran to Boone and pushed Stu away. She pulled Boone into her arms and dabbed her blouse sleeve against his bloody lip. "Are you all right, Boone? Why are you laughing?"

"Him and me. So much in common. I think … we can be friends."

"What? Never!" Stu made ready to kick Boone but Boone made no move to stand up and fight back.

Emily put herself in the path of Stu's boots, taking one good kick but bearing it in silence. Stu turned away, sullen, his eyes on the horizon, as if he contemplated a future away from them.

Boone caught his breath and sat up, with Emily a silent comfortable brace next to him. "Your pa and you fought over Indians. My pa was an Indian and my ma wanted me in the white world. So my pa and me fight over whites. You and me … both on the same side." Boone struggled to his feet and held out his hand. "My accident of birth is not worth us fighting over. I think in time we can be friends."

"You mean…" Stu stared at Boone's hand, thrust out steady at him. "You really did shoot the Indian to save me?"

"He had no right to get on you that way."

"You gotta understand, Boone, I don't feel this way because I want it. And Emily's the only family I got."

"No, Stewart. Ma's still alive. She's back east with Billy --."

Stewart took Emily's hand. "No, she ain't. I might not have been home here, Em, but I kept track. Ma and me exchanged letters. When I got to Atchison I found a response to a letter I sent a time ago. Ma's dead, typhoid, trying to help in an epidemic. Billy died, too. That's when I knew I had to find you."

"Letters? She wrote me letters. But then she stopped … oh Stewart!"

Boone felt the same loss that overtook Emily, but loneliness set in as Emily and Stu held each other, alone in their grief. After sobs and quiet talk, Emily broke free and ran to Boone. They exchanged sobbing kisses. "Boone loved them, too, Stewart. He was like a son to them."

Stu stared down at his dirty boots.

"Boone, our supper's getting spoilt. Stewart, will you stay and join us?"

Stewart glanced at Boone, at the hand no longer held out. "Sure. I'm still here, ain't I?"

Emily grabbed the two men each by an arm, and walked them to the door. She pushed them inside and though neither spoke, Boone hoped that someday, in the near future, he'll be proud to call Stu brother.

CHAPTER SIXTEEN
The Conflict

Stewart agreed to take over Boone's bunk in the barn and Boone agreed they could build on an extension to the house so he could move in before the winter winds hit. Boone allowed himself to move into Emily's bed but refused to treat her as anything but a sister until they were properly wed, which Emily refused to put off any longer than necessary. They first discussed having children and Emily said she wanted as many as she could have.

Boone was afraid to ask it but knew he must. "Do you think you are able?"

She was tidying her sewing project materials after making her wedding dress during this question. He watched as she paused, her body tight in contemplation. Finally she turned with a laugh. "Boone, don't dare doubt it! I might not be able to chase after them as a mother should, but everything else in me works."

Though they did not have Stewart's blessing, he agreed to mind the horses and the house while Emily and Boone rode off to Amarillo to get married. Boone felt like a nervous Lysander all the way there. He again had that odd sensation of being watched -- not followed but watched. Different than Stu, who he caught sight of in the distance -- here he had no physical presence to blame.

Northwestern Texas was in an uproar following Lincoln's election which led to secession, which led to a southern secessionist war, or war of northern aggression, as some called it. Boone wasn't even aware war had been declared while on the drive, and the three of them talked about it into all hours, when finally they were talking. Emily told Boone and Stu she would have voted for Lincoln, if allowed, and Boone finally admitted he was too young to think about it. Stu gave her a hug for her Union upbringing. Boone told her about his mother's fears, too, of the Missouri Regulators. But he didn't know which way he would have voted.

They both refused to let the war touch their happiness.

Emily made herself a maroon dress with gold lace trim. She'd started working on it when Boone was still on the drive. He bought them simple gold wedding bands, and the justice of the peace reserved them five minutes to do the ceremony. Emily only giggled when Boone admitted he would be 17 in a few months as she readily admitted to her age of 24.

When they went to the hotel, however, they found there were no rooms available. Giggling, they took their horse blankets and walked to the edge of town. They ran inside a hay shed that stood apart from any occupied dwelling. Emily was every bit as tender and eager naked in his arms as she was doing any chore -- every new move she made felt like a blessing to them both.

"Oh, Emily, I love you so much. Please don't ever leave me."

"Never will I willingly, my love."

"I'll follow thee, and make a heaven of hell, to die upon the hand I love so well." Boone no longer felt like the nervous frightened kid who once ran away from the only woman he knew.

They dressed again and ran back out of the shed. Not spotted. In all innocence they walked back into the heart of Amarillo. Boone tried to buy her a cake and some champagne but was told the town was out of supplies because of the war.

When they got back, with a little extra sugar and coffee begged from homesteads along the way, Stu greeted them as though nothing had changed. Days of married life slipped into winter as Boone and Stu worked on the addition to the house, and read the news, waiting to hear the war end as it began. They often fought over breeding stock, the right way to break horses, and a myriad of other chores. But when spring arrived, Boone came to feel they were brothers after all. Boone had flung himself into the fence to get off a nasty animal about to flip itself backward and land on him. The fence nearly knocked him out, but Stu pulled him out of danger at the risk of taking a few blows himself.

They were having a nice breakfast one spring morning, laughing over the follies of their breeding efforts, when Stu grew somber. "You caught that wild buck awful quick the other day. What's your secret?"

"It's not a secret."

"Oh, you injuns always got secrets. I suppose you don't want to tell me, neither."

"I'll tell you, if you ask proper."

Stu got down on one knee in front of Boone. "Tell me, you ornery cuss, or I'll bust your balls."

Boone laughed as Stu stood again. "Best way is to follow them to water. Watch them drink until they've had their fill. They can't run as fast with a belly full of water."

"Huh. How'd you learn that?"

Boone wasn't sure. "I suspect one of the ranchers I worked for."

Emily came out with more crepes but both men said to save them for supper. She didn't eat breakfast with them because she didn't want to interfere with "men talk."

Stu watched her walk back inside. "Say, Boone, what you see in her, anyway?"

"What you mean?"

"Well, she shouldn't have kids."

"She never said that."

"You can tell by watching her walk. More pronounced as she gets older."

"We talked about it, and she never said she was worried she couldn't. But it doesn't matter if we don't. There's something special about her. She puts up with a lot, but she won't put up with the wrong. I like that."

"She's a good Christian woman. She don't cotton to knowing spirits in trees and rocks."

"I wouldn't ask her to."

"What do you believe?"

"My mother was raised Christian. But she told me that she preferred to believe in the rain, the stars, and the trees. In the plants, and the buffalo, things we can feel and taste and touch. At the same time, never take anything for granted. Always say please when hunting, and thank you, when you kill." He remembered a quote. "A noise of hunting is heard within. All the fairies run away." He chuckled. "Hunt in silence. And always with gratitude."

They looked up at the sound of horse hooves and stood as they recognized their closest neighbor who lived a good ten miles south riding hard and anxious. "Hey Willie, you look plum withered. Missus okay?" Stu called as Willie pulled his horse up.

"Letting everyone know General Robert E. Lee has taken the field against General McClellan. Lincoln can't find enough to volunteer. Go to Houston if you favor the South, or Leavenworth if you favor the North. War's getting too real!" Willie rode off again, intent on spreading his message across the countryside.

"Oh no. War a year old and just getting worse." Emily stood behind them, one hand over her mouth and the other drifting down to her belly. The three looked at each other and none found the words. Things had been building in this direction since the war started. Lincoln felt sure it would end in 90 days. Emily once begged Boone to turn down the job as a Pony Rider because of the dangers. What will he say if she tells him not to enlist? So far he hadn't thought about it, too happy in her arms every night, and too young, besides.

"I think there are some ponies in the east corral that need attention. I'll get back to sewing those patches if you men get busy."

But no one moved. They had become a party of strangers, fearing to voice their thoughts.

The two men began to walk, but stiff, as though their undergarments had lost the stitching and dropped down between their legs. Emily had nearly gotten inside the house, when she looked over her shoulder to see Stu turn and give Boone a shove. She ran back to them.

"How can you fight to defend slavery?" Stu yelled at Boone.

"I don't defend slavery! It's the state's rights that's at stake. I would have voted for Lincoln. But I think maybe the states should be allowed to secede. They'd come back begging after a year or so. It ain't worth fighting for."

"You're just an Injun. You don't know anything about government."

"It's not gonna last. You'll see. No one should fight just to keep slaves. No one can be that wrong."

"Lee's in it now. It'll last."

Neither of them noticed Emily until she got between them and told them both to shut up. "It's a fight for Union and has been all along. They say this can't be two countries. I say why not? It's been two countries for the longest time anyhow. The South is making it official."

"Emily, you can't --."

"Stu, you been in Missouri with us. Why, we went running out of there because of slavery and the South wanting to keep its plantation system, with them northerners saying the South has got to get into their progressive notions or die with slavery. This country's gotten too big for one government. So let two try it. Boone is right. It's not worth a fight."

"Emily, this country is not divided in half. It's fractured. We could end up being six countries, not two. I'm for Union." Stu went to the horse barn, with Emily behind him and Boone following. Boone remembered how grateful Stu was that he had his own room in the house, when the worst of the blizzards hit and snows got so cold and so deep some men froze to death walking ten feet to the barn. How could he give all this up now? Or maybe he just felt he was in their way.

"You're a Texan," Emily reminded Stu. "You know Texans favor slavery."

"I also know Texas had been an independent country and didn't survive that way."

"Oh, I know well the war our Pa fought so hard to stay out of." Emily laughed but without humor. "This isn't our war, Stewart. I ask you to stay."

Boone stood next to her. "A man has to follow his conscience."

Emily turned on Boone. "A woman is a man's conscience!"

Stu finished cinching after walking the horse two steps, and jumped into the saddle. "You'll thank me when Union is preserved, Em."

"Please don't, Stewart. I'm afraid I'll never see you again."

"If you don't, remember. I do this for you and Boone -- and your family." Without further word he rode off.

Boone pulled Emily close. "Can't make a man stay against his will, Em."

She buried her tears in his chest. "Please promise me you'll stay, Boone."

"Leaving you would be too hard, Emily. What did he mean by family? Are you --?"

She nodded and placed his hand on her abdomen. "Stu guessed this morning."

"Can you still handle the chores?"

"You want to get me a slave?"

They laughed and he gave her a hug, careful and mindful. "Stu was wrong! He said you couldn't have children." *Uh-uh, Stu said shouldn't.*

Emily patted his cheek. "We will have many babies, Boone."

Boone watched her clump back to the house. No way to explain how life can change so quickly. He watched as Emily grabbed the door of the house and slumped.

"Emily." He felt no surprise that she was about to lose that baby.

CHAPTER SEVENTEEN
The Decision

Boone believed he caused her pain with their fight until she told him she hadn't felt well all morning. Boone held her hand as she dozed, the precious "potential life," as she called the loss, buried deep away from prying claws. He hadn't washed his hands and let his tears trickle hot and steaming down his face with the blood he'd rubbed there. How badly he wanted a family. *She has to be right. Each time her body will get more used to the idea. Each time. Unless ….*

"Boone? Are you crying?" Em forced herself awake, as she often did in the middle of the night when she sensed his upset.

"Just worried about you."

"Oh, don't. Maybe I take longer than most, but my body is getting ready. Could you get me some water?"

As Boone turned from her he envisioned the way Emily walked, with that hitch in her hip that made her seem lop-sided, like an overworked old mule. As he pumped her water he saw those two crosses again, and Emily's closed eyes as he buried her. The glass dropped out of his hand and shattered on the hard wooden floor.

"Boone!"

Boone fell to his knees and scooped up the glass but Em cried hard now -- she had been hit by water and a shard of glass. Hit by pain he couldn't share. Boone crawled over to her, crawled into her arms and together they cried until together they fell asleep.

*

Robbo's hardest ride ever -- over rocky crags and down cliffs and Boone feared at one point he broke the faithful pony's right knee but the horse got up again and kept going. That stallion they chased didn't go much faster in this terrain and

Boone had the advantage of planning various responses. The gorgeous paint was bigger than any wild mustang he had seen before. He'd been after it for months, even had a name picked out. Diablo. He heard the name somewhere and didn't know the meaning but liked the sound.

The horse pranced in frantic anger when it realized that Boone had chased it into a box canyon. "Whoa, boy, whoa." He had his rope out and as he nudged Robbo closer realized the horse had been owned once -- a gelding. Maybe never really tamed or turned sour from abuse.

Boone got the rope around the horse's neck after two tries and wrapped the other end of the rope around his saddle horn. The horse whinnied, rose up and lunged at Robbo, knocking Boone to the ground. Robbo didn't have a choice as Diablo ran off -- Robbo's saddle still tied firm to the other end of the rope.

"Oh no, you don't!" Boone pulled his gun and ran after them. He found the two horses over the next ridge. A Comanche stood over the wild horse. He had the noose so tight the horse had fallen, unable to breathe. Boone watched him work with the wild horse as he walked slow and easy toward Robbo, now roped to a tree.

The Indian loosened the noose and Diablo snorted, struggling for air. Boone thought sure that horse had been killed. The horse rose, trembling and in full lather. The Indian stroked its nose, ears and forehead, then put his mouth over the horse's nostrils and blew air into its nose. He threw a thong around the horse's lower jaw, mounted up on Diablo and rode toward Boone, who now had Robbo behind him.

They made a few attempts to communicate, and Boone, in surprise, felt he understood about half the words. As Boone mounted, the Comanche rode off on the now tamed horse, pull his own horse behind.

*

In a typical frantic emotion, Emily pawed one more time through the garden. Winter was fast heralded on the wind and she didn't like the emptiness of the cellar. Or the emptiness in her heart. She hadn't heard from Stu since he left. And then there was loneliness, with Boone off sometimes for days on his harvest of horses. He was determined to get that one that kept escaping, obsessively so since her miscarriage, as though her lack of energy was his fault. Boone promised her they'd keep trying, and yet he found more reasons to be away.

And no one settled around them yet. Confounded war stopped everything.

She came to a major decision, one more resigned to than inspired in, one that Boone prodded at her to consider. As she became more accepting, found two more squash she had overlooked. But then, living with Boone, she was no longer surprised by the mysteries in her day, or the way the world provided what she was finally willing to accept.

She just couldn't accept not providing Boone with a son.

*

Boone rode into the yard with a poor excuse for a wild stallion on a rope. This critter was probably fifteen years old and halfway back began to limp. But he didn't want to return empty handed. He had taken longer to get back than he wanted, but Robbo developed a limp as though in sympathy, so Boone slowed up. When he got into the yard he jumped off Robbo and bent over to look at her legs again.

"Boone! Is that it? You got the great Diablo?" Emily came up behind him with an expression of disbelief, wiping her hands on her apron.

Boone roped both horses to the fence. "Yes, but it wasn't easy. I'll tell you about it, woman, if you fix me some food."

"I will, and then I'll tell you my news."

"You can tell me yours first. Mine's more a story." Boone stopped to wash up in the barrel of rain water they kept outside. "Sorry I was gone so long." He grabbed her with wet hands and kissed her, making her giggle with furtive struggles.

"You know I fret. But you make good money on those beasts, so I can't complain." Emily led Boone in front of biscuits and a glass of water and got out her cooking pot. "Not sure about that one, though," she said with a nod at the horses outside. Boone liked his meat pretty raw so she didn't need to rush. "I have decided we can move to Kansas."

Boone gulped the water in his mouth and looked up. "Now? You were so against it."

"You change your mind again?"

"Not change, but…" Boone also made a decision out on the trail. "Why did you change?"

"Tired of waiting for people to catch up to me. I want to go where they are now."

"Yeah." Boone filled his mouth with a biscuit. "It's a good notion then."

"What?"

"What? Oh, let me tell you about the horse. You know I've been chasing Diablo for months now. I had him roped and secured but then he came at me. He reared up like he wanted to knock me and Robbo right over. All so fast, I didn't have time and I fell --."

"Out of the saddle you?"

"Yeah, me out. And they were roped so Diablo ran off and Robbo had to follow. And I leaped up after them, ready to shoot Diablo if I had to. Oh, but they were fast and they'd found a deer trail and I got so scared that I was never gonna catch them, ever. But then I started to laugh. While my breath is being jerked out of me all hot and hard and still I laughed. Ha ah Ha! Because I could see where the trail led and I thought to slow up but since I didn't know Diablo well I kept going, see! And then I heard a splash!"

"The river?"

Boone nodded. "They went right in and I keep going because if you ever saw two horses fight in the water, you know it's not … and that stopped me laughing, but I still run, all this time. I got to the river…" Boone took a drink of water, followed by a bite of biscuit, and wiggled his eyebrows at her.

Emily stomped her foot and turned away. "I saw a barn swallow today."

Boone almost choked on his biscuit. He regained composure with some more water. "So there they were, splashing around and around in the water. Robbo is good in the water and I could see he had control. Diablo appeared panicked, liked he never swam before. And there's Robbo just swimming around in circles so Diablo couldn't get back to shore. I whistled, and Robbo started toward me, so I jumped in the water and got in the saddle and when we got on shore, ole' Diablo had little fight left."

Emily eyed him like she knew he was funning with her. She nodded at the window. "So that's what's left of poor old Diablo after you took the fight out of him?"

Boone laughed, he couldn't stop and finally Emily joined in. Then he told her the truth, and how ole Gramps acted relieved to be caught. "Can't get good ones all the time. I figure he'll be good for you to learn to ride." He looked over at Robbo. "Except both horses are limping, and there's nothing wrong with their legs."

"Maybe Robbo is punishing you."

"No, she's not that much like you."

Emily smacked his chin and stood to stir the beef and carrot stew. "You fret over that horse too much."

"If you met Bill Roberts, you would understand." Boone pulled out his knife and made an etching in the wooden table. "See this?"

Emily looked at the now permanent carving in the table. "What did you do that for?"

"Watch yourself, woman, or I'll have the whole table carved like this before long. These symbols came to me in a dream, and I became obsessed with them. When Bill helped me to figure out what they meant, the obsession vanished. Now they're part of me. See this? This is sunset, this arrow means going around, and this means moon. So he says this means sunset goes around the moon. He thinks that's who I am."

"You? A sunset as a boy?" Emily frowned. "Well, you had an awful burden to carry back then, living alone." She ruffled his hair. "Not anymore though. I wish I could meet this Bill Roberts."

"Maybe someday." Boone rubbed at his eyes. That vision of the two crosses, one large and one small, clouded them. He didn't want to think the symbols were a curse, but he had to go around the moon now and hide for a time. "When you're settled in Kansas I'll enlist in the Confederate army." He squeezed his eyes shut and waited, but the blow-up did not come. When he looked at her, she remained frozen at the stew, her back to him.

"Why?" She spoke loud and resolute. No tears indicated.

"Sharpsburg battle at Antietam creek took a lot of good men, and now they face twice as many at Fredericksburg. Stu's right about Lee. But they've lost New Orleans and now Vicksburg is threatened. They need more men there to --."

"What can one Indian do?"

"Now, Em, no one person can make a difference. But I could try to pick up more along the way."

"Why?"

Boone squeezed his fists at his side. He heard his mama scream at him to run. "It's hard to explain."

"Try. You don't leave here if I have a single question."

"I'll answer them."

"You've been planning this for a while. And this is why you want to move to Kansas. Boone, we've never kept secrets."

"I know." *Stay and make those babies.* He shook his head. "I know how you feel. But if I tell you about my past you might not understand. Not a secret, Em. Just something I've not known how to share."

Em pulled in a deep breath as she sat next to him. She took his hand. "I want to understand everything about you." She brushed his hair in back of his ears. "You need to cut your hair. You look like a savage."

He pulled her hand to his lips. "I hope you can still love me. My mama was murdered by my father, a Kiowa."

"I know. But Boone --."

"I vowed on her grave to kill him."

Em's hand slipped from his to cover a gasp. "Oh, but you were just a boy. That's a normal reaction."

"Maybe. But the desire keeps growing. Maybe if I get to kill someone, legal, this urge will go away."

"Boone, I thought I knew you as well as myself. You could never kill anyone."

"My mama didn't deserve to die."

"Neither did my father. Boone, we can't choose the life we're given."

"But we live the best we can by making choices." Boone stood. "That's what I'm doing. I'm going around the moon and will come back a sunrise."

"You're not 18 yet. They won't take you."

Boone took out her tablet and pencil. He wrote the word '18' on it. "It's to put inside my shoe. So I'm not lying if they ask if I'm over 18."

"Boone Tyler, if you weren't so smart I'd --."

"You see? I'll sell my stock, find a buyer for this spread, get you to Kansas and then enlist."

"Good."

"Good?"

She stomped her foot when he laughed. "You'll never get everything done before the war ends."

CHAPTER EIGHTEEN
The Enlistment

Boone got their ranch and stock sold and moved them to Kansas in early November, in time for her to have help and protection from the winter winds surrounded by the townsfolk of Atchison. The war hadn't ended, to Emily's chagrin. Boone headed east before he got bogged down in prairie snow.

Their parting was bitter and sorrowful -- and tender.

While getting settled in Kansas, Emily bought every newspaper, both northern and southern, sure they would hear that the war had ended. But when Boone brought home two traveling companions, an ex-slave and an Indian who had been with him to repel an attack by a mixed batch of men called the Home Guard, she knew she had lost him. Boone had tasted victory and they were ready for more. They fought this Union attempt in Kansas and Oklahoma territory and wanted to chase those "cheeky devils," as Arnie, the black fellow, called them, north again. Emily didn't ask Arnie how he could fight for the Confederacy. She had gotten too used to accepting what she didn't understand.

She wept bitter tears watching Boone ride off, even after he promised he would return. She felt something was in charge of saving his life, but she didn't know what. She only hoped that something would continue.

*

Boone found a few more Indians to recruit on his way east, but no Whites. The five of them got good at running and hiding as they headed for the Arkansas post, where Louie, the name the Kiowa gave himself, said they could sign up with Confederates. Boone felt back in his element, in the wild, and wondered if he could ever return to Emily.

Maybe in time the two of them could accept a childless life, but nothing felt quite so hard to accept as that. He wanted nothing more than to give children the home he never knew. And Boone just couldn't stop bedding with her. He missed Emily the moment he kissed her goodbye, leaving late because he wanted her to stop crying first. He finally told her he'd rather die than not make it back to her, making her laugh.

Those weren't *his* crosses he drew. Staying away for a while meant she could maybe grow stronger, and her life put at less risk, than with him there.

As they headed south they found more grasses for their horses, and each of them had skill in hunting and making fire. Boone rode Robbo free as the wind, but pain cut deep into his gut when he remembered Em's face as he rode off, pain he released in the sudden rain showers that cleaned off their dirt.

A couple fellows brought rifles along but ammunition posed a problem. A couple of times they found a dead soldier and buried him after taking all he had. Their bigger need was finding food. Boone pointed to the geese and ducks overhead and once borrowed a rifle to take a quick shot, but none of the fellows helped him find the downed bird. Turned out they couldn't eat anything with wings. They wouldn't let him borrow a rifle again, once they realized how 'white' his diet was.

Boone looked forward to being a soldier so he could get his own rifle. They all thought him odd for carrying only a knife but the few times he owned a gun it broke down and he couldn't find anyone to fix it, and couldn't afford the ammunition.

They needed a Confederate camp willing to sign them on. Before they got to the Arkansas post they found one but the commanding general hemmed and hawed about protocol and expediency and his total inability to allow a Black to enlist. They told the General that Arnie had been a Cherokee slave but that didn't sway him any. "Jeff Davis would have my hide." The men just thanked him and rode on. As they rode off Boone saw a soldier there reach into his mouth and pull out a tooth. That unit was about starved to death, but what made a man lose a tooth without losing hope?

Boone missed his Shakespeare and found his memory of his favorite stories disappeared like wounds on skin. So along the way, as he got to know his "troops," he created poetic lines for each. A Cherokee from Indian Territory just wanted to see Georgia and called himself George. "Oh, George of the highlands he never goes." Two Southern Cheyenne hoped to see the South beat off the threat of that powerful northern government. "Wherefore art thou fatherless country." The Kiowa Louie was a gregarious fellow who got closer to Boone than Boone liked. "Back off, damned spot." He had the smell of Boone's father on his breath. "Oh, thou would-be king of stench." One of the Cheyenne kept his distance after Louie made a big deal of Boone's half-white blood. "The single foil of trouble in double."

But he kept the lines to himself, and they all got on well enough.

Arnie the ex-slave spooked Boone just a bit. He'd leave for a day and return without a word spoken. Boone wasn't surprised when they came upon him, shot up five times. Overkill. Didn't matter by what side. Both sides had a reason to hate a Black that fought for the South. Boone had tried to get him to go home but Arnie said he had nowhere to go. Said he would die rather than be cut loose into a world that wouldn't accept him.

Boone sent Em letters whenever he could, but not near often enough. Telegraph offices seemed to shut down when they saw him. When he did find one open, they charged him too much no matter how few words he used. All he got off one time was "Doing fine." Not cold and hungry. "Found some friends" another time, not that they were angry and vengeful. Emily once told him she was glad they were always honest with each other and he always gave her good cause to believe that. But since he lied about why he enlisted, other lies followed. He spent a lot of time thinking about ways to make a family with her without risking her life. Maybe he'd find a little Confederate orphan to bring home.

By the time they reached what they recognized were Union log huts, they lost the sullen Cheyenne. He said he would find his own way because he figured Boone would only turn northern on them. The other Cheyenne, Joe, didn't talk much and Boone wondered if he spoke English. Boone knew that *he* wouldn't turn Union, but also worried that he'd have to shoot at Stu.

Louie pointed out that the Union soldiers openly openly identified themselves with flags. Boone supposed this kept the Union forces from shooting each other. All those huts, and the campfires that were kept aflame against March's cold night, seemed so inviting that Boone wondered if maybe he *could* side with whoever fed him. Maybe being a half-breed on the run had ruined any sense of loyalty.

The four men sat in a line at the top of the hill, looking for Confederates.

"I've got a bad feeling," George whispered. "This was supposed to be a Rebel camp."

Joe raised his nose. "Gunpowder. Big battle here."

Boone noticed a large area freshly dug. Graves.

Louie nodded in that direction. "We're too late."

"Good thing or we would be under that earth, too." Boone sat back. "Any idea where another camp might be?"

"Not the worst problem. How do we cross that river?" Joe's voice drifted like the wind and then he too disappeared. The three men waited, but he did not return.

"Well," Boone sighed. "We got one shot at this. Pretend we're Union until we get across. Say we're headed for Butler at New Orleans to sign up."

George shook his head. "So you turning Union and making us believe something else? We'll all be dead because of you."

"Not turning. Just improving the chances until we get over the river. We do some good acting, we might even get them to give us a boat."

Louie put a hand on their shoulders. "We're Indian. We do not take sides. They'll let us through if we pretend we know nothing about this war."

"Will that work?"

"Can you swim?"

"Like a fish." In all honesty he believed he could easily cross that river, even with these high rains and as cold as that water was sure to be.

"Good. In case being Indian doesn't work."

*

They drew fire as they dove into the water but only George went under. Boone and Louie nearly drowned trying to reach him. Boone survived because he could hold his breath a long time and was surprised to see Louie climb onto the shore as well.

They pulled themselves up into the brush and, well hidden, lay panting. "Next time," Boone said, "we try my way."

"No next time."

"You quitting?"

"You too."

"No. The Rebel camp will be on this side. I'll go without you. Go home."

Louie shrugged and followed Boone through the brush.

"Why are you here?" Boone wondered if Louie knew Boone's father.

"Keep moving, stay warm."

Boone felt it more than coincidental that they were the only two left. Almost like Louie protected him. *All difficulties are but easy when they are known.*

Louie talked as they ran. "My people are good people. We do not deserve what they say, that we butcher without thought. We think. We pray. We hope every day that we are the people. Live day to day to please the great spirits. And each other. We never lie. We never kill without reason." He grabbed Boone's arm. "I am here because the Great Father in Washingdown thinks he knows better for us. That is all."

Boone nodded. "Did you hear them say the cavalry corps was at Grenada, Mississippi?"

"Yeah. Know where that is?"

"No."

"Then we better keep going."

Boone looked back across the Mississippi where their horses had been captured. No going back for Robbo now. He hoped the horse was well treated, and that when he felt ready to go back, Robbo would be waiting for him.

CHAPTER NINETEEN
The Confederate Indians

Boone and Louie found Grenada after several wrong turns. Once Louie risked an alligator attack and got covered in mud to get Boone out of harm's way. "It was only looking to scare us, that underwater panther," Louie said.

They signed on at the headquarters camp and were given horses, fairly overridden mules but all that could be spared. They were forced into maneuvers where they had no idea what they were doing. Boone caught on quickly but they weren't accepted as soldiers of the Rebellion, just a couple more bodies with guns to throw into the fray. Boone didn't expect to get much accomplished with this rifle, either. Louie said everyone in the tribe had better than this, although he hadn't produced one of his own to take along.

They weren't so much stationed at Grenada as they were stuck out in the countryside of Grenada, left to scrounge for food. They often snuck off to Jackson and begged on the citizens' mercy, where Boone found his best opportunities to telegraph home to Emily. He had no money but begged for sympathy. At least Jackson folk seemed more pro-Indian. Many of the townsfolk gathered when soldiers came to town and walked with them out into the countryside, as though for protection, yet chatted to each other as though on a picnic.

Boone wondered if they knew they could be shot as easy as any of them.

Louie came to hate Jackson for reasons he'd never share, and never went to town with Boone. One soldier who called himself Bunny said the town was safe enough, but powder keg and siege waited for any southern city and no one knew what General Grant was up to next. The whole area boiled like a kettle on hot fire as winter gave way to the first bursts of spring that April, 1863.

Boone composed yet another letter in his head as the army moved closer to the heart of Jackson, where its new telegraph lines fed the citizens like rows of shimmering wheat. "My dearest. So many days have passed and now I feel like a soldier. I look for Stu every day, not with my gun but with my heart." He got his telegram sent because of his gray cap and pants, taken from a dead guy, along with a few silver pieces in his pockets.

*

Their commander, General Nathan Bedford Forrest, concocted a new plan to tear up Union railroads but Boone's company stayed behind. The ride up to Tennessee demanded the most experienced soldiers. Boone's company captain, Davis, decided on a little diversion for his men. Since they were surrounded by Rebel states, and they couldn't disturb the flow of resources on the few rail lines they had in this area, Davis heard of a Union camp wagon to steal. The fellows in Boone's company were anxious to go. They knew hunger as well as their first names.

Louie had made himself favorable in the captain's eyes by teaching the men stealth to take supplies from the blue bellies who thought nothing of destroying southern food sources. The generals referred to Boone's company as the "misfits" and Davis hoped to earn for them a little respect with this raid -- though chances were good they would eat all they took.

They tied their horses off and, following Louie's lead, crept into the brush close enough to the camp to get smoke in their eyes, then followed his directions to spread out. Louie nodded at Boone and leaped onto the back of a dozing blue belly supposedly on guard duty. He wrapped a hand around the man's mouth and slit his throat before the man uttered a sound. Louie laid him on the ground, waved them forward and gave his war cry.

"Yeaaaa Aaaahhhhhh!" And the rest of the company joined as they leaped out of the brush.

The Federals scrambled to their feet and fell just as quickly. Within moments those closest to the supply wagon were dead. The Davis Company Misfits grabbed the wagon and ran off before anyone else arrived. Louie had their escape route so cleverly planned that no one figured out how a wagon could up and disappear.

*

Boone awakened from a full and contented nap with a telegram shoved in his face. He sat up. "Emily."

"I long every day for you walking back into the yard of the home you barely know. My new friends are helpful, and this time our darling child made six months before coming. Born a few months ago. Too soon, too soon! She gasped and fluttered her eyes at me before expiring. Oh, but we'll have a child yet, you mustn't fear. And I am recovering nicely, with the help of friends. But you must come home. I have buried Sugar Lee close to the maple tree. You know, the one you said will live forever? You will love living here, Boone. Come home."

A little girl? Who almost … after Boone cried himself out he sat up. There was Louie, sitting watch over him. Boone wiped his eyes and folded the telegram up. He wondered if she lied to get him to come home. No, not Emily.

"She is sad for you."

"No … worse than that." Boone told Louie about his wife's deformity and intense need to have his baby. "She needs me to stay away."

Louie sat next to Boone, looking thoughtfully across the swamp. "You should go back. She needs you. She must have that child. Or she will not live happily, no matter how hard you try to save her."

"I can't just leave here. I'll be shot for desertion."

"Not if they don't catch you."

"No. If I leave, I leave honorably."

Louie nodded, his teeth gritted in pain only he understood. "We will find you a way."

*

The heat warmed them as Boone galloped with the rest toward the enemy's line. He wiped sweat from his eyes, and looked behind him but couldn't see Louie,

118

couldn't tell one rider from another. If Vicksburg had been conquered, they had to salvage as much of their beleaguered army as possible.

He worried about Louie. He wasn't old, but not as young as some and seemed to be slowing down.

Another musket ball whizzed past his head. They had been warned that they might even face artillery fire. He was glad for this old plug because Robbo getting shot up would have been too much to bear. And glad for the revolver he took off that last dead guy, which he pulled and started firing but those foot soldiers disappeared again.

Blasted skirmishers. Like devils from the underworld, they were. Boone danced around with the rest of the cavalry, seeking a new direction.

He couldn't say until much later what that explosion was but suddenly he was flat on his back, ears ringing, his horse struggling to stand on what was left of its legs. Boone turned over on his back and put a bullet into its brain. He scrambled backward until he bumped into another horse, reloaded, and shot that one. He saw that its rider had a chunk of saddle cinch iron embedded in his skull and put him out of his misery by pushing the iron through. He saw other men he knew, some unhurt but dazed. Where was Louie? A huge mound of ground lay to one side with dead men laying in various pieces in and around the exploded dirt. As the smoke cleared, Boone saw some of the wounded trying to get up or crying for help.

"Louie!" Boone didn't see him anywhere.

The blue bellies rode toward them, their mission to finish off every Rebel who dared to live. Boone couldn't tell which way to go. One rider came at him from another direction but instead of shooting him, leaped off his horse and grabbed Boone's arm. Boone could barely see from the smoke and dust choking up his eyes but on instinct got up into the saddle. Death was death and saving was saving and maybe the twain could meet.

The rider jumped up behind him and yelled at the horse to move. Gunfire followed them and after a moment Boone realized, even with a ringing headache and inability to see, that he was alone in the saddle.

CHAPTER TWENTY
The Deserter

Boone waited until the Union Army had moved on and ran back to look for his rescuer. He found Louie half drowned in his own blood, but somehow still alive. "We lost Vicksburg?" were Louie's first words. Boone got the bleeding stopped and made Louie comfortable with water but he didn't give Louie very long anymore. Still, this horse meat should sustain him -- sustain them both.

"I dunno. Don't look good. Why did you do that?" Boone carved a piece of horse meat off the fire for Louie. He wondered if any of the rest of their company survived.

"Do what? Save your hide? It's what brothers do."

"Hold still. Don't want you to start up bleeding again."

"You gotta kill me, Boone. You can't stay here."

"Don't talk crazy. I'll get you out of here."

"Boone, one way to keep Emily from dying in childbirth. If you want it."

"I do!"

"A root. Of the Bur Bur plant."

"The what?"

"The ... plant my people know. You make a tea, she drink after every time you have sex. She'll not be pregnant."

Boone shook his head. "I want children. So does she. She just needs ... time."

Boone gave him some more water, but Louie rejected another offer of food. "Then allow her that one child. But use the plant, if that seems unlikely. Before you lose her. You suffered ... enough ..."

Boone spit out a piece of bad meat. "Louie, did you know my father?" In the long pause that followed Boone thought Louie had died.

"Yes."

"Tell me about him."

"Were good friends. Followed you. Watched you grow. But I stood up against him in council. He … called me foolish. He was a good man, Boone, but he tries too hard to be friends with whites. Most accept him but I know him better. I believe he needs to die and I believe you need to kill him. But Boone. Your mother lied to you. He must tell you secrets he's told no one, before you kill him."

Boone realized that his mother protected him the way he tried to protect Emily -- by not being honest. "Did you want to kill me? For being his son?"

"I did. But could not. Because …"

"Because you want me to kill him?"

"You will lead the Kiowa. Protect them. Protect their future. He lets the whites push us around. Whites will listen to you. You speak their language. You will learn what he cannot."

My son is no savior! "I owe it to Emily to stay out of that world."

"If her fate is to die, even the Bur Bur plant cannot prevent it."

Boone picked up a stick and poked the fire. "We all die. Some day."

"Some of us can choose." Louie pulled his knife and, before Boone could stop him, sliced his throat open.

Boone sought comfort. *A man that apprehends death no more dreadfully than as a drunken sleep.*

*

Boone found the remnants of his cavalry company on patrol in a corner of Vicksburg. They were glad to see him, especially Clint, who was half Indian himself. Clint told Boone that he had been given up for dead and everyone was surprised he'd returned.

The reformed company included four men who survived the battle and three new recruits, all old men. They were short two horses and had to share. The camp was the most abysmal Boone could imagine. Nothing in all his running days matched this appearance of unholy hell. If this wasn't a swamp, he didn't know swamp. A small patch of land dry enough to sleep on and still they rose in the morning with water in their veins. One of the old fellows developed croup but he could still use his rifle well enough. Biggest challenge was in keeping their weapons dry. Learning to sleep with the coughing and intermittent sounds of shell, mortar and gunfire getting closer all the time got easier in comparison. Food? They told Boone they only ate what they could steal. On occasion a supply wagon headed their way but was waylaid either by civilians or deserters. Alligator became feast and men challenged each other to the kill. Just another instance of kill or be killed.

Boone no longer felt he could make a difference here. But how to get out? Why did he even return? They thought him dead anyway. He looked up from the sputtering campfire to see Clint try his hand at fishing. Boone had filled his head with stories of huge sturgeon and walleye and how good they tasted and Clint preferred that to gator wrestling. Clint looked thinner than usual -- they all did -- and they needed hope of a future to cling to.

"Got me an idea."

"Yeah?" Clint pulled his line up to disappointment.

"Brownsville." Boone figured Clint would come along if he went to south Texas.

"What about it?"

"Important Confederate post. Let's ask for a transfer."

"They need us here."

"Vicksburg's gone."

"We all said that before. She's holding."

But no matter how many of Admiral Farragut's ships they sank -- and Boone had been commended for sneaking explosives on the Indianola -- they couldn't seem to break the Federals' hold on the Mississippi River. If they lost Vicksburg would the South lose the war?

Boone felt himself a realist. The South was doomed and Texas needed saving. And he needed Emily.

"Uh-huh." Boone saw a thousand fish leaped out of the swamp and recognized the vision. The fish turned into horses and Boone, fat and happy, herded them with ease, but then a thousand Comanche were riding them and ran him over. Unharmed, Boone stood and raised a hand and the horses returned to him, with the Comanche swearing eternal bond of friendship to the Horse Man.

Clint interrupted his daydream. "Besides, I want to rank first. If I can rank, I'll get a good position in Brownsville. Just you wait."

Boone missed Louie. He didn't have any illusions, like this one.

*

The weather was muggier than usual for mid-April. Before long they ignored chiggers and stripped to the waist. They were all expert swimmers and fishermen, but they didn't stop to think of food. They followed orders and fought where they could to try to get to Vicksburg and help those who they heard ate rats. But they didn't have enough soldiers to hold the line before Opelousas, not near enough, and while many other southern town civilians often picked up the battle with their soldiers, this town just signed an agreement to let the blue bellies in.

Boone's cavalry got back in time and fought its heart out on the banks of the Red River to protect Port Hudson, most of them dying in the process. Boone took a defensive position where Sam told him to, in the bushes to continue firing where no one saw him to fire back. From there, he watched Clint fall.

After the Federals rode over them toward Port Hudson to accept the Rebel surrender, callously over the top of the dead cavalry, Boone crawled over to Clint, who stuttered in broken breaths. "I'm ready. Let's go. Brownsville. They'll give me medal for this. Ready. To go…" Clint spit up a great wad of blood and died.

Boone and the remainder of his troops abandoned their horses and scurried through the underbrush to join the ranks of the Rebels who were hidden behind their stronghold at Port Hudson, to find they did not welcome new mouths to feed. The Colonel sent a couple of his Negroes out to tell the Federals that the Rebel enemy was too strong for them. They always trusted Negro reports in the past, but exaggeration worked on the timid generals, not this Grant who had them in a stronghold siege.

Other Arkansas men joined in the clamoring to eat or leave. But they were told to be patient, as more men were coming with food. When they didn't arrive, Boone asked for permission to go out and find them, or food, or both, before they lost all of Louisiana and the Mississippi, too. He met with the Colonel and got a million instructions for what to do if he was captured and by the time he angled his escape, the Union ship Essex began bombarding the fort.

Boone slipped away like a weasel, and on sight of the Union forces, realized all was lost. He never looked back.

*

Emily looked up from the sweat of her weeds and blinked away the heat as she heard the wagon approach. Time for the berry wagon already? Boone had been gone nearly a year and in that time she named every wagon that came in. There were times Emily felt Boone no longer existed except in those hastily worded missives.

She at first worked in Atchison at the grocer and that made her feel accepted. She even attended the local church, not to learn their theology but to make friends. She nodded at the preaching but added nothing to the conversations. She didn't hate religion, just continued on a path of growing disbelief ever since her mother left. She and Boone didn't discuss their beliefs but they felt the same -- that belief in the afterlife was both private and sacred.

One matron befriended Emily out of pity for her man being in the Confederate Army "fighting against Union!" and for her sad deformity. But most had Rebel leanings. Boone left her pregnant so Emily accepted the friendship and planned to return as good as she got. She had the best corn, beans and squash garden any of them had ever seen, and a canning secret that made her the talk of this prudish town. She received all manner of goods in exchange for her offerings. More dried elk and buffalo than she would ever eat. She even took in their produce and canned for them.

Truth be told, she couldn't stand any of these people and no longer worked in town after the baby died. They took her to be grieving and helped her to heal. Although she occasionally kept up appearances by going to church, she no longer nodded at the sermons. But she kept selling her canned goods. After the first visit to church following the burial of Sugar Lee, two ladies noted her absence of emotion during the service. "That child robbed her of God."

This made her insides laugh. No child will be born of her that wasn't meant to be.

She had been grateful enough when these ladies tended her following this third loss. She came close to dying herself, but she would never tell Boone that. They fed her so many liquids she felt at times she floated away. Then they forced her to pretend to agree that perhaps she wasn't meant to be a mother. But enough was enough. She could handle her own and then some, with her niche that fit right in to the town's economy, and stopped going to church altogether.

Let them gossip, she thought, they'll still want my goods.

She recognized Ames in his wagon with his bucket of blueberries. He drew to a stop and waited silent for her approach. Usually a talkative man but in a tense and stuttering away, as though he didn't want to give her a chance to respond. Now she met the berry bucket held out to her in silence.

She put the bucket at the edge of her garden and poked around for three nice-sized zucchinis. There were times that she preferred an even exchange of raw goods, especially when her hands were red and raw from canning. Ames would accept her offer, or perhaps not.

Ames pointed to his floorboard for her to set the zucchini down.

"Are you well today?"

He seemed to reel at the sound of her voice, as though he'd just received a curse from the devil. He picked up his reins and looked out over the trail. "Nice doing business with ya." He whipped the reins to force the horse into a trotting departure.

She turned back to her garden, but caught movement out the corner of her eye. When she turned back to the wagon saw that in its place stood a scruffy bearded fellow who looked older than anyone's years. As he straightened and smiled at her, she screamed.

"Boone!" She started toward him at a trot. When he didn't move, she slowed up. "Is it you, Boone?"

Still he did not move.

She reached him and, hesitant, touched him. "Boone."

"Emily…" Boone fell to his knees. He wrapped his arms around her legs and sobbed. "I've deserted."

Emily got him into the house but she didn't know how, because he could barely stand. From his prone position on the bed she fed him water and bits of food, knowing he would soon have much to say. As he slept she stripped him of his rags and checked for injury. Verge of starvation, she figured, and dehydration. She cursed the world and the government for doing this to him and so many more men. She crawled in next to him and held on tight.

*

Boone awoke several times to eat and drink before he woke enough to get up. After doing his business outdoors, he joined Emily on the porch. She knitted furiously to keep her mind off the stories he would tell.

He sat next to her, eyes on her cornfield with entwined beans and squash. "Looks good."

"Yes. I've done well here, Boone."

"But you lost another child." He ducked his head into her shoulder and sobbed, until she pushed him away and wiped his tears.

"Come now, it's past time to mourn her." She cheered him with a tender kiss on the mouth. "Do you want to talk? Your few grams were so short."

"If I knew where to start."

"Let's start at the end and go backward. How did you come to be in Ames' wagon?"

"Arkansas River. I found a raft, made it stronger."

Emily didn't like how Boone didn't look at her. He gestured more with his hands, too, than he used to.

"Floated for days. Water, raw fish."

"But you were so dehydrated, Boone. We're not that far off the Arkansas River."

He gave her a look she didn't recognize. More than fear but less than hate.

"Men on shore, firing at me. Like a game. Finally I had enough." Emily put cake and coffee between them and he gained strength in the sweetening. "I swam over to the opposite shore and ran up to high ground. Right into a band of volunteer blue … ah, Federals. They grabbed me, made me captive. I tried to convince them I'm Indian, with a tribe, but that made it worse.

"Boy," the captain says. "What makes you think being Indian makes you any better than being a Reb?" "Yeah," says another, and he gave me a shove and I was so tired that I naturally fell and couldn't get up. "Yeah, and we know Indians fights with Rebs cause they're always losers. So we're holding you prisoner until this war is decided, and then maybe we'll have a war and wipe out your people, too." Well, Em, I thought I was done for, I mean, I see them eating and drinking and I get nothing but another blow alongside the head if I utter a sound. So I kept myself from sleeping and first chance I got I slit my guard's throat and ran off."

Emily bit down her shudder. He had no emotion at all.

"But without any chance to grab food. And then I couldn't remember anything anymore, not my name or where I lived. I don't know how I got on that wagon, Em."

Emily wrapped her arms around Boone. She couldn't tell where her trembling ended and his began. She pulled his mouth to hers and sank into his taste, his warmth back in her life again. His hunger for her grew to match hers for him, so with little coaxing she got him inside onto the bed before they embarrassed the neighbors. Emily hoisted her skirt and ripped off her panties, and Boone wore only a pair of wool trousers that he gratefully slid off. She rode him as skilled as any rider refusing to be bucked off. Before long both cried out each other's name. Emily laid against his chest and listened to his heart, clinging hard even as she felt death in the wings. How could she feel so mortal at a moment like this? They were finally together again.

"Emily? Will you pack me some food?"

She looked down at him, startled. "Why?"

"I made a promise. To a friend."

*

Boone rode off to find the Kiowa and a plant to put in her tea. He could tell she wasn't strong enough yet. He should have died in that war. Because now he has to lie to the one person who deserved only his truth.

*

Three days passed and the only visitor Emily had was her monthly one, robbing her of yet another child. She sat in the garden, waiting for the heaviest to sink into the ground, that special magical ingredient she didn't share with her neighbors -- her own personal touch of fertility. Boone had returned but was gone again. Crazy? Maybe. She heard war did that to soldiers. She had not heard from Stu, either, not once. All her babies died. All her babies. And now here she fed her blood to the corn. Maybe she was Corn Mother. The thought made her giggle. Maybe she was crazy, too, and any baby of hers would be born crazy. Killing it was Nature's way and she accepted that.

When the corn rows rustled she wrapped her arms around her legs, ready to scream at whoever for disturbing her privacy. Boone stood over her, smiling down at her. He swooped her up in his arms and carried her inside to make love to her, as the mere thought of her monthly friend made him passionate. Afterward, with her blood on his hands, he ran outside screaming.

Emily caught up to him rolling on the ground, the bloody hands over his eyes, crying. She gathered him up in her arms and held tight, and his sobs turned into sighs. "I'm sorry for whatever happened to you out there."

"Not ... what happened. What will happen."

128

"What do you mean this time?"

Boone rolled away from her. "Maybe … maybe I will learn how to tell you."

Emily wrapped her arms around Boone. Together they watched the sun set behind the cornfield as the slivered moon made its appearance.

"There I am," Boone whispered in her hair.

"I know," she responded. "Oh, Boone, I know."

CHAPTER TWENTY-ONE
The Lost Lies

In the days that followed them into another long winter where Boone turned 19, he struggled to rise in the morning and couldn't get to sleep at night, and every chore hurt every muscle. At least he had his Shakespeare, and Emily read with him to help him fall asleep at night.

Every day the horses reminded him of Robbo. He had hoped Robbo got loose and found her way home ahead of him, but Robbo had never known this place in Kansas. She might be waiting for him in north Texas. But knowing the war's brutal need of horse flesh, Robbo was most likely dead.

A man lives on hope, so Boone conjured the plan of moving back to north Texas to buy back Emily's old homestead. He didn't think Emily would mind, except for the chore of moving again. But at least in Texas he might enlist with a volunteer company and erase this stigma of being a deserter. Moving to Texas meant possibly moving into potential danger, and as he wrestled with weeds to find ripened harvest he also wrestled with ways of keeping them both safe, including the idea that he'll never have children anyway and Emily didn't care that he was a deserter.

In the days since he returned home, he found a Comanche tribe to ask about the mysterious plant, but no one could figure out what he was asking for. He found one who spoke a little broken English, who agreed to meet Boone once a week and teach him to speak a brand of Kiowa-Comanche. After weeks of communication he brought Boone the plant he wanted but cautioned him never to share this native secret.

Boone told Emily that he traveled once a week to learn Comanche so he could get a job as an Indian agent -- an idea always on his horizon, as many with blood in each world were able to communicate in both. Others were distrusted because of flipping loyalties but Boone never lived in the Indian world for that to concern anyone.

Boone twined new rope in the barn as he remembered lying to Emily to get her to drink the tea. He realized, as he stomped the life back into his right foot, that he needed new boots and that he must be honest with Emily. She seemed so well settled in Atchison and talked every day about the fine family they would have. As he twined the rope he saw himself putting a noose around her throat as he made love to her, and as he stomped his foot, patted down more dirt over her grave. Sam scolded him for his worry, but Boone had to be honest. All Sam cared about was making love to her.

The barn went dark as he closed his eyes against a sudden headache -- and that's when the screaming began, screams so loud that he thought they came inside him. He ran out and saw Emily in her cornfield, trying to scare the deer with her screams, but the deer seemed resolute and ready to charge at her. He didn't have the rifle on him or they would have had fresh meat for supper. Together they got the deer out by separating and threatening to surround her. At one point the female appeared to turn on Emily to run her right over, but Emily did not back down.

"So Boone." She leaned against him, laughing as the deer ran off. "You know what they say about deer in a cornfield."

"Yes, Em." He grabbed her hand and pulled her to the porch. "Let's move back to Texas. I can't stay a deserter. Now that Vicksburg's gone, Texas could be next."

"Boone, you want to move where the fighting is? What kind of world would that be for our children? And what about your Comanche lessons and dreams of being an interpreter?"

"Always will be more Comanche around." Boone knew this was not necessarily true. "I would not take you where the worst fighting might be, like Brownsville or Houston, but where protecting Texas is, like Austin or San Antonio. Or maybe we could buy back your old homestead in north Texas, although there have been warnings there of war against Kit Carson. So I think more south this time.

I thought I could join the Union, maybe help you find Stu, but there's a chance I'd be shot as a spy." He took her hand because she almost seemed to smile. "I want to make you and our children proud."

"Boone, you do not even have to try. I am always proud of you."

"There is more." Boone decided to start the hardest truth of the story. "I met a man in the army. He knew my father. He died."

"I'm so --."

Boone placed a hand over her mouth and shook his head. "He told me that my mother lied about why she had to keep me safe from my … from Kae-gon. When I was five, I started asking questions. She wouldn't answer them. There were times when she tried to rid herself of me. I think I understand why now."

"Rid herself … oh, Boone, I'm sure she didn't … mean …" Emily wiped a tear.

"The first time I met my father, he was with some others. They rode up and grabbed me, took me to their village without Mama. I think I was three. I wasn't scared, though, not at first. I thought it was fun. I didn't know until after they brought me home again that he was my father and he threw me back for being too small."

"You remember what happened to you when you were three?"

"Sure. Don't you?" But Boone didn't wait for Emily's response. "I don't think they took me very far, but it seemed worlds away. They showed me how they lived and I was shy at first because they seemed so loud. I wasn't used to all that singing and dancing, the horse races that stirred up the dust everywhere. I don't remember anything too specific … except someone's spirit bag got wet and he needed a ceremony done so it would be sacred again. That was the only time I saw a fight, where one said that kind of ceremony was nonsense. I also remember my father saying I will need to be a man someday. When he brought me home Mama screamed and chased them off.

"As I got older, I thought that I wouldn't mind having my father teach me to be a man, and I asked my mother why she was so mad at him. Then she told me the story of how they met, how gentle he had been with her. He kept visiting her in secret until finally she agreed to move to his village and marry him. And then her father, an army general, stormed the village, killed a lot of people and took her back. Then when she ended up dead, I felt betrayed by everyone. Louie made me see that I cannot *just* kill my father. I have to listen to him first."

"And maybe talking to him will give you a reason not to kill him. You have feelings for him, Boone, I can tell. But Boone, what do you think your mama lied about?"

"I don't know. That's why I have to talk to him. Find out. It feels important now. And Emily? Sometimes I say or do strange things. Because … my twin brother Sam is in my head. He died at birth, but now he's in my head. I tell you because … I hope then he'll go away."

"Oh, Boone." Emily hugged him. "That war was terrible for you, wasn't it?"

"No he's been in my head since … even before Mama died. He's like the opposite of me. When I think one way, he thinks the other. Maybe he's my Indian half." He took Emily's hand and played with her fingers. "Louie also told me where I can find a plant to keep you from having children, but that I should let you have that child. It's my choice."

Emily jerked her hand away and stood. "*Your* choice?! You fed me abortive tea!?"

"Not for several days now. I wait until a week after your ceremony to start to add the leaves to your tea. And then I figure a week before your next one when I stop."

"You! You keep me from having children?" Emily stomped out into the yard and then back to him, ready to hit him but flapping her arms away again, back and forth, her limp more distinct, although for a moment he thought she walked without limping at all.

"Just until you seem strong enough. Emily, I want a child with you, too!"

"Boone, I'm 30 now, And if I ever become a mother, if my body is ever ready, it's now. *Now*! You have no right to deny me! You don't want to be father to my children, fine. I'll find someone who does. I'll leave you, Boone. Please don't make me because I love you but I will, right this instant, I swear I will. Because my love to have a child is stronger. A child … your child …" Before he reached her she fell to her knees, sobbing. "Oh, I am good for nothing."

Boone pulled her into his arms. "You know that's not true. I just love you too much to bear the thought of losing you. You are good for so many things. But your body, Em, isn't made for some things. If you have a child, you could die."

"You don't know that." Her tears flowed fast and furious and she hiccuped as she talked. "I'm sure I can give you a son. I'm sure."

Boone held her close. "My vision, Em. You gave birth and you died. You and your baby. I don't want to lose you. We can find children in need of love."

She went limp in his arms. Thinking. Accepting. Coming to terms. We all have limitations, he told himself, and she needed time to plan this new future now.

"Tell me what you saw in your vision."

"Two crosses the first time. One big and one small. Another time, I saw your face, your eyes closed, in the grave, and threw dirt on you. Oh, Em, don't ask me to see you buried."

"Two crosses?"

"One big, one small."

"That could be anything."

"But then your face --."

"All people die someday, Boone. It doesn't mean I die in childbirth. And it doesn't mean the child I carry will die."

"But Emily, the chance --."

"We take chances every day, Boone, just by living. Life is meant to be lived. I won't be denied, Boone. I won't drink your tea again."

As she stomped back out into the garden Boone closed his eyes. "How durst thy tongue move anger to our face? How dare the plants to look up to heaven, from whence they have their nourishment?"

He had no choice but to love her until she died.

CHAPTER TWENTY-TWO
The Orphan

Boone and Emily packed up their Atchison homestead as much as they could while they waited for a response to the 'for sale' sign. She had ignored him during the process, not letting him anywhere near her, but finally her passionate nature overwhelmed her. Boone feared what that meant. He never could resist her advances but tried using Shakespeare to keep the need from completion. "Let villainy itself forswear't. I must forsake the court; to do't or no, is certain to me a break-neck. Happy star …!"

He failed.

One morning as she washed plates Boone told Emily his biggest fear -- that he wasn't meant to settle anywhere. She took a deep breath. "You fight your need for a home, Boone." She suddenly slouched and cried out, "Oh Boone! I want to trust you again."

"I will never get in the way of your happiness, Em. Never. Please believe that. My agony is nothing compared to watching you in yours. I want a child as much as you do."

The next day a buyer arrived with an acceptable offer for the homestead. Everything they could bring had to fit in just one wagon. Boone used his work horses to pull the loaded wagon with one bunk prepared for them to alternate for rest. He tied his new riding horse, Aldo, to the back -- a good horse, but not Robbo. He thought of selling the saddles he bought after getting used to riding bareback in the war, but he needed saddles for the horse ranch he wanted in the future. He helped Emily up into the over-stuffed wagon and put a hand on her knee. "It's already November but if you hang on tight I'll make good time, and at least we're headed south."

"I can hang tight to you, Boone. Just don't ever leave me behind." She threw her arms around him, forgiving him, loving him and Boone wanted this moment to last forever.

He got up in the wagon next to her and gave a last look at all they were leaving behind --her good trade, his new Comanche friends and the dream of going back to his old home near Leavenworth. He looked up at the clear blue sky, a day made for travel and new dreams, noted the distance of the mountains and calculated making it near there to bed for the night.

"Hyah."

*

Boone pulled the wagon up short when they saw the debris in the trail ahead, by this time fully into Indian Territory. Part of the overturned wagon still smoldered from a weak fire set in the corner that also took half the canopy and bracing. Boone put a cautious hand on Emily's knee and jumped down. After looking around the wide open prairie landscape, Boone ran to the wagon. He found two men, brothers by the looks of them, and a woman, not yet dead. She grabbed Boone's hand.

"Charlie. Find Charlie."

"Who shot first?"

She shook her head slightly, eyes unable to focus. "My son, they took him?"

"Who?"

"Indians."

Boone sat back on his haunches as the woman's hand went limp. Indians? None of the people had been scalped. Mama told him a story once about how Indians learned to scalp from Easterners who were offering ransoms on Indian scalps. Boone picked up a rifle near one man. He sniffed the barrel and stuck his finger into the nozzle. He nodded as he rubbed his finger and thumb together. Even if they didn't fire first, they had time to fire back.

Boone felt Emily's hand on his shoulder and stood, still holding the rifle.

"What did she say?"

"They took her son. Or someone. Named Charlie."

"Who? Indians?"

"Maybe."

"What can we do?"

Boone wrapped an arm around her shoulder. "We get away from here."

"Boone! You're not a coward. Not since you were 12. And not even then."

"I don't want to put you in trouble. I shouldn't have brought you, Emily." He guided her back to the wagon. "We don't know what happened here, or what's still out there."

"Can we at least bury them?"

Boone looked skyward. Already they weren't going to make Las Pegras before nightfall. Emily crouched down by the woman and sang softly. She was gonna get her way on this one. He searched the wagon for food and ammunition and found it pretty well stripped clean.

You don't want to blame Indians. You are becoming ready to meet your father. He still has to die, Boone responded to Sam.

*

Boone couldn't sleep that night. He thought Emily felt as haunted as he, but finally he heard her light snores. He needed a dog that would sense and growl when danger was still far enough away. But he heard dogs could lick your hand one minute and bite it the next. Could those two crosses be for him and Emily? They left three similar crosses behind them, off the trail. He closed his eyes, wanting nothing more than to get to sleep, but felt that every chirping animal within fifty miles had lodged with them here in this small grove of trees alongside the creek. A couple of times what sounded like a twig snapping was just another croaking critter.

He forced his eyes shut but sleep was far out of reach. He stood and walked over to the horses. His senses itched. He turned back. Someone crouched over Emily. In total stealth Boone ran back and leaped. He knocked the fellow sideways so quietly Emily never stirred. He grabbed the man -- no, lad, maybe 14 -- by the neck and held tight.

"Please, mister, I don't mean no harm."

Emily sat up. "Boone? What --."

"It's okay, Em, I got 'em." He pushed the lad up against a tree. "What you doing here? Why were you looking at her so close?"

"I thought … you's Indian. I thought maybe you took my ma. Is that my ma?"

Emily came up behind them. "Are you Charlie?"

Seeing the moonlight on her face he cried in disappointment. "You see my ma?" Charlie was thin and shaky with a huge nose and wispy stubbles where a beard might someday be. He blinked hard and reached up to rub his eyes but instead rubbed his cheeks or chin. Boone's eyes watered for his mama and Emily's in response.

"I'm so sorry. We buried them back there, where you were attacked." Emily wrapped an arm around his shoulder. "Stay with us," she whispered. "We'll be your family."

"No! You're wrong! My ma needs me." But he didn't push her away.

"Sorry, son. But she's telling the truth. We buried 'em." Boone felt sudden pride for allowing Emily to have her way. "Back where your wagon burned. You'll find the rocks and crosses off the trail, best we could do."

"No. You're lying!"

"Please, Charlie, listen." Emily tried cuddling him against her in a motherly kind of way.

Charlie pushed himself away from her. Boone put a hand on Emily's shoulder to stop her, first from falling and then from following him. "We're on the southern trail into Texas, boy, if you want to catch up."

Charlie faded into the light of dawn so quick they wondered if they imagined him.

Emily turned in anger. "How could you let him go?"

Boone turned to the cold fire to stir the embers. "Come on, let's fry up the last of those eggs before they spoil. We'll take us this early start."

*

Comanche horses snorted and pawed the ground as men armed for war surrounded them. Armed for war, or the hunt -- Boone saw no sign that they were responsible for Charlie's current misery. They weren't wearing newer Eastern goods. "We're friends. Friends." He glanced at Emily as several of them rode close. "We can pay your toll to let us through. We can give you food." He could tell they understood him. One raised his spear and sounded threatening. But he responded with some choice Comanche phrases that Boone never learned.

One man jammed the tip of his spear against Boone's neck, as several others on Emily's side reached out to stroke her hair. "Don't be frightened, Boone. I know what to do." She climbed out of the wagon, nearly falling to the ground.

"No, Emily!" But the spear against his neck broke skin, drawing blood. He didn't dare move.

Emily started toward one in her usual awkward manner. The Comanche were in awe as they watched her. Boone understood then what his mother told him once. They revered the deformed as people chosen to bear special powers. He felt the spear tip weaken against him. When she stumbled and fell -- on purpose, he could tell -- two of the men jumped off their horses to help her.

Boone shouted in clear Comanche. "Leave her be! Her power is mine." All heads turned to him. Boone knocked the spear away, feeling no pain as he stood in the wagon seat. "We'll take no food from the Comanche." He watched as the Comanche exchanged puzzled glances. The one with the spear reached to Boone with his hand and wiped the blood on Boone's neck, as though seeing him for the first time.

"You are as us? Or half?" He spoke in clear English. The warrior turned to the rest, using Comanche again. "We can use them." He turned back to Boone. "You stay. Help us fight to keep whites off our land."

"Are you dog soldiers? Siding with Cheyenne anger?" Boone noted the sashes made of buffalo skin and porcupine quills as bead work, what he heard they called "dog rope." He put up his hands. "I can do more for your people in peace where I'm going. The Big War in the East will end soon. Gather your people and be ready. They will come west. I will help finish the fight, then return to find my father. Kiowa chief Kae-gon."

At this the man backed off. Boone wasn't sure if he was Kiowa or Comanche anymore. The spear with Boone's blood raised skyward as the dog soldier shouted, and the others responded the same. Still shouting, they rode off.

CHAPTER TWENTY-THREE
The Confederate Meeting

"Boone, let's stay here."

Boone looked around the open prairie. "Here? There's nothing here."

"Okay, let's find the closest town, or a fort."

"Emily, we're still in Indian Territory."

"Is that a problem? Maybe we could find an Indian baby to adopt."

"Oh, dream on, woman. All right. I'll find some kind of well-traveled trail. I promise." Boone moved the wagon on. He didn't admit it to Emily that he didn't know this territory very well. He pointed off to the east. "Looks like the trail goes that way."

As they headed due southeast, Emily told him about how John Ross and his Cherokees came through Kansas on the way to Fort Leavenworth while Boone was gone. Ross and Stand Watie had divided Indian Territory into another Missouri, and not only that, but the Confederates promised Stand Watie that if he fought well for the South, his people would get all the money that the U.S. government promised him, and his own state, besides.

Boone chuckled. "What would they call it? Watopia?"

"Shame, Boone. So Stand Watie has many warriors of Cherokee, Choctaw, Chickasaw, Seminole and even some Comanche fighting for the Confederacy, although many remain neutral and some support Union. But they did not fight each other. And Boone, he has a lot of half-breeds in his army, as well as full white and full Indian. The Confederacy won't allow him to recruit full bloods, though. Amazing thing, prejudice. Anyway, Watie isn't even half Indian himself."

Boone had long ago ceased being amazed by what Emily knew and remembered, her mind an iron trap of knowledge. "Sounds like you want me to join them."

"Now, Boone, you know I don't like you fighting." She looked off into the distance. "I wonder if we'll ever see Stewart again. How will he find us?"

"I don't know." His voice belied the hope that Stu was still alive.

"Oh, look!" She pointed off to a hill in the west. Several elk watched them.

Boone pulled out his rifle and halted the wagon, but they fled before he had good aim. "I do need to hunt us some food, Emily."

"You wish me to camp here and wait?"

Boone jumped down from the wagon after handing her the reins. "Keep following this trail. See how the rocks bend to the north? Stay south of them and head for that tree-lined river, and then follow the river south. I will catch up to you." He untied Aldo and mounted before turning back to her. "You use the other rifle if you have to. It's loaded."

She squinted up at him. "Kill kindly, my love. We only need one."

*

Emily watched Boone ride off. She let her hand drift down to her swelling abdomen. Had Boone noticed? As close as she could figure, this child would be born in May. The war must be over by then. She prayed every day for peace and children, happy that together they decided to accept whatever came their way.

As she turned the wagon to follow the river she heard the sound of gunshots. She hoped he got in a clean kill. Her canned goods were less satisfying without meat. Ahead she saw riders and horses watering at the river's open sand bar. She pulled the wagon up and held her breath. One, already on his horse, wore that long black plantation coat with gray trousers, and as she watched, he replaced his black slouch hat on his graying head.

Stand Watie. Here in person, as though he had heard her mention his name. Not with his army, though. Just his guards.

She didn't tell Boone but she knew he and his warriors robbed anyone for supplies, so desperate were they for food. The Confederacy had so little to go around and ignored Indian Territory. When he saw her, Stand Watie didn't hesitate but rode up to her wagon, followed by the five men who surrounded him.

He sat looking at her, assessing her, and then waved at her wagon.

She nodded. "I can spare some." With her body already aching from the bumpy ride, she got out of the wagon. One of the warriors jumped off his horse and grabbed her arm. "Please don't. I said I would."

Stand Watie yelled at the warrior in Cherokee and at first the man seemed too angry to comply. Finally he gave her a shove at the wagon.

Emily grabbed onto the wagon's side and clutched at the pain in her abdomen. "No. Please." She screamed and sank to her knees as blood poured out to the ground. She lay writhing, clutched at grass and cried, looking for no help or pity from anyone.

Stand Watie gestured to his warriors when he saw the blood. In terror at the sight, they rode off, supplies forgotten.

CHAPTER TWENTY-FOUR
The Stand Watie Affair

When Boone caught up to her, an elk strapped behind his saddle, he saw Emily knelt over a small dirt mound. When he got close enough he saw signs that riders had surrounded her.

He leaped off his horse. "Emily!" Then he saw the blood and saw the pain in her eyes. "Where are you hurt? Come on, lie down."

"Not hurt, Boone." With throat dry she could barely whisper. She accepted his coat for her head and let him stretch her out. "Just … a bad flow this month. Perhaps we rest here a day?"

Boone gave the little mound of dirt a second's glance and went for his canteen. He gave Emily her fill. "Are you sure? Who was here? Did someone threaten you?"

"No. No threat. They were frightened off. I think … they heard your rifle." She closed her eyes. "Get me a blanket, Boone. I need to sleep a while."

Boone watched her drift off. The elk meat needed to be treated, so they might as well camp here for the night. With a grunt of resignation, he got to his feet to butcher and smoke the elk meat. She would need her nourishment.

She'll tell him more when she was stronger. He knew that much about her.

*

Boone walked back to Emily, the crumbling stone barracks and the red wood building behind him swarming with Confederate soldiers. "Fort Towson, Emily. The Confederates use it as headquarters and we are welcome to stay here for the remainder of the war, if I sign on."

"We have to stay in one of those stone rooms?" She shivered in her coat against the strong northern wind. Boone worried that she was losing weight.

"Guy named General Sam Bell Maxey is in charge and says they can open one for us, if in return you can help keep the men fed. We could keep moving, if you want. I can find Stand Watie somewhere down the road."

"No! No, this is fine, Boone. I would like the rest and get the chance to do some good cooking for a while. But where do they find the food resources?"

"Cherokee and Choctaw, believe it or not. I offered to break some horses, too, in trade for the room. They snatched that idea up, saying the soldiers here aren't much good with horses."

With winter fast approaching, Boone fixed up the shelter they offered with minimal effort. Too late in the year to plant a garden, but Emily showed off her prowess with the supplies they gathered from the local tribes and soon had everyone eating out of her hand. They appreciated Boone's ability to hunt, too, and catch wild horses.

So they settled in, although Boone was made to ride with soldiers nearly every day looking for Federals to shoot at. Other times they huddled near the fire to keep warm. Boone most often bit back his desires for Emily's warmth. To her credit, Emily didn't bother him about having a baby since losing the one on the trail. She finally admitted it when he told her she was getting too thin. And now that weight refused to grow back.

On the day Boone alone manned the fort, they were surrounded by Union General James Blunt with some troops from Fort Gibson. Boone tried to remain hidden. They found no one to fight, nor were any inclined to post their flag in this territory. Emily wandered about freely and told the Federal soldiers that she was an Indian captive and preferred to remain that way, and asked after her brother. They didn't bother her much because of her limp and her inability to smile at any of them.

Before they rode off, one of the soldiers rooted Boone out and held him at gunpoint. "You're one of Watie's men, ain't ya? We didn't come all this way for nothing. If you can't give us Maxey, give us Watie."

"Sorry, I'm neutral in this war. Just hired hand."

They grabbed him and pinned him down. "We got us a message for Watie, and you're gonna deliver it." And the beating began.

*

Boone came to in darkness and feared he'd gone blind. He felt a warm softness on his face and pushed away but still couldn't open his eyes.

"Easy, Boone," Emily's voice had swollen with tears. "Who would do this to you?"

"Horse threw me." He tried to sit up but his ribs hurt too much. "Federals said I had to give a message … to Stand Watie. Even when I ain't in it, I am. Accused of being with him. Just because I'm half Indian."

"Well then." She dabbed warmth on the bruises on his chest. "When you find Watie, you help him kill those sons of bitches."

*

As Boone recovered, they heard that Blunt and Maxey's forces had tangled out in the hills, and only a few Rebels stumbled back to hold the fort. Boone told Maxey he had to find Waite and deliver a message, and Maxey wished him luck. As the chill settled in their bones in the fading winter of 1864 due to lack of firewood, Maxey looked like an old man waiting to die.

"I wouldn't mind staying, sir, but my wife is getting antsy."

Maxey ran a trembling hand through his long black hair. "Well, we could still win if Lincoln ain't re-elected. But if the Democrats can't do no better than that McClellan, I don't hold much hope for our side." Maxey sat back with a cigar, hoping to regain some of his vigor. "I got nowhere else to go. I want to thank you, Boone, for the horses you broke for us. I don't know that we could have lasted. And your wife's cooking and preserving skills. Gotta tell you, I've wanted to try her other skills as well. Best to get her away while you can."

Boone walked away, as the distaste for army generals worked through his mouth. He remembered his grandfather and the move across the Mississippi when he was two. His grandfather ordered men about, men who sometimes pawed at his mama, and his grandfather didn't stop them.

Emily stared at him from the doorstep of their shack as he approached. He pulled her inside with him. "We've got to go, Emily. There's nothing left here for us. Let's go find Stand Watie."

"And then what? Boone, you're not fully healed yet." She touched his still swollen and bruised face.

"I'm fine, woman. If we don't find Stand Watie, we'll go to Austin. Come on, we can be out of here in an hour and in Texas as soon as we cross the bridge. Maxey agrees it's best we go."

"But Boone, I don't want to go. Don't I get a say in this?"

"No." He feared mentioning she'll be raped if she stayed.

"No? That's it? No? Boone, do you know how hard it is to homestead in Texas? You have to have money. You can't just walk in and stake out a piece of open land. It's not like that there. Do you know how much my papa had to pay for that dirt farm he had? Here the land is for the taking, because…"

"Because I'm Kiowa? Emily, look at me. I'm white! My mama wanted me to be white! If I stay here I don't know what I'll turn into."

"And if I let you run away again --."

"I'm not running away!"

"You are! You always run away. Boone, for once, let's face things standing still."

In a fury he seldom felt Boone swept all her cooking goods from the table to the floor and ran out of the shack. He ran to the shed where the animals and wagons were kept and found Aldo. He had to stop and catch his breath because his ribs still hurt so much, felt dizzy and had to clutch the wagon. As he turned to pull the wagon back outside to hitch his horses up, he saw the door blocked by a soldier.

"What you doing?"

Boone pulled himself up in an attempt to look strong. "Wife and I decided to move to Texas."

"In March? Might find some of the route blocked."

"Texas is right over the river."

"You running away? Deserting us?"

"No. I'm going to join Stand Watie."

The soldier, drunk from what Boone could tell, grabbed his arm. "You don't want to do that." With a cocky grin he pushed Boone back. "But hell, I won't stop you. Just leave that nice little wife of yours here. We'll take good care of her." He turned, cackling.

Boone grabbed the soldier and gave him a jaw-cracking fist to the mouth, knocking him against the shed's stone wall and out. He turned to see Emily staring at him. "We have to go."

She turned and went back into their room.

When he had the horses hitched up he waited for Emily. Finally he opened the door, expecting a shoe at his head. But she sat at the table, shawl and bonnet on, and all the goods in the room in sacks, the one trunk filled but not closed.

"Stay not thy compliment. I forgive thy duty." Emily pointed at the trunk before he could respond with surprise. She'd never quoted at him before. "You can check and see if I forgot anything. Anything that's not broke, that is."

Boone took a quick look around and in the trunk. "You did great." He held a hand out to her but she picked up two of the sacks, keeping one arm free as always for balance. "I'll get the rest." Emily nodded and walked out. Boone watched her, amazed.

He bolted the trunk shut, hefted it, and grabbed another bag.

*

Emily and Boone got across the river and into Texas in total silence. Night was coming on when Boone finally spoke. "You heard, didn't you. You weren't safe there."

"I like being settled, but I want to feel safe. I'm sorry I didn't trust you." Emily started to cry. Boone stopped the wagon and they threw their arms around each other. "Promise me the next place … promise me, Boone." She sobbed so hard she hiccuped. Boone kissed her tears, her lips, her neck. He got out of the wagon and lifted her into his arms, still kissing her. He laid her in some soft grass, and they made love and fell asleep, still crying and kissing.

Emily woke early the next morning, with a start. "Boone, look what we did, out in the open like this. We better get moving." She jumped up, fearing the wagon had been stolen.

Boone leaped up after her and took her in his arms. "We're all right. We don't have to rush."

"Where are we going?"

"First settlement we see that has a doctor and a mercantile, we'll stop, Emily. I promise. Rebel or union controlled. We won't take sides anymore."

"If that's possible." Emily tended the fire while Boone hunted fish in the river. She figured he must have gone a ways down river and didn't hear the riders coming. She recognized them. Stand Watie, this time with at least 100 of his soldiers.

He recognized her. "You fine?"

"Yes, yes, thank you. My husband would love to meet you. He wants to join your army."

But he pointed to her wagon. "Food."

"Oh, yes, sure."

Off in the distance, they heard the pounding of more hooves, and at the same moment Boone flew up from the river, a fish in each hand and water raining off him into the wind.

"The Union company is coming!" Boone shouted at them. "Emily, get under the wagon!"

The Indians dispersed in many directions, finding so many places to hide so quickly that Boone felt a new admiration for them. There may be many half-breeds but they were every bit as cunning as he expected of full bloods -- and felt shame for any notion otherwise. He saddled his horse and leaped on, riding off to meet Blunt's Federals heading their way. When they saw him, they began to fire.

Boone rode back to the wagon to defend only that which he knew was sacred, and no one else. No more taking sides.

Out of what seemed like air Watie's men erupted, arrows flying so hard and fast that the soldiers never had time to reload but fell out of their saddles one after another. Boone leaped out, too, taking advantage of his position to knock a man off his horse with a spear and rammed the spear into his chest. Another rider shot at Boone but missed and Boone leaped on the back of the horse and slit the rider's throat -- all the while aware that Emily watched, keeping herself and the baby they just made safe.

Almost before they were aware the battle had begun, the rest of the soldiers rode off again, while hurling threats at Boone. They saw, in his wagon and white wife, the side he chose against what should be his nature and cursed him. Boone felt the curse land down on him as he helped Emily back into the wagon.

As they rode off, Boone and Emily waved at Watie's men, who were too busy with robbing the dead to pay them much mind.

Except for Watie. He stood in the saddle and saluted Boone.

CHAPTER TWENTY-FIVE
The Father's Lesson

Boone scooted out of the house that early a.m. Summer went quickly once they settled in Austin. Emily took great caution with her growing pregnancy, and Boone often collapsed into bed long after dark for all the chores he took on, along with building his horse ranch. At least here he didn't fear the winters, but the crops had started to go fallow, so he looked forward to a rest of sorts over the winter months. He stopped to view the rising sun and said his quick prayers to the east, praying for Emily's strong heart, constitution and completion of her desire to give him a healthy child. They were both cautiously excited, now that they lived in the vicinity of a doctor. Boone ran for him that morning, as Emily couldn't get out of bed for the pain. The doctor confirmed her labor and shooed Boone out of the house.

He heard his horse's whinny and went to the stable, but their loving nuzzles couldn't take his mind off Emily's pain. Not even his most beloved Shakespeare stirred his mind anywhere else. As Boone brushed the gelding's mane, he imagined holding his child, soft, sweet and innocent. He hoped the child would look like Emily -- her kind blue eyes, her bright red hair and especially her white skin. He concentrated on her strength and sent her his spirit.

Emily felt sure Boone would understand, while holding his newborn, what drove Kae-gon to kill his mama to get his boy back. In her four years with Boone, forgiveness was the only demand Emily has made of him that he hadn't fulfilled.

They had talked about Sam, too, and she agreed that Sam must be his Indian side. She liked the part about Sam not wanting to kill his father. Lynelle had loved Boone's father enough to marry him in secret. Emily said that he had been surrounded by love, including the brother in the womb. She reminded him that his mother may have wanted to die rather than lose him.

She told him she never wanted to outlive another child. The pain she wore for each of them was the worst imaginable. "Ahhhhh!"

"Hold it steady, woman, steady!"

How could he hear them? How could he not? He couldn't hear the soft support offered to her by the doctor or his assistant but only the loudest of sounds. Emily should be given less than her share of pain, as she'd had to put up with so much all her life.

Again he thought to run in there, and again, he reminded himself that she needed to focus.

Emily had professed great pride in him and told him he created a good legacy for his children. Watie called on him again and again and Boone always responded. Now, with Lincoln re-elected and a child to care for, Boone would not fight again. He had lived every day with the belief that Emily would lose this child, too. He hadn't wanted to feel the child's kicks at first. Finally, when she passed seven months, he bonded with the active womb movement and did not leave her side again, except for chores and at harvest.

As he thought back over his life, he could not believe he was not yet 20.

They settled when they found a ranch abandoned close enough to Austin. Texas laws were different than other states and territories. The state, when annexed to the U.S., claimed that as a state Texas had the right to all vacant and un-appropriated lands in its borders, so Lincoln's Homestead Act didn't apply. Boone had contacted all the state officials about this abandoned property and found that he only needed to pay the property's back taxes, which amounted to two of his breeding stock.

Emily made friends and put her canning skills to good use in nearby Austin, even as she grew big with child and took care to rest often. Boone caught wild horses, broke and sold them to the highest bidder, mostly to the Union army who occupied the area after the fall of Brownsville. With the war still on, they were often hard pressed for food. Meat they had plenty with Boone's ability to bring down whatever ran on four legs, but they scrounged for other goods. His crop harvest was not as healthy as hers had always been.

He recalled how tired she seemed just yesterday. Yet she thought only of him and questioned his silence in front of his favorite breakfast. She insisting on keeping her cooking chores. Boone took a spoonful of gruel. "I think how to set you free when you tire of me."

"I shall simply take my baby and run, the way your mother did with you."

"Don't tease me, Em."

"Look how nicely you turned out. Should I not wish that for your son?" Her eyes sparkled as she kissed his bronzed cheek. "Will you accept the blacksmith offer to run the shop this winter?"

"No. Too many hours. I can't leave you alone that much."

"Do not spoil me, Boone. You know I will outlive you." She told him to have seconds. "You need your strength. I need your strength."

As he watched her, he thought her pregnant shape made the limp she lived with all her life almost disappear, as though the weight had evened her out somehow. But her face drooped even when her eyes sparkled, giving her that tired look.

He wondered how she would keep up to a child. She acted comfortable with that deformed gait but sometimes in her sleep a moan would slip out. He made her rest as much as possible, but she often grew restless and irritable. Last night she shooed him out of the house for peeling her potatoes after watching him reduce them to spuds. "Not like whittling a stick!"

He should take ownership of the blacksmith shop, but how? He would be away from home from dawn until dusk, and then out with the horses. But they did need the income.

"Ahhhhh!"

The cry tore Boone from his chores to peer out the barn. He stared at the tarped window, where the black covering loose and flapping over broken glass reminded him of the bird a few weeks back. Emily had called him inside with a screech and he hurried, picturing her on the floor bleeding to death. But she stood alongside the window where the tarp had come loose at one end and pointed down.

A sparrow fluttered on the floor. Boone crouched down beside the bird as it flapped to get airborne again.

Emily put a hand on his shoulder. "I heard a loud smack and the tarp loosened and the poor little thing fell to the floor. Maybe it just wants some warmth."

Boone sat cross-legged on the floor.

"Aren't you going to take it outside?"

"We'll see if it gets the use of its wings back. There is a saying about a sparrow. If it comes into your life and leaves again, you will be graced."

Emily patted her bulge. "We already have been."

"See how it's trying its wings. We will let the sparrow go before we scare it too much." He cupped his palms around the bird and got to his knees as Emily opened the door. "Awoh! It bit me."

"Let it go," she consoled him.

Boone threw his hands upward and the sparrow was airborne. They watched as the bird flapped its wings a few times. Its wings collapsed, and the sparrow dropped dead to the ground.

Boone and Emily stared as though wishes might bring it back. "I think it was old," he told her.

But Emily went to bed and stayed there the rest of that day. Boone sat with her, giving her all the reassurance he had. Finally she wrapped her arms around Boone. "At least he chose us to die with. That makes us special. Right, Boone?" Boone realized how afraid she was. "Are you sad you stopped giving me that tea?"

"Oh, my girl." Boone kissed her abdomen. "You gave me a reason for my life. I had to give you one, too. Before you, I was always running. Before me, you had a dream. Before you I had a dream, too, but a dream is not as strong as a reason. A dream is a cloud, where reason is a tree."

"But you worry, Boone, because a tree can be felled."

"We have our reasons. We will grow stronger, our roots deeper." He would not admit his fear. Not to her.

Boone led Aldo back into the stable and called Tio over. Many more children Emily wanted! He'd gotten her used to the idea of adopting, so that had to be what she meant. He could only brush horses at the moment, certainly not keep thinking this thought of having more children. He felt like that sparrow just before it hit ground -- a useless flapping of wings. A few of his mares had given him trouble birthing. Once he even got on his knees and plunged his hands into the horse to grab hold of baby hooves. The thought of doing that to his wife ... "Thy scarlet robes as a child's bearing cloth I'll use to carry thee out of this --."

"Boone! Come now!"

Boone dropped the brush and turned, whacking his left knee into the barn post. He swore under his breath and limped into the house, his breath coming out in cold spurts as he imagined Emily stretched out on the bed -- writhing, screaming, bleeding.

Boone peeked in to see Dr. Bradshaw packing his bag with the tools after his assistant washed them in a bucket. He went to Emily's bedside and brushed the hair off her cool forehead.

"I had to cut the child out. Her deformity went too deep. There was no way to know."

"She'll be all right?" To Boone she seemed barely to breathe.

"That'll depend on the strength of her heart."

"She has a very strong heart." Boone nodded down at his wife. Her face was pale -- her hair like fire on the pillow.

"Emotionally, perhaps. But physically?"

Boone looked around the room. "The baby?"

Dr. Bradshaw's mouth set in repressed sorrow. "Too much trauma. A boy."

His assistant, a young girl, gasped and busied herself with her gray cloak. "We did all we could." She ran outside sobbing.

The doctor picked up his bag and pointed to the corner of the room. A box had been fixed as a bed, lined with the softest cotton clothes Emily could spare. On those clothes the dead baby lay wrapped. Boone couldn't see its face.

"If Emily wakes, she'll want to see the baby. I hope you have the courage. To do what needs to be done." Dr. Bradshaw gave Boone's shoulder a shake. "Be strong." He walked out the door. The sound of his "hyah" pulled Boone from his stupor and he ran to the door.

"Wait! How do I care for her?" But the doctor said "if" and Boone knew the answer. He looked back at her, so still and peaceful. *Run, Boone, run!*

Boone knelt down beside Emily and brushed her cheek.

As she stirred, Boone pulled the baby's box to her bedside. He reached for the cloth, and after a short prayer for courage pulled the cloth off his boy's face. He looked just like Emily, the round little cherub face, tuft of golden-red, almost invisible hair. His child used its last heartbeats inside his mother's womb. Not a bad way to die, if one *must* die. Boone stroked his boy's cheek, feeling as a father would without knowing he knew how. Hot tears rolled down his cheeks. How badly his father must have missed him. How hard to let his boy go at age three when he had the chance to keep him forever. But a young one needs its mother.

Boone picked the boy up as though he might break. Emily will want to give him a name. He pictured his boy squawking and kicking for his mama's milk. With trembling arms he pressed the baby's forehead against his own cheek. The dear boy's eyes were closed, and he was still slightly warm and moist from his mother's womb. Boone didn't want this last sane moment to ever end.

Emily stirred and her eyes blinked open. "Boone? Have we?" He pulled Emily's blanket back and laid the baby inside her arm. She looked at the bundle against her breast. "Oh, he's beautiful! See how nicely he sleeps."

"You can tell … he's a boy?" Boone felt the pride destined to collapse back into that aching loss that would never let go.

"Oh, yes. We did it, didn't we? You must … have more faith in your wife."

"Yes, you were right." He turned away to blink back tears.

Her eyes squeezed tight in pain. "Did you name him?"

"No, dove, I saved that for you."

"Well, I hoped ..." Her head sank back against the pillow. Boone held her hand tight, willing her to stay with him. "I know you want more children. But I ... think I need some ... some rest first." She looked so dreadfully white, her eyes without sparkle.

"The name, Emily. What do you think, now that you've seen him?"

"Such a cherub. Peter Nicholas suits him well, don't you think?"

Boone kissed her hand as she gasped for breath. "Yes."

"Find him ... a Kiowa name, too. Forgive your father, Boone. And forgive me ... for..." Her hand reached up to touch him but faltered in mid-air and fell again. Emily left him to be with her son.

Boone collapsed down on both of them as sanity drained away.

*

Boone dug graves in the woods near the pond where Emily loved to sit and listen to him read. He turned the page to their favorite passage from Romeo and Juliet and sat down next to them. "Oh, swear not by the moon. The inconstant moon. That monthly changes in her circled orb." When the woods darkened, he closed his book. Her last words and thoughts were for him, of his future without her. She wanted forgiveness for leaving him.

But Boone couldn't see that future. *You killed her. You killed them both!* He collapsed with dry racking sobs on their graves, tearing at the dirt as though to dig them back up.

When he could sit again, after all the moisture had left his body, he picked up a stone. On the boulder near their grave he etched his symbol, the sunset that shoots around a crescent moon. He refused to give the graves crosses.

His mother tried to reach him. "You are not going to drown, Boone. Keep swimming. Keep breathing. You are meant for better things."

Boone shut her out and ran. He ran straight for the sound of Sam's screaming.

CHAPTER TWENTY-SIX
The Madness

Boone ran from the graves, taking nothing with him but a knife, believing that homestead had been cursed. He felt like a twelve-year-old again, running naked, vowing to kill the father in him. He followed his nose to a campfire of meat cooking and used his knife to cut off all his hair. He wasn't white, or Indian. He was erased.

He held the knife out, ready to kill for meat.

"Boone! It's me!" Long Ear Jackson saw him staring at the food. "You don't have to kill me. I share." They sat without words and Jackson handed him a piece. "Why you here? Where's that pretty wife and child? Oh, I am sorry. This is why you look so miserable. Well, join with me. Watie sent me away, said I was becoming a madman. Let's be two madmen and go to Mexico where we can rob, steal and plunder the vaqueros and trade wagons. Good kind of life for fellows like us with nothing left to lose. Maybe we even marry down there, eh?"

Stay away from your father. Go with him. This is your sunset.

"I'm no one." And with that thought, with the words of the first crazy man who'd tried to make him in a slave in his head, Boone's last lucid moment disappeared and he gave his life completely to Sam. Sam was instinct for survival and all that mattered was losing the pain of being human, a half-breed and Emily's killer. For the longest time he had no idea that a fellow named Boone Tyler still existed.

*

Months passed, and still Boone did not know who he was. In lucid moments he felt the weather must be hot because he lost most of his clothes and the burden of living as a civilized white man along the way. They were on foot much of the time as one horse after another died in his relentless drive away to get away from himself.

They stole wherever they could, rode them to death and were on foot again until they found another to steal.

You don't belong anywhere. Be wild. Stay wild. Not Indian. Not white. You're no better than an animal.

In Boone's formerly sane mind Sam was all Indian and he was all white. As Boone's madness set in this began to change. Boone became the Indian and Sam the crazy white man who didn't know where he belonged. Sam's face was Emily's face, and his mother's face, and then the face of every white who ever hated him. "You're letting me down. I freed you to do the right thing. How can you fail? Don't you know what the right thing is? You have to listen to your soul. Your soul has no skin color, Boone. What's wrong with you? Aren't you the man I loved?"

Boone laughed at Emily's voice inside him until she went away. Soundless, voiceless, he found someone else to tell him what to do and where to go, how to live again.

Long Ear Jackson's laugh. He spoke a cackle without words. Boone rode in circles around it, trying to figure out what he was doing. He robbed wagons. Stole food and horses, always following that cackle.

But then Jackson disappeared and Boone was surrounded by Kiowa. Not Jackson's cackle now. Sam's laugh.

He rode with the Kiowa across the border into Texas, and back into Matamoras, and then … there was a woman. With a beautiful little boy.

He stopped hearing Sam's cackle when he saw the little boy's hand on his arm. He wasn't blonde. His name wasn't Peter.

And Lee had surrendered to Grant.

CHAPTER TWENTY-SEVEN
The Army Job

When he walked his ragged old mule to the buildings on the horizon Boone did not know where he was, but at least he knew who he was. Sam's voice finally quieted as he headed north on the roads of civilized travel. He ignored all along the way, even those who called out a greeting. Several times he was accused of being a Confederate. *Do not show fear. Fear will ruin the mind.* He thought maybe that was Shakespeare, but maybe not. He stopped at the fort's gates and adjusted the heavy pack behind him, and responded to a small squeak. "Soon now."

As he got closer he saw what appeared to be an encampment of natives surrounded by soldiers. There were some meager attempts at farming in the rough rocky soil, but most of the natives appeared uninterested, except in the horses where several were laughing and riding in the corral, as though pretending to break what appeared to be aging and worn mounts. Children played with sticks and balls in a game he could only assume was improvised, and most of the women had some busy work in their hands, mostly making clothing.

When he reached the fort he told the guard with short words that he wanted work as an interpreter, and the guard waved him in. Boone didn't know what the guard saw under Boone's heavy hat to hide eyes deepened with time's response to rage.

When he saw a blanket-wrapped native whittling, he cleared his throat. "Water."

With the thirst quenched -- barely, as the water was bad -- he asked the old man his tribe. Navajo. And where he was. Boone was surprised to learn this was New Mexico Territory. *Where was Aldo* was his a frequent litany. He came to the gradual knowledge that he worked for some vaqueros who needed horse stock gentled but what else he had done after leaving Emily was lost in his mind's dark recesses.

The Navajo handed Boone some corn kernels, for the thirst, before walking away. As Boone munched, he understood. Emily had to die to set him free. But to be truly free, he must never love again. Not even Bark, who was cooped up in Boone's pack waiting to be fed. He clenched the corn in his fist. Bark needed to be freed. The baby raccoon had been lost and crying for its mama, so Boone adopted it. "I understand you, little one. But you cannot stay with me for long." A month later, Bark wouldn't leave.

Boone walked to the mule he didn't name and found himself corralled by soldiers.

"You're an Indian?"

Boone had nowhere else to go. "Half."

"Navajo?"

Boone laughed, but not in a funny way. "Kiowa."

"Yeah?" The soldier nodded to the Captain. "Want me to go for General Carleton?"

The Captain got up from his chair in what Boone read as disgust. "Yeah and take him with you."

"Don't mind the Captain, we ain't all like that." The soldier, whose name was William, led the way. He had a panting agreeableness to his voice that made Boone wonder if that's what Bark would sound like if he could talk. His tightened fist with the corn signaled him as someone looking for trouble. "So what's it feel like to be half Indian?"

"Like half the world hates half of you and the other half hates the other half."

William shoved his hands in his pockets as though dejected. "Yeah. Guess so." They walked on. "Ain't half that hate half, though. Not like you think. I come from Wurttemberg. It's a German kingdom in Europe. They call me a Dutchman. Many hate me here, too."

"World's complicated." He showed William the corn in his hand and strode over to his mule, with William traipsing behind him. Instead of giving it to his mule, he opened his pack and stuck his hand in, with William peering over his shoulder, puzzled. He pulled his hand back out in a second, wet and slightly red from the nibbling. With no explanation offered, he nodded at William and as they walked on, wiped his hand on his pants.

William seemed unaffected by the cold air -- seemed winter was always coming and forcing him to get a year older. *How old are you now* but Boone didn't care. He instead studied their ragged and harvested fields and figured they didn't get much this year. Their crops looked yellow and wilted, and then he remembered the taste of water. Alkali. Bad ground that no amount of Emily's fertilizer would cure.

Thought of her brought tears back but he didn't notice. Brown, half grown corn stalks, not tussled, dried up nubs. Patches of pumpkin vine there had given up crawling. He didn't recognize what else they tried to grow and failed to harvest.

"Not much of a farmer, myself," William said, noting Boone's sadness.

The Navajos sat, just sat, blankets clutched around them as though trying to hide, staring at nothing. Others, he figured, were out hunting, risking their lives to exist on Comanche resources. And then he wondered how he knew who the real land owners were.

"We gotta ride to Carleton. He won't come here. Some says he's afraid to."

"Ride?" Boone couldn't remember the last time he owned a horse. "My mule is slow. Someone … robbed me."

"Maybe Grant will come. Or Sherman, now that he's got nothing better to do. Maybe he can get you to help."

"Me?"

"You talk Comanche, don't you?"

At the stable William pointed out a horse for Boone. Not much but with four legs and Boone figured as long as it wasn't mule, he could make it move. "I gotta let my raccoon go."

*

162

William took him up into the mountains of Santa Fe. General Carleton, the architect of the Bosque Redondo, had his headquarters at Fort Marcy. He sent out word of all kinds of gold and silver strikes in the area to get whites to settle in the territory. But Boone had seen displaced Mexicans, people with crosses and virgin statues, who were in better shape than these homesteaders. Leftovers, William said, misunderstanding his comment, who don't realize this wasn't Mexican land anymore.

William talked but Boone entered his own world again. He wondered how he might react to meeting Grant or Sherman. Sherman was in charge of the western troops, but Grant was in charge of the whole army. Sherman brought Atlanta down, but Grant was the butcher at Vicksburg. Boone felt his fists clench. Slavery had to end, he knew that, but all of a sudden? What about the people who still felt them superior? Could they suddenly change? Boone wondered how ex-slaves were enjoying that freedom now.

He had been on the Santa Fe trail once before. He was nine and his grandfather took them to Santa Fe for his mother to meet a man. Halfway there Lynelle disappeared. They found her walking back to Kansas. "Not anymore. Ever."

"Ruin't," the General told Boone before they found her. "By your father."

Boone never learned for sure if his grandfather was dead but stopped caring. He could still try to find Samantha. He should find out about Stu, too, by going back to Emily's old homestead. But Stu might accuse him of murdering his sister, the way his grandfather could accuse him of murdering his mother. "Our remedies oft in ourselves do lie, which we ascribe to heaven. The fated sky gives us free scope ..." he forgot how the rest of it went and hated that he forgot. Boone noticed William was out of water and offered his canteen.

"You don't need it?"

William shrugged. "Had some water last week." He chuckled but Boone didn't get the joke. "We got a couple more hills to cross. Should find a stream for the horses, anyhow."

163

Had some water last week. That triggered a memory, sending him back into Mexico. Why would he have robbed silver shipments? Had he been forced? He had watched for trains, wanting only water as a reward. How much more might he remember? What did he *want* to remember?

He reached behind into his pack, now without Bark, who Boone sensed followed along on his own somewhere, and pulled out a harmonica -- ornate, good quality silver. As he played while climbing that last hill, William stole appreciative glances. Boone got to look around this old city of Old Spain. Lots of signs of Pueblo occupation -- that's what William said those adobe houses belonged to.

Carleton wasn't at the fort but they were told Sherman could arrive any day now. For the next couple of days, after William left him alone, Boone wandered. He liked looking at the buildings as the ladies liked looking at him. Most seemed to think he belonged. He wandered to the vendors to buy sweets, or corn, or tamales, at first alarmed by and then grateful for how much money he found on him. William said the Pueblo were religious but everyone sold goods, even on Sunday. If he didn't watch where he walked he tripped over another animal loose in the street and someone would ask him to buy it. The smell at some of the stands meant the meat had sat untreated a little too long, although the seller insisted anything he sold would cook up just fine.

And the noise and the fighting were outrageous. He saw several horse races in the streets, which made him laugh until he nearly got run over. Garbage tossed in the river, defecation and urination on sidewalks, streets, roads. Just everywhere. So much whiskey that the smell soaked into that of dead meat. Drunks were a constant as were their obscene songs.

Boone found Santa Fe vibrant and alive, surrounded by a ring of mountains and a desert that bloomed in November. The water wasn't the best, but he had learned in Mexico to use lemon to kill the alkali and strainers for better purity. As a potential interpreter, the army gave him a loft in the fort's barn for sleeping.

William found Boone polishing his rifle early one morning in the fort's livery stable and took him into town. "General Sherman will talk to you."

Sherman stood over a Mexican and barked orders at him to clean up the sludge from the front of his shack. "You'll infect your horse. Hell, you'll infect all our horses! Clean it up! I'll make you pay next time!"

"Can he do that?" Boone looked around but didn't see anyone likely to stop a bulldog like Sherman.

"No. Not his place. But he was this big hero in the war, and out there he's like a…" William struggled for the right words.

"White man in a buffalo herd?"

William laughed, a bit of a snicker. "Or Indian on a cattle drive."

Boone didn't find that near as funny.

Sherman scraped his boot on a stone that had come loose in the street. Boone figured he might feel a little embarrassed to be caught with horse manure on his boot. The man, so ruthless on Atlanta, seemed rather small, not much bigger than William but with an expression fierce enough to control a wild fire.

He also seemed -- Boone wasn't sure but he also seemed defeated. Like he didn't want to be here but didn't know where else to go.

William gave Sherman a salute. "Damned Dutchman," he muttered as William sauntered off. He placed an arm around Boone's shoulder. "Between you and me, we should have encouraged the Belgians to send soldiers, or maybe the Swiss. Anyone but the Prussians. Useless lot. What tribe you with?"

Boone couldn't puzzle that last statement about Prussians out and didn't hear the question directed at him.

Sherman took a step back. "You don't speak English? Not much good to me then, are you?" He looked around as though to give William a good tongue lashing.

"Yes sir. Here for a job. I can work with Indians, sir."

"You can work … you a half-breed?"

"Yes sir." Boone met Sherman's stare and didn't blink.

"Fur trapper father?"

"No sir."

Sherman waited. "Well, guess it's not my concern. What you speak besides English?"

"Kiowa. Some Comanche. Some Mexican."

"Huh. Just what I'm looking for. But you knew that, didn't you?" He didn't wait for Boone to answer. "Who recommends you? What experience you got?"

"Talking with 'em, is all." Although Boone couldn't remember talking to anyone at all in the past year.

Sherman ran a hand through thin, unruly hair. "Then let's get you some." Sherman walked them back to the fort where he threw salutes back and forth. "Captain Mulroy, get yourself and William and this squaw-man back to the Bosque. He's going to stop those Comanche raids on the Navajo."

CHAPTER TWENTY-EIGHT
The Army Instructions

Captain Mulroy introduced Boone to Major William Rawley, the commander of the Bosque Redondo. Rawley took Boone to help with construction of an aqueduct because they experienced flooding due to the recent rains. Boone hadn't noticed getting wet, making him wonder over the current state of his sanity. The flooding was more due to hard ground in the lowlands, and they could control that with some ditch digging. This work took longer than they expected, and then all the people of the Bosque went into winter quarters. They had nothing more for Boone to do that year, as raids and scrounging for food kept everyone busy, and Indian agents and army soldiers got into arguments about who should be in charge of the Bosque that never got them anywhere. Boone continued to relish his saner moments and the real world again but never gave a thought to his future. Sam had gone blissfully silent with Boone's lack of planning.

Boone went on several expeditions after buffalo that winter. He tried to teach these soldiers the Indian method that he learned from the Comanche. No use of firearms because that frightened the buffalo and made them stampede. With silent arrows the buffalo sometimes forgot why they ran. In early 1866, after another day of lumber hauling, Boone was called away from his sweaty chore and taken into council with some Navajos.

"We attack the Comancheros," Navajo leader Barboncito told him, in competent English.

"Why?" Boone meant this question for any of them, including the white officers in council, but Barboncito responded.

"They trade with Comanches. Comanches take from us, trade to them. We want to get our goods back."

"Between here and Fort Bascom," Major Rawley said. "That will be your territory, where you will find them."

"Alone?"

"You will go out as one of them and gain their confidence."

"I can dress as I wish, but I can't disguise myself as someone they'll know."

Rawley threw up his hands and sat back. "Barboncito, can you explain to him how to take this seriously?"

Barboncito stood in front of Boone, his hands clasped behind him. "The government gave us this land to settle and to farm. These soldiers stay with us because we keep trying to go home to our land at the Four Mountains."

Rawley sighed but otherwise kept his impatience swallowed.

"Here we are tormented, the little we grow is stolen no matter how many keep watch. We are always hungry. We go out to hunt and again we are tormented. We ask to be left alone to take care of ourselves."

Boone nodded as Barboncito took his seat again. "I long for the day you can return to your own homeland. But when I talk to Comanche, I go as myself and not as one of them."

Rawley took up the talking stick. "Alone?"

Boone had to laugh. It felt good to laugh. "I'm used to being alone. And I have nothing more to lose."

Rawley followed Boone out. "Convince their chief to meet with me in council. Bring in his warriors, too. Tell them we want to make a deal. Not a treaty. A deal. Don't rile them. Don't call them trespassers. One wrong move and they will cut you down. You were raised in the white world, right?"

Boone stopped at his horse and checked the cinch.

"Say they see a stranger coming. But that stranger has his hands hidden. What do they do?"

"Invite him for coffee?"

"Hey, man, these are savages. They don't ask questions. They just kill."

Boone turned, humor gone. "They are human beings."

"Okay, human beings who kill. You ride toward them like this." Rawley held up his hands, palms forward. "Only way you'll get past first glance."

Boone hesitated. "Now I have a condition. If you want me to be successful at this."

"Think you can make demands?" Rawley sighed. "What?"

"That copy of Shakespeare you keep in your office." Boone jumped into the saddle and waited until Rawley returned and willingly gave up the book. He tucked it securely in his saddlebag, already feeling more civilized. "Now, just so I understand. You want me to act like a whipped dog and tell them to come to talk. Are you someone they can trust?"

"Just be someone *we* can trust." Rawley slapped Boone's horse to get it to take a step.

Boone pulled back and looked out across the unforgiving but starkly beautiful landscape. "I need to pack some supplies. How far is this Fort Bascom?"

"Far enough. Head north and east. You'll find wagon tracks and people to supply you along the way. Just pick up some water and rations for the day." Rawley held out his hand. "Good luck, son."

Boone stared at the hand. "We'll shake when the job is finished, not before."

CHAPTER TWENTY-NINE
The Comanche Raids

How many days and nights since Emily died, Boone couldn't count. But only three days since he left Fort Sumner and he ran out of places to stop for food and water. After two more days without food and little water on the trail he spotted his first Indian tracks and got on them.

Stay in the white world, Boonie. You'll never survive in your father's world. He couldn't escape his mother's words, no matter how far he rode. "I wish I had a third world choice," he muttered as the wind washed the tracks ahead. He thought he might be back in Texas, especially after he saw the sign 'you're a Texan now.' Horse tracks parted from wagon wheel tracks, with no sign of a scuffle.

He saw a feather drift like a lost bird -- a long white feather with black in the tip, perhaps an eagle feather, and alighted to catch it. His horse reared up and ran off in its thirst to find water on its own.

"Good luck!"

Boone chased after the feather, going forward, not backward. He tucked the feather in his hair. Where he ended was no longer up to him.

*

How much sand, scruff, sun, to kill a man? Boone could no longer open his mouth. He found a scorpion under a rock, sucked it dry and ate all but the tail. Most of the time he crawled, because standing led to falling. He still found an occasional track. What did they use for water? An underground spring? Boone dug and got more dust in the face. Even as a boy on the run, he never met climate like this.

A change in the landscape ahead -- more rocks, rising up, leading to a gully, perhaps. He didn't smell water. Some odor not related to sand and cactus. He tried to stand, to look into the distance, but fell again. He flopped on his stomach as the world blackened around him.

*

Boone fought the pinpricks on his skin resembling the touch of many hands. "Leave me be!" he screamed but no words came out. He didn't exist past a mound of pain. Water ran from the sky and he rolled onto his back, mouth opened, to catch some. He was surrounded but no human threat held fear like dying of thirst. He squinted up to see drops of water coming down from a pouch held over him. When he got as much as they offered, two of them threw Boone on a horse. They tied him on and rode off.

He didn't know where they ended up, some kind of box canyon of high walls with one way out. They stretched him out and gave him food and water but he didn't think anything could make him feel whole again. He didn't recognize any of these Comanche or the few Kiowa who ran with them, but they were distinguishable by their tattoo marks. He had to think hard to remember how he got here.

He listened to them talking around him, surprised at what he could understand. A few of Comanche knew some English, so that helped, but for the most part, Boone understood. He seemed to have retained much of what he'd been taught.

When Boone saw one ride in with a Navajo basket and another with a blanket, he found his voice. He gave his attention to the old chief, the one who bore the sacred feather stick. "You are the people who I owe my life. You are also the people I was sent to find. May I sit in council? I offer no harm and hope to receive none in return."

"We are all hunters in this party. Seeking that which the land provides. I am here to bless the hunt as my eyesight has long left me."

"I am half breed. My father was a Kiowa. Kae-gon." He used his father's name as a badge of honor, although the honor tasted foul in his mouth.

Old Man shook his head, as if disbelieving Boone's story. "We will sit in council and invite you as a guest. Because we saved you and now must know why."

Boone spotted two young boys out perhaps for their first hunt as men and he envied them. He guessed them to be that age he was once. But then, he, too, learned to become a man early.

The men gathered at midday in cool canyon shade to cut and cook what they caught. Even April weather got hot in this desert. Boone watched as some fashioned arrows out of local shrub and picked out rocks for arrow tips, some needing a little hammering to make a better point. Other stones were used as they were found. One handed Boone an arrow he had just finished and told Boone to keep it. The stone tip was crooked and the shaft wasn't that straight. Boone thanked him. He finished eating before the others and drew his symbol in the dirt with this new arrow. He stared at the symbol wondering if he'd drawn it wrong and realized what bothered him. One of the Indians had an arrow with an iron point. Comanchero trade.

He heard these men were deadly with their arrows and that made them the most feared on the plains. Comanchero trade meant that these Comanche and Kiowa were desperate enough to go against whites and Navajos. Several of the men were antsy to go out again, but Old Man waved them to stay. They sat with their backs against the wall as they listened to the half-white-tongue speak his council.

"Am I supposed to hold a stick?" As some laughed, one pointed to the arrow he clutched. "Okay, with this arrow I speak the truth to Comanche and his brother Kiowa. With my Kiowa heart, I swear --."

"He will still be talking when we bed for the night," said a voice from the wall. Another round of laughter.

Boone tried another tactic, fighting the need to quote Shakespeare. "Tell me how good your arrows are. I have heard legend about the Comanche. Not sure what to believe."

One man jumped to his feet. "I can shoot five arrows with one bow and kill a man as far away as that rock!" He pointed at a rock Boone guessed to be twenty yards away.

Another jumped up. "I can shoot ten before white man reloads his rifle. And hit him that far away!" He pointed to a cactus bush, about thirty yards off.

The men erupted in wild conversation but Boone suspected they didn't exaggerate much, even about feats on running horses. He fingered one of the shields lying near him. Thick, triple-layered buffalo hide. And their spears, so deadly against buffalo, worked just as well on a soldier.

Old Man waved for everyone to sit again. "Why did we find you near death?"

"I was sent by soldiers at Fort Sumner to talk peace."

"Soldiers who dragged those Navahones to Bosque?"

"Ah, yes. It took longer to find you than I had water to look. My horse thirsted, too, and ran off." At this he heard snickers. "The soldiers want you to come to the fort and talk so that there is peace between you and the … Navahones."

"Navahones don't want peace. They fight the Utes and everyone around."

"We do not care to sit in council fire with white soldiers."

"Our last attempt and they shot at us before we could say anything."

Old Man held up a hand and turned to Boone, waiting.

Boone cleared his throat. "They want peace. There must be a way to find it."

"For this we saved his life."

Old Man held up a hand as laughter erupted again. "Do you, Kiowa son, know these people you talk for?"

Boone had to work for whites but he began to wonder what he really wanted with his life. "They want to know boundaries of Comanche land. And how to ask you to stop raiding from the Navajo … nes." He waved at the goods now spread on the ground.

One young man jumped to his feet. "They already know our boundaries!"

Old Man nodded. "My son Kejones speaks true."

Boone faced Kejones direct. "They want you to stop trading with Comancheros. They cause problems for Navahones. Can we talk on this?"

Kejones sat again but Boone saw anger stilled his tongue. Old Man continued the talk. "We get many goods from Comancheros. Many are part of our family, half our blood. They deal with us honestly, but the Navahones try to stop them because they are angry that we get goods to fight them for being on our land."

"But you cannot blame the Navahones. They were taken there against their will."

"They were put by white man, yes. You think it unfair we attack them? They attack us."

"But if we could stop --."

Old Man made a sharp chop at the air with his hand to silence Boone. "When you go to someone's house, do you attack the host who gives you the rabbit to eat? We share with people who act like they are the guest. Not like they are the host."

"But … the Comancheros are illegal in this country. They are Mexican."

"You say they are illegal? White man say they are illegal? They are half breeds, like you, and they say they are not illegal. Who's right?"

"You say they are half breeds? You call them this?"

"You can think with two sides. This is good. Listen to the right side. You join us."

Boone felt his mind drift back to Mexico. Comancheros, Mexicans … half breeds…

She looked so unique, with a round head and prominent nose, her eyes small but with a huge glimmer of life. She was one of the few in the village still with full Mayan blood, and he wanted to get to know her better. He had no interest in her beyond talk, no interest in any woman, though she was young and ready for motherhood. He walked with her as she told all manner of strange and wonderful myths, when suddenly three Spaniards on horses rode up and got between them. They picked up this woman and pushed Boone over, trampling him with their horses as they rode off with her.

When Boone found her again, she had been ruined, but her family treated her kindly as the child inside her grew. Mexicans. People created out of the violence of one group over another, a people calmed by their belief in the goddess and given the virgin Mary in exchange for docile behavior. Mexicans. Half Spanish, half Mayan or Aztec or ….

"They have put the Navahones on our land. We take from them what is already ours." Old Man lit his pipe and handed it to Boone to shake him out of his memory. "They built a fort in our land, near our water and shoot at us to keep us away. They want us to come to them now? So they can kill us? I say let them come to us."

"They have. I am here to tell you they wish to know how to keep the peace." Boone puffed on the pipe before handing it back. "You are honest. There must be ways to keep the peace." He must have smoked in Mexico, as this didn't make him choke. The men looked at each other, puzzled, and Boone realized he had used too much English. "I mean…" But he couldn't find the right words except to call the soldiers liars. He wouldn't give these Comanches any more reason to make war. Not only because they saved him. He realized he'd been a fool to trust the soldiers. They didn't treaty with the Comanche and Kiowa for that Bosque land. They just took it. Because they didn't care about the Navajo.

"I delivered a message." Boone felt at peace as he said the words. "They expect you in council. Make whites your friends and you will find they have an honest side." Boone stood and Kejones stood with him. Boone couldn't meet his eyes.

Kejones grabbed his arm. "So you have chosen your side?"

Boone looked up at the sky. "I have to believe we can get along. Because the whites are so many more than *all* the tribes if they were living as one." He started to walk north, to put the Bosque as far from his life as he could. He had not gotten far when Kejones brought him a horse and enough food and water for two days.

After telling Boone a good direction to follow to say near water, Kejones watched Boone mount. "I wish you well on your journey. I would like us to meet again."

Boone clasped arms with him. "I'd like that, too." He rode off. There was one future he wanted, and the trail could be a long one.

CHAPTER THIRTY
The Confrontation

A whistle blew at the new Cheyenne station that early spring of 1867 and Boone's wild-eyed, frightened reaction mimicked his horses, as none of them were accustomed to the sound. So much civilization rising from rails. Cattlemen were taking over, too, with miners and speculators, all pushing the original natives aside, making his mother's dire warning seem more prophetic, even here in Wyoming Territory.

Now nearing in his 23rd year, a time of healing and hard work with some luck thrown in, he was finally realizing his dream owning a horse ranch. He was still dirt poor, but for the first time he'd manage to breed horses. One mare was pregnant and he hoped his stallion would work magic on the new wild mare soon. Then he could finally geld that stallion and train him to sell. Maybe kings rode stallions, but he'd never be one.

Hard long road to get here. With burgeoning memories of Mexico that he fought and tears for Emily that he did not. Sam emerged again to keep him company, often with Kiowa words of wisdom mixed with his Shakespeare. Finally Boone could appreciate both. He read a newspaper once with eagerness that held the words of peace spoken by Satanta, chief of the Kiowa, to General Hancock. "I have no bad hidden in my breast at all," and then condemned the army for interference in his land. Either the interpreter had little sense or his father's family was as mixed up as Boone's. Their desire to fight remained, even as so many whites moved west. He often wondered where his desire kill his father went after all this time. When he dug hard, he could find it.

He was still Hamlet, after all these years. Hamlet with a madman for a dead brother.

Boone thought he understood the white world. Emily told him all about the Revolutionary War. He knew the reason for the revolt from Great Britain and understood the revolt of the South not so long ago. Without a strong federal government and its desire for progress and now its need for taxes, there would be nothing in this country but small petty kingdoms all wanting to do things their own way. The break from Britain had been over taxation, but at least here, paying taxes meant they had a say in the government. The Kiowa didn't want to belong to the government and that made the Great Father mad.

Boone felt pretty voiceless, though, because here in the territories, they weren't allowed the vote, and statehood seemed pretty far away because they would not include Indians or half-breeds in the population tally.

Impatio nudged him for more oats and Boone happily obliged his Indian pony. After re-reading some Shakespeare, it seemed all people had savagery in them. "I'll not fight with a pole like a northern man, I'll slash. I'll do it by the sword."

He wanted to help whites and Indians get along, but how? He didn't want to help whites make Indians dependent on them for food. People want to be treated like people. And like him, they all want to make their own way, their own life. Is the country not big enough for both?

The work he did for the army along the way got him enough to buy this homestead that was little more than a shack, with the land included as part of the Homestead Act. Several acres of land turned into some grazing field with his coaxing, the shack accepted several add-on rooms and still stood, and the capture of wild horses came one at a time, but right away. The horse the Comanche gave him turned out to be a prize. Named Impatio, this horse helped corner the first young colt that he trapped and tamed back in Colorado Territory, while still homeless. The mama horse had tried to get her colt back while Boone slept, but some critter that turned out to be a raccoon made so much noise that Boone awoke, and captured the mama, too.

That hadn't been the first time raccoons helped him out. Bark had been the one to bring him back to sanity. Maybe Bark followed him. He would wake to find someone's saddlebag had mysteriously showed up at his campfire surrounded by raccoon tracks. Or he would be dying of thirst and come upon muddy raccoon tracks. Always raccoons. Some people trapped them for their fur and tails, but he would never kill a raccoon. Maybe he had been a raccoon in a former life -- a philosophy he heard about and accepted without question.

"Aye, but that's a colt, indeed," Boone said aloud, enjoying the sound of the Merchant of Venice as he shoveled hay in the outskirts of this western merchant town. "For he doth nothing but talk of his horse and he makes it …" He frowned and pressed his lips tight at his loss of words but then shrugged and chuckled. "I fear he will prove the weeping philosopher when he grows old!"

Some of his neighbors thought him foolish for feeding his horses like the Plains Sioux and Cheyenne did on the grasses, but that gave his horses better stamina. He still spoiled them with oats and hay bought from hay farmers, on occasion.

He heard horses coming down the road from the direction of the train station. He kept his head down as he filled holes in the corral's ground by impacting wet hay. He always feared the next stranger he met would be his father.

Louie told him, "We followed you, watched you." Was Kae-gon out there right now?

He grabbed Impatio's rope to pull him inside the barn.

"Hey, fella, any of those horses for sale?"

Three riders, Southern outcasts was Boone's first thought, were astride the lowest level of horseflesh he had ever seen. Boone figured they weren't on that train, as those horses appeared near ridden to death. One of the horses was a pudding foot, another whey-bellied with soft neck, and the third, though Boone couldn't say for sure, looked dead in the mouth. The men were in bad need of shaves and clean civilian clothes. He stared at them maybe a minute longer than decorum allowed as he wondered if he would recognize Stewart.

"Think he's deaf?"

"Dumb for sure."

They regarded his thin, dark and hawk-like appearance with distaste. "Boy, you got any manners at all? We asked you a question." This aggressive one, blonde with heavy jaw, leaned over his saddle, eyes spitefully nasty.

"Sorry, none full broke yet. Check back in a month if you're still in a need."

Another, squat and red-haired, pulled a canteen off his saddle horn and took a swig. "Oh, you're a wise ass redskin, eh? Maybe you don't know how to handle a horse. Maybe you gotta have white folk teach ya." He gave a yell, spurring his whey-belly hard to make the poor animal run around Boone's corral. His two friends joined in with riotous laughter, and the three of them got Boone's four nearly tamed animals into a frenzy.

Boone attempted to get himself between the corral and the marauders, but found the pounding hooves and dust they stirred impossible to penetrate. He ran inside his house and grabbed his rifle. When he ran back outside he raised the rifle, and noted through his sight that Blondie had a gun aimed at his head. Boone cocked the trigger, holding steadfast, heart racing, as the riders rode up around him.

Blondie broke the tension illuminated by the sounds of horses' frenzy. "Which of us do you think would be quicker to shoot? See, I killed men before, in the war. I have no qualms killing an Indian, and will get no punishment, neither. But you, killing a white? How long will you last?"

Boone kept his aim steady. "I killed in that war, too."

Red pulled out his rifle. "Try killing all three of us before we get you."

Boone's rifle lowered as the men on horseback laughed at him. The one with the gun aimed at Boone's face cocked his trigger and narrowed his aim with one eye squinted.

"Boone? Aren't you going to introduce me to your new friends?"

Boone opened his eyes and looked over his shoulder. Amanda sat as pert and fresh in the family buggy as a summer rain in a rose garden -- one who wished him to play Petruchio to her Katherine, though very less than shrew-like.

The three riders plastered silly, half-sopped grins on their faces and the weapons were lowered. Boone figured they hadn't seen a female in about as many rain-less days this late April. Blondie twirled his pistol before holstering it. They moved their horses forward to stand like dead weight in front of her buggy. The odor of roses dissolved into the smell of old ragged clothes and dirty horses. "Afternoon, miss. He a friend of yours?"

"That's right." She squinted up at him, made uneasy by the sun and the horses still riled and squealing behind them in the corral, waiting for Boone's calm attention.

"We was just teaching the young buck the right way to work up his stock. You know, teach 'em some respect." Blondie stood ahead of the redheads Boone figured were Irish and brothers, while Blondie sounded Prussian. He pulled his canteen. "Will show you some, if'n you've a mind to accept." He took a swallow of what by his grimace wasn't water.

Boone leaped up and grabbed the man's arm, pulling him to the ground like filth needing to be buried. "Get off my land. You're trespassing."

Blondie reached for his gun as he rolled on the ground but grinned at Amanda and stood, hands up and empty. "Got some spunk in ya … your lady friend, is it?" He dusted off. "Lady like you deserves a proper man."

"Well, that ain't you." Boone itched for a good fight.

"Come on, Clem," Big Red said from behind him. "This Mormon bitch and her half-breed buck ain't worth the time."

Clem jumped on his horse but paused long enough to tip his hat to Amanda. "Ma'am, can't say I think much of your taste in men."

"I say the same to you," she replied.

"What you say, Matt?" they asked the third, who hadn't uttered a word.

Matt raised his fist in the air, gave a loud whoop and rode off. Clem followed him, but Big Red aimed his gun at Boone again. "Better not ride out alone in the dark. I hear the rattlers are right nasty around here."

Boone turned to Amanda, giving them his back as a response.

Big Red kicked his horse into a gallop to join his retreating friends.

Amanda closed her eyes and her puff of breath lifted the brim of her bonnet. She jumped down from her buggy. "Boone, you were sore outnumbered. You oughta know better than to mix with their kind."

Boone sighed as she stood close to him. He brushed some of the dust off her cheek. "I don't much like mixing with *anyone*. You know that, Miss Amanda."

"Well, Mr. Boone, I know you are a few years older than me and widowed and all, but there are a few things I could teach you. Like how to show a man your back right off. Aren't too many around here who stoop so low as to shoot a man that way."

Boone wrapped an arm around her shoulder. "I like your concern, Miss Amanda." He cleared his throat and looked into her eyes. "I really do."

They held the gaze a moment until his horses' snorts made him turn. Boone went into his corral to calm them down. "They might not shoot a *man* in the back, Miss Amanda, but to them, I'm Kiowa."

Amelia giggled.

He stroked Impatio's nose. "What's funny?"

"This time of year you could pass for any man who works outdoors, Boone. You gotta think white to be accepted, that's all."

"Would you like a drink of water before you finish your ride? You know I love your company." When she nodded he took her arm. "Did you ever notice how the setting sun is so much easier on the eyes than its rise? Do you suppose the sun tires, just as we do?"

"Why, Boone, that's near poetry. I think it's a fine sunset, and easy on the eyes so we can appreciate it. I'd say your love of Shakespeare is making you a romantic."

Boone guided Amanda inside his house and pumped her some water. He didn't tell her about the Kiowa part of him, his symbols, but he got a sudden thought about his sunset symbol meaning that even as a boy, Boone had tired of life. Maybe Amanda could help him get over what needed getting over. He'd sure like her to try.

She drank noisily and sighed as she handed the glass back. "My, that is fresh and sweet-tasting. Boone, can you stop by tonight for a little song?"

"I don't reckon … I need early sleep tonight. Tomorrow I have to work on Luster. The big race is next week and he's got fine potential."

"You entering the race?"

"Monty, over at the blacksmith, said he'd stake me. I still work for him sometimes. And prize money means I could keep Luster and fix up my ranch when I sell the other three."

They shared a conversation over their cool water, easy talk as though those three men never existed -- about planting gardens and the best way to salt beef to last the winter. When conversation dwindled, Boone walked Amanda to her buggy, absorbing her rosy closeness. At the wagon, he held steady as she stood on tiptoes and kissed his cheek.

He took a chance and kissed her back, short and tender, on the mouth.

Amanda gave him one backward-glanced smile before waving goodbye. She made him feel like he was 12 and running away from what needed standing up to.

He came to realize that feeling helpless was what love was all about.

CHAPTER THIRTY-ONE
The Sense of Wild

Boone pulled Luster with a gentle coax into the secondary corral, away from the other horses. Already Luster's nostrils flared, edges of his eyes widened and his ears flicked back, forward, back again. Boone breathed at him, a memory of the first day they met, when he'd successfully applied the rope taming technique he'd once observed. He'd finally gained enough muscle and confidence to try. The horse realized, receiving Boone's breath as they stared eye to eye, that Boone held the power of death over him. Not a power Boone wielded lightly, and though the horse's sense of wild wasn't gone, the stallion at least stopped rearing up on his hind legs. Progress. "Easy now. I understand you. You just want to let loose. But we have to control our passion for the proper times."

Boone eased him toward the feed bin. The saddle and blanket were draped over the corral fence. Luster sniffed at the mixture of hay and oats and looked back at Boone before starting to nibble. Boone slipped the horse blanket on the roan's shapely back and then, with a little more force than just the day before, threw the saddle on. Luster stomped a back foot and threw a wild eye at Boone but buried his nose in the feed bin again.

Boone had been careful of the mixture he put in the bin because the horse will soon get his dander up and he didn't want to give the pony anything that might interfere with his blowing off some steam so soon after eating. Boone tightened the cinch and slipped the bridle over its face. Luster backed up and tossed his head but Boone matched his movements to get the bridle smoothly in place.

The horse didn't like being taken from his feed, but this was all part of the process. He seemed a little less miserable about the idea than even just yesterday. This time Boone tried his luck with a riding saddle instead of the breaking saddle. Luster wasn't broke yet but close enough for Boone to chance riding him in that race next week. He still needed breaking to halter and saddle. For a prize of $500, Boone would risk getting tossed in front of a crowd. He could finally afford a new roof on the house and barn and maybe even some new dishes and pots, so he could cook like a civilized man for Amanda.

Lucky for him he couldn't remember the last time he was tossed. Just the last time he lied about getting tossed.

He wished they would have a horse-breaking contest -- he'd win for sure. And that was no ego talking. Many men walked around with busted backs, all hunched over, or on a permanent limp, but he felt as fine and straight as the day he was 12. After a decade he didn't feel busted up anywhere. Not physically, anyway. Heck, why have a contest like that? They might just as well hand the purse to him now.

Boone stroked Luster's neck as the memory of his mother hit him fast and hard. Had so much time passed that all he remembered was her death and not how she lived? What would she be like now if she had not been killed? Shouldn't that make him more willing, not less, to go after the father? "Truly then I fear you are damn'd both by father and mother." The Merchant of Venice used to be one of his favorites, but now he found new meaning everywhere.

He walked the horse to the water bucket for a short swallow where he tightened the cinch again. After Luster had enough to clear his throat for the snorting that would follow, Boone walked him again and checked the cinch one last time. This should be the last time Luster needed the distraction during the saddle-up. This time they will ride until Luster liked it almost as much as Boone did. At least they didn't have the heat of summer to contend with, as races were most often run in the spring for that reason.

He will win that race, too, because Luster will still have that sense of wild in him. His mama told him that would save his life someday -- his inborn sense of Kiowa wild. *Live with the whites but think like an Indian, Boone.* Maybe Sam's voice was now his mama's. Boone patted Luster's neck and mounted.

Luster pawed the ground a moment and leaped, front feet ripping the air.

"Come on, boy, you can do better than that." Boone tightened his legs as Luster blew, arched his back and then circled, while serenading Boone with grunts and snorts, pin-wheeling and then dove at the fence to rub him off before kicking the lid off again. Boone nearly turned himself inside out as he fought not to let Luster win. Finally he grabbed the horn because by the Good Lord and dust in the belly Luster was not going to whip him. No one could see his disgrace in grabbing the apple, anyhow.

Ever so slowly but quicker than the day before, Luster wearied of the fight. He tore at the fence a few more times and stood by the feeding bin -- panting, sweating, pawing the ground. Boone coaxed him forward with a slight kick of the stirrup and a shift forward in the saddle and Luster started to walk, in the right direction, too. Boone made the horse walk a few rounds in the corral and the horse jerked his head against the reins but not as much as Boone expect, and stumbled once but otherwise behaved, though chomping at the bit. Boone jumped off, knowing the work still ahead but sunholler if this horse wasn't going to be ready on time.

He walked the horse out of the corral, checked the cinch and leaped up into the saddle again, willing himself to feel light in weight. "Come on, let's ride." He gave the horse a gentle spur to the side and Luster jumped from standstill into a run. Boone rode him faster, harder than ever before in his life and yet so smooth he felt he was flying -- up into the sky, up through the clouds. The horse had perfect instincts for the ground under its feet and though not as responsive to the reins, seemed willing to go where Boone wanted without being told. Boone didn't need to turn back. Luster will tire eventually. Winning meant getting to the finish line first, but not necessarily stopping once they got there.

*

Boone got the horse with only a little fight to head back to his ranch, with its instinct perhaps of knowing easy food and water as its reward. Boone walked him the last half mile so Luster would cool before they reached home. Once in the corral, he took the brush from his left vest pocket and brushed the horse's neck. The horse snorted, this time in pleasure, as it waited for food. Boone spent so much time with horses he knew every emotion and cadence of their breath.

Boone left the horse saddled and took the bridle off so it could eat. He stretched his back out as the corralled horse walked to the feeder. Many men ruined themselves at an early age with their breaking, but Boone didn't believe in the blindfold 'em method. Boone created his own way of making them human dependent. Not let them graze until they know who the food comes from. Luster now needed to learn to respond better to the reins, not to bite the bit or throw his head up so much.

Boone dipped his hand into the horse's water bucket and cleaned off his face. When he looked back up, he squinted and wiped the water off his face with his dry hand. Smoke! Coming from Miss Amanda's! He threw the horse brush down and leaped over the fence.

On the way he grabbed the old buffalo robe that had been airing on the line, with nary a ribbon left attached, and ran like the wind.

CHAPTER THIRTY-TWO
The Fire

"Come on, come on, get 'em out, get 'em out, come on, Richard, I can't contain it!" Randy hit the barn with water from the trough, sending Richard inside the barn to open the stalls.

Beside him his mother Genevieve, a husky lady, shoveled dirt against the fire, at the same time digging a trench to keep the fire from spreading. Amanda filled buckets with water and kept them coming, as fast as she could without dropping or spilling too much.

Boone focused on helping Richard, after hearing Richard's mumbled shouts and the animal squeals inside the barn. They had stampeded into stalls in the far western corner as flames licked the eastern walls. The one exit was on the northern side. There was a mare, a colt filly and a prize bull with heavy horns. The bull was dangerously close to the mare, its eyes wide with fear, mouth foaming.

"Get behind!" Boone yelled at Richard. "Don't stand in front of them!" Richard had roped the mare and tried to pull her forward. "We got to get the bull out first."

The bull had pressed itself against the far wall. Knowing he had no time to lose Boone waved his buffalo robe in front of the bull's face. The bull pawed the ground and slammed his horns into a wood post at the mare's front haunches. The mare whinnied and tugged on the ropes. Boone threw the robe at the bull's horns with a short but sincere prayer. The robe landed square on the bull's horns and over its face. It grunted and tossed its head but the old and worn robe held, partly pierced by the left horn.

Boone ran to the side of its stall, double-fisted and slammed his fists into the bull's hind quarter. It jumped and ran straight through the burning wall, the blanket catching fire at the edges. On the outside Randy managed to dodge the bull just in time. The bull raced off into the open range, blanket smoldering. Boone ran out and saw that the bull dropped to its knees and rolled, working the blanket loose. Then it stood and munched grass as if nothing had happened.

Ma ran after the bull and put the fire on the smoking blanket out with her shovel before coming back to tackle the barn again.

"Get behind the mare!" Boone ran back to see Richard apply the same method to the horse's rear haunches but she wouldn't move. Boone scooped up the colt and ran out the door, and sure enough, the mare followed behind, pulling Richard on the rope with her. Boone and Richard got the two horses safely installed in the corral and turned back to help with the barn.

But Randy and his mother had given up. Gen Johnson, a pioneer fighter since her young days, threw the shovel down. Boone noticed, too, that the fire took over the northern section but would be out before long. The barn was half rock, and lucky too, or the fire could have been a real inferno. At least no other buildings were in danger now as the fire's intensity had dwindled.

Gen held a sweaty palm out to Boone. "Boone, I don't know when we've had a better neighbor. My animals could have died without your help." She nodded at Richard. "And my young son, too." Richard was 12, an age Boone knew well. She walked up to what was left of the barn's stone walls. "I don't know where we'll keep the animals now."

"I can help," Boone said. "I know where there's a stone quarry. We can rebuild the barn all of stone. Maybe with a tin roof, if you can afford it."

"Oh, we couldn't ask that time of you. You've enough to do all on your own."

"I'll help anytime." He winked at Amanda, who looked exhausted and dirty but smiled back at him. "You better get your seeder bull corralled before it wanders off."

"That was something," Randy said, laughing. "The way that bull barreled out of there, a fiery blanket over its face!"

"Buffalo skin," Boone said in a quiet tone.

"The beatingest thing I ever saw!" Richard said.

Amanda took Boone's hand. She stood on tiptoes and kissed him on the mouth. "We owe you so much."

Boone chuckled with that sad sense of relief that when one thing dies, another is born. He never felt comfortable visiting the Johnsons and only came to help out when they needed help. He used to cough up dust from the cattle drives and not talk much to drovers, but here he was, coughing up smoke from a fire and feeling as natural as at home. Mr. Arden joined them from down the way, bringing more water, which he used on the dying embers. Mrs. Johnson declared the day an event and invited all to stay for lunch. She had been tending a big pot of chicken stew when the fire started.

"Do you know what caused the fire?" Boone asked. Silence answered him as they all looked at each other. "Not a lightning storm. Maybe green hay? Although I don't know if you got yourself hold of any this time of year." Boone felt like kicking himself. They didn't need any blame seeking right now.

Amanda grabbed Boone's arm. "Oh, let's be grateful the fire's out and the stock is saved. And go have us some of Mama's great stew."

Boone stared at the ground. "I'm sorry. I think I better --."

"Oh, don't you say no now, Boone, not after you practically saved our lives!"

Boone looked into the smiling, grimy faces, and for the first time could even meet Mr. Arden's eyes. The old fellow didn't seem so bad now -- friendly, almost. "All right. Guess I did work up a hunger."

But some nagging doubt would not leave him, and he found himself avoiding Amanda's eyes the rest of that visit. He wished the whole time he enjoyed their company that he could come up with an excuse to ride back home.

Something wasn't right about that fire, but he just couldn't figure out what.

CHAPTER THIRTY-THREE
The Lost Dream

Halfway home Boone stalled up. His buffalo skin. That was the last of his mama. He never even got the blood out. Maybe after all this time he no longer needed the skin, and it came to a good end. That fear of love seemed to have fallen away after that fine lunch and conversations. All he had to do now was win a race, and he'll feel ready to ask Miss Amanda to spend an evening with him. He will buy her the biggest longhorn steak …

As Boone rounded the trail that gave him a clear view of his own corral, he stopped dead. The corrals, both of them, were open and empty. Luster, and his three other horses being broke to sell, were gone. His legs turned to lead.

Somehow, he'd gotten lost. He just had to turn around, walk back up the trail, figure out where he walked wrong.

He ran to the corral. Even Impatio was gone. There was no fire this time, no sign of culprits nearby, nowhere to run to. He checked the corral for signs of tracks. Sure enough, lots of 'em heading off to the west.

Boone grabbed a corral post and snapped the wood loose from the ground. He knew what had caused the fire and what happened to his horses. He went into the house and opened the dusty old trunk where he had stored his Mexican life. He pulled out a holster with two pistols. Only a few bullets, but that will be enough. Just enough.

*

Boone walked back into Amanda's yard. He saw the barn's burnt-out shell and froze, fists clenched at his side, worried over how he might react when one of them said something sideways to him. But he needed a horse.

Amanda was hanging out the linens and ran to him. "Boone! I was coming get you. Mama doesn't think we've done enough for you yet." She noticed his holster and frowned. "We realize that you probably don't eat well, living by yourself, so we want you to come for supper every night." She touched his arm, aware of his tightness. "Why did you walk again?"

"I need to borrow a horse."

"A horse! My goodness, Boone, you have a lot of horses. Well, you'll have to talk to Randy about that. That's men's business. Come on in, I've made a pitcher of lemonade and you look thirsty."

Boone opened his mouth as Amanda pulled him toward the house but didn't know what to say that wouldn't make them feel guilty. He mustered no more than a one-sided smile for Mrs. Johnson, who sat on the porch scrubbing out the freshly plucked chickens.

"I'm afraid he might say no to me, Mama, so you ask him."

"Boone, we want you to be our guest for supper every evening, or at least every evening you're free, starting tonight. We want to get to know our neighbor better."

"Sit down, Boone. I'll get you that lemonade."

"Oh, honey, Boone's a busy man. He's probably got a lot of work to do. Did you come back because you forgot something, Boone?"

Boone wandered to the side of the porch and looked out at the open field. "Yes, ma'am. My … the buffalo skin I threw over the bull."

Amanda came back out with the glass. "Boone asked me if he could borrow a horse, Mama. I said to talk to Randy."

"Oh, Randy and Richard are out hunting material to rebuild the barn. I think they're carrying a guilt for the fire."

"Can you imagine, Boone!?" Amanda poured the lemonade from a pitcher set out on the porch. "Those brothers of mine rolling up bible papers behind the barn?"

"Is that … what happened?" Boone tried to keep sarcasm from his voice.

"Well, they won't admit as much. But what else could it be? We haven't had green hay in there yet this spring."

"They will deny doing any such thing, of course. Especially after the way their papa died." Gen smiled sourly at Boone. "Amanda's father had a great liking for smoking tobacco. He fell asleep once with a burning one in his lips, is as close as we could figure, like he usually did, with his shirt pulled up against the cold." She shivered and turned back to her chicken gutting. "We lost our homestead and my husband that day."

"Sorry." His words of consolation fell lifeless from his lips. "I … do need a horse."

"My, well, I guess that would be all right. For how long, honey?" When Boone didn't answer right away she continued on with sudden nervousness. "You have a horse ranch, don't you, Boone? Why you need one of ours?"

She would be happy to know that her sons didn't start the fire. But he couldn't stand the thought of her sympathy. "I'm sorry … just … a little trial I had in mind. I have to go. Thank you for the supper invite, but I *am* a little busy."

"Well, all right. Tomorrow evening then. Don't say no, we'll expect you." Gen tossed the chickens into a pot and turned to go back inside as though the conversation had never happened.

CHAPTER THIRTY-FOUR
The Four-Legged Bargain

The horse tracks Boone followed seemed to mimic the train tracks, as though they were seeking rapid getaway. They'll look for buyers with easy cash along the route, so he checked every ranch along the way and found all horses well-guarded, as though the snakes had attempted trespass there, too. But Boone didn't stop to ask, fearing the barrel end of anyone who didn't stop to ask.

Boone detoured off their tracks onto Cheyenne's main street to find a cheap horse at the livery. The town grew quickly once the train station established here, with eight mercantile shops, 24 houses and a sheriff's office. Three new buildings were going up, and at least half a dozen people saw the one they called a half-breed walk into town on foot. He made friends with a few people who, at first, wanted nothing to do with his kind, until they realized they didn't know what his kind was.

He figured the outlaws were headed in the direction of Fort Bridger, but Boone wouldn't cross those foothills on foot. He went to the bank and closed his account, assuring the banker that he needed the investment to win the race and would re-open the account as soon as he won. Boone's reputation in town as an honest businessman paid in his favor. But closing his account didn't give him enough for even half a nag.

His mind kept swimming with how he could have prevented this. Maybe he should have demonstrated how his stock wasn't ready to be sold. But how could he, after the way they riled them up? Any good horse would act that way. Maybe he acted as though he thought himself better than they were. Maybe all kinds of things he could have done.

But no amount of guilt lessened this killing mood. He felt as trampled on as when he found his mama dead.

As he walked to the blacksmith shop Boone heard the sound of a buggy with a familiar squeak behind him. "Boone! I didn't expect to see you in town."

Boone didn't want Amanda to get sour thoughts of him, but she alone deserved the truth. "My horses were stolen. Happened when your barn was burning. I think they set the fire deliberate to get me there. Now I'm following the trail they left behind."

Amanda sat back in shock. "Oh, Boone. Who would do something like that? You mean those three bums who were riling them at your house?"

"Don't know who else. They wanted to hurt both of us."

"Oh, Boone. Please come back with me and we'll give you a horse."

"No, I don't want your ma to feel bad. I'll get me one in town."

"Then what will you do?" Amanda had to get her buggy going again to catch Boone's long strides.

Boone grabbed hold of the buggy frame, making her jerk the animals to a stop. "Please, Amanda. Your family has already suffered enough. I'm on my own now."

"But, Boone, I..." Amanda looked away, appalled by what she saw on his face.

"I'm sorry. It's my fault. I'll fix it." He felt relieved that she did not follow him any further.

Boone told himself that Luster wasn't ready to race anyway, that his horses wouldn't have brought him the money worth the work, that he could take Monty's offer and become a junior blacksmith in his shop. The shop needed new paint and some timber to replace where the wood hadn't been properly treated. Monty had asked for his help in the past but Boone was always too busy.

Monty was bent over the anvil, shirtless, wearing the black apron that kept sparks from most of his skin. The way his shoulders were slouched made him appear lacking in everything but mental willpower.

"Hiya, Boss."

Monty had stopped to wipe his brow with his dirty gloved hand and turned with a lazy grin. "Boone! I expect a couple fellers for their special order on these shoes that ain't ready yet." Like him, Monty was a half-breed, but a black mama and white father -- plantation owner, no love required. Monty had more white features and a more one-sided attitude. He said his people called him a muley, meaning black and white halves. "What brings ya by? Needing a new bellows?"

"I got me a string of bad luck. Horses all got stolen. Need a mount to go after them."

"Oh." Monty threw the shoe he worked on to the ground. "Thought maybe you came here to help me. You just wanna *be* helped. Well, I ain't got a horse to spare but can't say as I blame you for asking." He spit a wad of chew to the ground. "You don't deserve the trouble."

"Can you pay me to fix your wood and paint?"

Monty wiped at the brown dribble that leaked out. "A few dollars is all. Let you sleep here and feed you, too."

"That'll do. I'll just need a day because I got to keep moving." Boone set right to work.

The next morning he had $3 more and a hopeful stride to the livery. Inside the stable filled with the smell of horse flesh, Boone didn't see Chas anywhere. He went from one stall to the next, calculating how much Chas would want. Rent one, maybe, but he wouldn't trust Boone to bring back whatever he rented out. Chas didn't trust him.

Boone kept a respectful distance as he inspected the animals. The first animal was a shaggy black thing that attempted to remain standing on shaky legs, its nose grazing the ground for no particular purpose. It wouldn't last two yards, much less as many miles as Boone needed. Apparently a cribber, the way its stall had been chewed up. Not worth any price.

The second stall was empty, and the third held a mule that appeared nearly broke in half, its back swayed, its eyes wild, belly bulging. The next two stalls held actual horses, but the price would be too high for either. The fifth horse was possible

195

but its hooves needed work, and its mane was tangled. It also bore an army brand, so could be skittish, not necessarily old.

Boone opened his fist and counted his coins as he stepped toward the anvil and cold fire pit. Chas was too cheap to use a blacksmith.

"Eh? What you want?"

Boone turned to the face the old smithy, a full black man who admitted his real name was Charles. He liked the sound of Chas, said it made him sound fancy. Boone didn't know much else about the man, not even if he had been a slave. Only figured he had the right not to like most anybody.

The old man chawed, too, more subtle than Monty. Boone smelled the tobacco but never saw him spit. "What you doing in here, boy?"

"Ah, I need a horse. To rent, or to buy --."

"How much you pay?"

"I thought maybe to make a deal with you. I got my horses stolen. If I get them back, and I will, I will give you your pick." Boone winced. Anyone in his right mind would take Luster.

"I get your word and nothing more?"

"Ah, I can sign over my homestead to you."

"Don't need it." Chas turned away.

"Wait! Surely we can come to some terms. Your stock here ain't that good."

"You trying to sideswipe me?"

Startled, Boone shook his head.

"Let me see your coins."

Boone didn't realize the coins jingled in his fist. He opened his hand.

"Huh. Seven dollars? Well." Chas swallowed hard. "Guess we don't do business today."

"Isn't this enough to rent a horse for the day? If I don't find what I'm looking for, I'll have him back here this time tomorrow."

"Can't be sure of that without security." Chas stared at the coins in Boone's hand. He walked over to the third stall and turned back to Boone. "Tell you what, though. I do have one animal. It ain't much, but for whatever coins you got there you can have 'em. It's got four legs, anyhow. I seen some with less."

Chas motioned the mule. Boone gave him the coins. "Much obliged." Boone reached out to scratch the animal's neck and the mule bit him. "Hey! You varmint. What's its name?"

"Crabby." Chas laughed and dabbed at his chin with a red kerchief. "Let me get you a bridle. Don't know if he'll take it, though."

*

Boone used to think there wasn't an animal he couldn't break, handle or tame. Then he met Crabby. Only part mule, Crabby was three parts pure she-devil. Chas didn't have a saddle that would fit her but let Boone have some tired-out bridle and rope halter. Boone had to fight her to get the bit in, because she bit back without hesitation.

"Think she'll hold my weight?" Crabby was wide enough all on her own and those spindly legs might not take kindly to more weight. Boone swung a leg over and sat, his feet touching the ground. Crabby staggered.

"Maybe you oughta carry her," Chas said with a snort.

"Come on." Boone shifted his weight forward and slapped her butt. "Walk on." But Crabby didn't budge. Her snout lowered to the ground as she fell asleep. "Four legs are no good if she don't know how to use 'em."

"True enough." Chas removed his hat and wiped his forehead with his kerchief. "Get off and pull her for a bit. She might get the idea. Been stabled a while. Probably forgot how."

Boone pulled on her to move forward, and just as the bit seemed to loosen she took a step. She stopped again, and Boone had to pull hard to get her to take another. By the time he had walked a mile down the street to the saloon, his arms were as sore and tight as wet leather drying in the sun. Before he got her to the hitching rail she decided she wanted to lope and he had to dig his heels in to hold her back. He tied the rope tight but with enough rein for her to reach the water trough to drink.

In the saloon Boone asked for his canteen to be filled with water. He wanted a shot but hadn't the money to pay. The bartender seemed unwilling to take the canteen from him until he caught the eye of someone behind Boone.

As the bartender filled the canteen, Boone turned. Randy grinned at him with a hand out.

"Don't often see you in town, Boone."

Boone shook his hand but briefly. "I'm usually busy."

"Can I buy you a shot?" Randy waved at the bartender before Boone could answer. "I don't want you to buy back, though, because I have to be moving. Richie is getting us a wagon to pick us up a load of rock for the barn. We already wrecked the bed on one wagon."

Boone thanked him for the whiskey and slung the filled water canteen over his shoulder. "I wish I could help with the barn. I have to leave town for a few days."

"I wouldn't think of asking you to help. You've done enough for us already. Tell you what though, when you get back, we'll have us a barn-raising party." He laughed, downed his whiskey and bade Boone farewell with a slap on the shoulder.

Boone sipped his whiskey. He didn't normally drink, not liking how liquor made him lose his senses. But he enjoyed the taste of this one. When he saw the bartender eyeing him, he drained it, slammed the shot down and walked for the door.

A tired gambler in a worn white shirt and lazy black tie near the door grabbed Boone's arm as he headed out. "Why the rush?"

"I've got work to do."

"You mean hunting down some horses?" The gambler sat again and shuffled his cards.

Boone sat facing him. "What do you know about it?"

"Three men came in here day before yesterday, unclean, bad saddles, wanted to gamble. They sat at that table," the gambler pointed, "and I could hear 'em talk plain enough about what they did."

Boone stared into the cracks on the floor. "Why are you telling me?"

"Maybe I can help." The gambler put his cards on the table. "I retain a lot of what I hear, stuff that sounds unimportant, casual stuff. Like where they were hiding out." He indicated to Boone to cut the cards. After the cut he tossed the top several cards to the bottom before dealing.

"I can follow their trail."

"Play a hand with me."

"I don't have any money."

"Relax, tinhorn, I just need to limber up on an honest man."

Boone rubbed his nose with the back of his hand. "I never play."

"Even better." He dealt five cards to each. "Well, go on, pick them up. We'll play Five-Card Dead. You bet only on what's in your hand."

Boone reached for the cards as though they were on fire.

"Of course you realize those horses are probably sale-branded by now. Shame, too, the way you were fixing to ride the big one in the race next week." He smiled at Boone's reaction. "I hear everything in this corner of the room, friend."

Boone laid his cards down. "Three sevens."

"Thought you didn't know how to play."

"I know how. I just don't play." He played cards with Emily in front of the fire on cold nights. *To come at first when he doth send for her, shall win the wager which we will propose.*

The gambler laid his down. "Two Queens. Too bad you weren't betting." He shuffled again. "Let's try something more challenging."

Boone leaned over the table, grabbed the gambler's tie and jerked him forward. "Let's try being straight. You know something or don't you?"

"You sure are unappreciative."

Boone rubbed a hand over his eyes to stop shaking as he sat back again.

"That's better." The gambler dealt five to each again. "Five Cards Draw-em this time." He looked at his cards and pulled out three. "How many to pitch?"

"What?"

"Look at your cards and keep the ones you want." When he saw Boone about to toss all five down, he shook his head. "You have to keep at least two." Boone tossed one. "You are a greenhorn, are you? Okay." He dealt Boone one off the top and dealt himself three.

"Always played dead." Boone looked at his cards and grunted. "A straight. Funny how they just fell together."

"Yeah." The gambler threw down his cards with a laugh, not even showing his hand. "Funny. And you didn't suspect a thing, right?"

"Now give me my wager's worth."

"Fancy talk from a half-breed." As Boone started to rise, "A roadhouse."

"What?"

"I know where there's a roadhouse, could be where your rustlers took your horses. Heard them mention a ride about a day and a half west of here. And I know a place. Spring Valley. Abandoned this time of year."

"Thanks." Boone headed for the door but turned back. "Why you helping me?"

"Does it matter? Take my advice or don't." The gambler shuffled again. "Just get out of here so I kin breathe again."

Boone's hand went for his gun but he turned and walked out.

CHAPTER THIRTY-FIVE
The Campfire Conversation

A crowd had gathered in the street and many were laughing. Crabby stood with her front two legs in the water trough, lapping up water as dainty as a city slicker. Boone pushed through the crowd and pulled up on her reins. "How many times do I have to tell you. Bathe at home!" He nodded at people he knew and the crowd dispersed, laughing with him.

With back hooves kicking at the dust in the street, Crabby relented to his tugging and stepped out of the trough. She stamped her front hooves a few times and gnawed at her right leg before allowing Boone to lead her like a sassy dog off down the road.

When she had a good walking rhythm going Boone jumped on her back. She stopped and staggered under the load.

"Come on, Crabby, I don't weigh that much. Surely less than you." He urged her forward and she whirled on him, nipping at his leg.

"Sorry, girl, would you mind walking a bit? Please?" He slapped the reins and she took a step, rest, step, rest, for a while out of town before finding a one-step, two-step rhythm. Boone began to relax and found a handy bit of Shakespeare to fill his time. "Either they must be dieted like mules, and have their provender tied to their mouths, or---."

Crabby fell forward when her front legs collapsed. Boone had been feeling a little more human when he found himself rolling over the top of Crabby's head to the ground. As he stood again his head knocked into Crabby's nose like a fist to the jaw but she didn't bolt. Her brown eyes stared at him as though worried what he might try next, her nose air snorting gray curses at him.

"You a Shakespeare critic?" He jerked the reins hard and walked on. She trotted after him without resistance as he cursed the fates, the stars, the horses, the town, the railroad and everything in-between. He even cursed the gambler, because he could be walking into a trap.

But he saw by the signs that they traveled this way. Three controlled horses and several on loose rope. He noted the sun gave him time, but not a lot, and wiped the sweat from his brow. The mule brayed and tried to run forward but Boone held her back and mounted. For another two miles he rode on, at times nearly falling off as she ran swaying in a way he had never known on any four-legged before, even the first mule he'd had.

After those two miles Crabby tired, stopped, and when Boone didn't get the message, flopped to her side, sending him scrambling to keep from getting trapped. Boone was tempted to leave her there, but Crabby gave him such a big-eyed stare that he couldn't. So he sat down and waited until she wanted to walk again.

Turned out that wasn't until near dark, so he found her some grazing and water, started a campfire and tried to get comfortable for the night. He'd gone without food before, and he could again. But he wished he'd considered his needs beyond water.

*

A noise had him up with both guns out before he could figure out what he'd heard. He could see Crabby with head up, nostrils flaring. Wasn't a dream, then. Boone had plenty of nights out on the trail like this one. Most times the noise turned into an owl hoot or the wind cracking tree limbs together. He breathed deep of the creosote and pine and holstered his pistol again, when an Indian on foot wandered into his camp. Comanche by his dress, he walked bold to a place where the low light of the fire gave Boone away.

He pointed at Boone's feet. Boone handed his canteen over. The man just drank and stared at the dying fire. Boone picked up some sticks and leaves and got the fire going good again. *If this is my father, can I knife him right now?* His father lived many miles away, according to the last Kiowa he met. This man wasn't as big as Boone remembered, but then, he remembered the father from the size of a youngster.

"Are you lost?" Boone had to hide a laugh because a Comanche would not be lost.

"Are you?"

Boone thought at first the man only echoed his English until he realized the man emphasized "you." He laughed. "You know English?"

"I get by."

"You talk like you know me."

"I can see you."

Boone gestured upward. "In the night?"

"You're alone out here. Like me. Your horse is stupid."

Boone laughed and this time the fellow joined him. "I won't deny that!" Boone sighed. "Some men stole my horses." He leaned over, hand outstretched. "Boone Tyler."

The man looked at the hand and rubbed a palm across Boone's palm. "You can call me Gray Bear. Most white men are not able to say my real one."

"Try me."

Gray Bear shook his head. "Who stole? Were they Comanche? Cheyenne? Ute?"

"White."

"Ah. Good."

They sat enjoying the silence and crackling fire. "How did you lose *your* horse?"

"Did not lose it. Tied it up back there. Not sure I can trust you."

"Afraid I might ask you to trade?"

"Yes." They shared a companionable smile. "What will you do if you find them?"

"Get my horses back. Kill 'em so I don't have to keep watching my back." Boone saw the old man's gaze become fixed and unswerving at him. "What? You'd do the same."

"I will not stop you. Kill all the whites you like. Or don't."

"Do I know you?" A sudden gesture, the way he nodded, seemed familiar.

Gray Bear stood and found a stick by rejecting a few before he found a sturdy one. "I will sleep here tonight." He paced around, scraped at the ground with his feet to smooth out an area, and drew a large circle in the dirt while chanting under his breath. As Boone watched, he curled up inside the drawn circle to sleep.

"What's that for?"

"Protection. Keeps night devils away, if you say the words right."

"Really?" Boone remembered a few times since being on the run when he awoke to find some spider or reptile had taken a few nips out of him. Once a bite had gotten seriously swollen. Gray Bear handed him the stick. "Do I have to bless it?"

Gray Bear laughed. "You do not know a lot. And yet you've survived much."

"I don't know the words."

"You do. They are hidden in you."

Listen to me, said Sam. Boone concentrated, kept his words inside, and drew his circle carefully. "How do you know me? Are you following me?"

"Why would I?"

Boone pulled his bedroll into the circle and scrunched up to fit, wondering how to sleep like this. He didn't want this man to be his father. He felt too good to kill. Boone generally stretched out under the moon and let his body get used to the chill of the night air, so gradually his body left this circle.

"Are you Indian or white?"

"I was raised in the white world, with my mother, until I was 12. She saw what will happen to your world. I stay white to honor her wishes."

"This white world make you happy?"

"Not all the time." Boone traced his symbols in the dirt, even though he couldn't see them. "But I get by." He stretched out on his back, ignoring the circle. "Sometimes I dream of helping both worlds. You know, help them learn to communicate."

"Why you do not play the music?"

"What?"

Gray Bear held up a harmonica. "Found this. It makes music. A man alone at night, he plays music."

Boone reached over, hand trembling. He'd left it near the campfire. "You've heard me?"

"I've heard white men. Would love to learn to play this thing. Someday."

"You sound like you appreciate white culture. Why?"

The man's voice was hypnotic and mostly in tribal in response. Boone struggled to stay awake as he listened. "When the white man cooperates, life is a thing of beauty. When he only takes and takes, and kills when someone tries to stop him, it is a thing of horror, like the jackrabbit who can never stop running to eat because he will be eaten. Eventually he just falls over and dies. My people want to live as we've always lived, on the rich fat food of the earth, but every day they kill more buffalo and let good food rot on the ground so that our people will be destroyed. We try to stop them and they try to stop us from stopping them. We share the land as long as there is enough water to drink and buffalo to eat. When there is not, we move on. That is the way of things.

"Now we find the land gets smaller and smaller. Now your people, your white people, say they *own* it! You cannot own the water. It is there for all. What good is land to own if it gives no food? If you shoot your gun to hunt and scare the game onto someone else's land, you cannot go and get it? Land is not to own. Your people say no, this is *our* land. You belong *there*. You stay *there*. Go nowhere else. But no food is there. We say take your gold or other stupid goods and go back home. But they say no, they must *own*. And when they own, they kill all the buffalo and give us bad food in return."

205

"You must really hate the whites."

"Not hate. Just try to make them understand. Want this thing of beauty again."

"My mother loved my father. But that kind of love drove her crazy." He thought it was important for Gray Bear to hear that. He heard a coyote in the distance but before he had the chance to worry, he fell asleep.

He awoke in the morning to find himself curled up in his circle and the Indian was gone, his circle erased. Boone had slept, he thought, better than he had in years. The dreams were happy and peaceful, of him and Sam together as boys who swam in clean lakes and drank from an unending waterfall, under the guidance of a loving father.

Boone had to remember his horses to get going again.

CHAPTER THIRTY-SIX
The Mule Rider Attack

The moon rose full and blinding white, an omen over the foothills of the Rockies, before Boone found the roadhouse. The hideout was more like a hole in the canyon with a door, a wall of rock closed off by wood. The horses were likely on the bluff. Boone couldn't go up there unless he knew they weren't around to shoot him in the back. He pulled the mule to hide behind the scraggly pinion pine alongside the canyon wall. Crabby brayed and Boone clamped both hands over its snout. He looked back over at the door, and Crabby bit his hands.

"Ouch!" He clamped down on his own mouth and pulled both guns as the wooden door eased apart and Clem and Matt stepped out of the cave, guns drawn. Boone had felt awkward and uncommon when he first put on the holster, but now recognized them as a second pair of hands as he pulled his guns -- shades of Mexico he savored in Sam's memory.

"That's far enough." Boone stepped to his left, away from rock. He cocked both triggers, hoping to look as dangerous as he felt. "You know what I want."

"Hear that, Matt? Lover boy here thinks we know what he wants."

"Uh." Matt held his gun but the grip loosened as Clem put his back in the holster sitting loose on his hip.

"You wanna put them away?" Clem pointed at Boone's guns. "We can't do business like this." Clem gestured up at the moon. "Nobody's foolish enough to gunplay after the sun goes down. Moonlight can make you see things that aren't there. You're an injun, you know that. You people are superstitious."

"You leave my people out of this. I want my horses." Boone squeezed the trigger, pumping off a bullet that nicked Clem's shirtsleeve and embedded in the wood behind him.

"Hey, that wasn't very nice."

"Oh, look at that, you're right. I meant to hit you." Boone figured they didn't understand sarcasm. Probably never even heard of Shakespeare. "Sorry, guess I'm not feeling friendly. Ever play a game called Russian roulette?" Emily told him about a game her grandfather used to play until he shot his own head off. Boone had been thinking to just shoot them straight off, but a glint of compassion in Matt's eye made him think twice. "Throw your guns down. Then, for every time I ask and you refuse to tell me where my horses are, I shoot the rock in a different location. One shot is bound to hit one of us, eventually. That person loses." Boone cocked the trigger again.

"Hey, now, wait a minute."

"Where are my horses?"

"You don't know what you're doing. You'd take a chance shooting yourself?"

Boone fired at rock above Clem's head and Clem's hat flew off. Clem grabbed his head. Boone shrugged. "Just lucky. Now it won't be fair if Matt plays, because he can't tell me anything even if he wanted to. You know where the horses are, Matt?"

"Uhhhhh." Matt stared at Boone's guns, his own still out and loose in his hand.

"Then if you hit him, you'd feel mighty bad."

Boone heard Emily's voice. *He's right, Boone. Walk away.* Boone lowered his gun. "Matt, go back inside. This is between Clem and me."

"No, Matt. Stay out here and we're both safe."

"No, Clem, you're not safe, because I can just shoot you." Boone felt distracted by the way Matt studied him, a kind of quiet fascination. Clem drew his gun, meaning to shoot Boone down. Boone could have taken him, but never got the chance because Matt sideswiped Clem, knocking him to the ground. As Clem grabbed Matt's gun to shoot him instead, Boone angled his own shot and hit Clem in the chest.

Matt grunted and stood, his chest sprayed with Clem's blood. He held his gun out on Boone but shrugged and re-holstered it. They heard a shout from overhead and both whirled, looking up. When they saw Sinbad he had already drawn and neither of them got their guns out fast enough.

Sinbad shot them both.

As Boone fell he heard the sound of horse hooves and rolled to his stomach as the horses flew down from the bluffs and over the top of him.

*

Randy and Richard rode hard on the trampled grass trail in the direction the old Indian told them to go. It appeared this was the trail of the thieved horse stock, and they hoped they'd find Boone in time. Amanda had seen Boone with the gambler and told her brothers what the gambler told her. But the best part of their luck had been the old Indian. When they saw Luster and the other horses running free, the two young men rounded them up and herded them, still trying to follow the trail. Boone wasn't with the horses.

"That Luster's fast!" Richard shouted through the wind and galloping hooves. "Race is tomorrow!"

"I know. Keep looking!"

The trampled grasses gave way to more rock and all the horses slowed in response. Ahead, the sky darkened in an almost funnel shape, yet they couldn't feel any wind in the air.

"We gotta keep going!" Randy yelled.

"You stay with the horses. I'll follow the trail." Richard rode off, even though the trail took him toward the building storm.

Randy's horse danced, anxious to keep moving with Richard's paint, but Randy grabbed the rope off his saddle, looped it and after a few false tries got Luster roped. But with no trees in the area Randy had no choice but to rope the other end to his saddle and hope they would all stay put. He got off his horse and sat on a boulder with the prancing horses to wait out the rain.

While he waited, he wondered if the magic that Boone seemed to possess would have followed him out this far.

*

The wind and downpour of rain with clapping thunder brought Boone back to consciousness, along with the feeling of being gnawed on. He somehow managed to lay on his shoulder against the rock and though the pain made him pass out, the pressure stopped him from bleeding to death.

Crabby nibbled on his hair and brayed in his ear. Boone blinked and sat up. Dizzy, groaning, but alive. With two dead men on either side of him. Matt had been shot in the head.

His horses. He thought to look for them until he remembered the pain that made him pass out was as much from horse hooves as from the bullet in his shoulder.

"We gotta get out of here, Crabby. Think we can manage?" Crabby brayed and nuzzled his ear, then nibbled Boone's butt. "Okay, we'll give it a try."

Crabby seemed to have some energy, and Boone wondered as he rode her what she found to eat out here. He would pasture it. But every bone in his body hurt so much that even if she stopped he would still feel like he was moving.

"Just my luck, you energy, me none."

When she tried to jog, his head screamed the pain and he slipped from the mule to the ground.

*

Richard bent over him. "Think he's gonna be okay, Randy?"

Boone blinked against the rain and feel of water choking him. He first saw Crabby swishing her tail over him, and when her foot came up to kick him, someone jerked her away.

Boone was on his side, with Richard in front and Randy in back. "Looks like the bullet went clean through. Hurts though, I bet, huh, Boone?"

Boone tried to sit up but dizziness forced him back. "Can't …"

"How long since you ate? Get my bag, Richie." Randy helped Boone sit up and held him steady. Richard gave him some smoked jerk beef and held him while he managed some bites.

Randy started a bandage. "So…what happens now, Boone? You can't race like this."

"I know. My horses --."

"Oh, we got 'em for you!" But Richard caught Randy's eye and shut up.

"I took them to the local ranch while Richie came on to look for you. They're all safe."

"Sure appreciate that." Boone took a long satisfying drink and went back to chewing. He looked up into the rain, which seemed to be centered right over them. "Gotta find that Sinbad and kill him. Not safe, any of us, if he comes back. He's crazy. Saw men like that after the war."

"Don't have to worry." Randy sat alongside Boone and Richard sat on the other side, as though to keep Boone from toppling. "I saw him run, took a shot --."

"But he missed! Randy thought he was coming back to finish you, Boone. So when he sees Randy, he gets all nervous and turns too fast in the saddle, and he went one way while his horse went the other. Got his foot caught in the stirrup and the horse dragged him."

Randy nodded. "Left him back there somewhere, head pretty well taken off by the rocks. Vultures were looking hungry. That's when I figured to get the horses to the nearest corral and told Richie to find you."

"Oh." Boone looked over at the mute man and mourned him. "Well, good."

Randy stood. "Feel ready to ride? We'll get Doc to see to that wound before it festers."

They helped him into the saddle, but Randy gave him a longing look. "How do you do it, Boone? How do you manage to stay alive against all odds?"

Boone eyed the clouds, now moving off toward the mountains. "Sun sets, moon rises, all in its time." He patted his mule. "We'll send authorities back. So their families will know."

*

"You're a lucky man, Boone. A little lower and the bullet would've punctured your lung." Doc put the final strips of tape over the gaze and stood.

Boone winced as he buttoned his shirt back up. Doc fitted a sling over his chest and eased the arm into the looped cloth.

"To remind you not to use that arm for a day or two."

"He gonna live, Doc?" The two men turned to see Sheriff Wiggins in the doorway. He didn't come into the room. "We got the two at the embalmers. The third, not enough left to scoop up."

"Am I under arrest?"

"You know, you should be. Except I happen to know a little about those three. And none of it good. Since you did us a favor, I suspect we'll look the other way on this one."

Boone only grunted. He didn't ask for a reward, and none was offered.

"Did you really ride that mule for over twenty miles?"

"No, five. She rode me the rest."

Doc laughed. "Well, Boone, I'd stay off the critter another day or two. If that's Chas's mule, you're not lying about that."

"She's better. She still gets impatient with me, though."

Amanda poked her head in. "Okay if I see him, Doc?"

Doc nodded. "I'd say you'd be good medicine." He scratched his face with the back of his hand as he looked at Boone. "Gonna mix you some tonic. Take the edge off the pain." He patted Amanda's shoulder and left the room.

"My brothers got your horses back in our corral, Boone. So they're taken care of easier." She seemed embarrassed under his stare. "But you say the word and we'll bring them back to your place."

"Tell Richard to ride Luster in the race. If he wins, he gives me the money but keeps the horse."

"Richie? But … okay."

"Randy can have the pinto. I'll keep Impatio, and Crabby, of course."

"What about me, Boone?"

"Why'd you send them after me?"

"You were riding into an ambush."

"I suspect I knew that."

"I don't understand how anyone can dislike you."

"I like that you don't understand."

She sat next to him on the bench. Her odor bothered him but he stuck tight. "Can you tell me about it? You run like a man hiding a violent past, Boone. Should I be afraid of you, really?"

"What do you think?"

"I see pain. Beyond that, I see a man trying to understand everything that happens to him. Like you have a way of reaching into the heart of everything to find the truth. Someone like you should be dead, twenty times over. But here you are. My brothers were wondering on it, and now I do. How do you stay alive, living like you do?"

He brushed her hair off her face. "That's my biggest problem right now, Amanda. Staying alive to do the one thing I gotta do. Maybe it's Sam. Maybe he's the one that keeps me going. I could love you, if the time were different. But I have to follow the needs of a boy, and finish what I set out to do. Maybe then, I can come back. But I won't ask you to wait."

"Okay, now I don't understand you."

"Sunset goes around the moon."

"What?"

"Ever wonder where a sunset goes?"

"Well, it goes with the sun."

"The sun is one thing. The sunset is something else." Boone stood. "I'll keep riding until I figure it out. I'm responsible for the hurt of too many."

"Wait, you're leaving now?" Amanda stood and held his arm as he seemed to sway. "I don't think you're ready. Come home with me, Boone. At least until after the race. So you can collect the winnings."

Boone pulled her close and kissed her, soft and innocent but with as much love as he'd ever felt. Sam pushed him away again. *Find your father.* "I'll wire my address." Boone didn't tell her Richie can't possibly win on that horse. As good as he was, all the progress made with Luster was gone now. Richie had a better chance than Randy, but that gave him odds of next to none.

Boone let her help steady him out to the doctor's office. "How much I owe you?"

"I'd say two dollars will do it."

"My last horse, the gelding. Sell it, you'll get more than you need. My house will go to the next bum who wants it." He kissed Amanda on the cheek and pushed away. "Randy could have it, if he wants. He's near marrying age."

He walked out on the stoop, contemplating his direction. Boone saw the sheriff watching him. But he had nothing more to say.

And the sheriff, well, he just let Boone keep walking out of town.

CHAPTER THIRTY-SEVEN
The Train Job

Boone on Impatio followed the Cheyenne rail line eastward, thinking to go all the way to Chicago. Before he ran out of funds he got a room at a boarding house of a small rail station settlement in Nebraska, still smelling like the recent rail crew. He sought an address for his aunt by sending a telegram to the Chicago Theater Board, and spent the time waiting for a response by taking a blacksmith job. At least it got him close to horses again, and he could start building up his meager purse.

Finally he got a response with her last known theater address, and wrote her a letter.

"Dear Aunt Samantha: I am sorry that it has taken me so long to write to you. I do not know if I should. My mom, your sister Lynelle, told me you loved Shakespeare and did some acting in Chicago, so that is where I write to you. I know you might never get this. It will probably be hard to find me with a response, too, but I hope you will try. My mama died. She died when I was 12, back in 1856. I have been alone pretty much since then. I guess your pa died, too? I cannot live with my father, because Mama wanted me to live in the white world. I wonder, I guess, if you are alone, if you would like some company? Or if we could maybe just visit for a day or two? I would need to hear back from you, so that you can tell me where to find you. Are you still in Illinois?

Well, I hope this letter gets to you. I think it is important for us to know what becomes of our family. Maybe you have been trying to find us and this letter fills you with relief as well as sadness. I would like to meet you. Sent a response to this address.

Love, Boone Tyler

*

One day Boone met a Kiowa, Satank, who was on his way to join his son. He asked Boone to come along with his party so the whites would not murder them. Boone did, not sure that he could help, but was curious about Satank. He thought by riding with him he might witness the behavior that settlers had complained about. When the Kiowa saw the white wagon trains, they thought only to ask for food. They had ridden for days without seeing any elk. But as they approached, with hands up and no weapons drawn, the whites shot at them.

Boone was in the middle of hell, unable to take sides, and rode off, not waiting to see if they settled this without death. He went back to Cheyenne but his homestead had been torched to the ground and Amanda's homestead was vacant, the barn unbuilt.

He sat with tears of sorrow, wondering what became of them.

He took a job as a coal stoker on the train route from Cheyenne east to Lincoln, and from this boarding house sent another letter to his aunt, telling her to reply here instead. Stoking fires, traveling from place to place, often snowed up, without a thought to another day. Time passed and he received no response to his letters. Impatio was boarded more often than ridden and on some days seemed not to know who Boone was.

He hadn't asked Satank about his father. So he kept up with his Shakespeare and learned to play the harmonica. Or maybe Sam learned, because the melodies sounded like something a Kiowa would play. A man needed to know where he should be by this age, and he was here, doing a white job that stirred up Indian tempers.

As Boone played his harmonica, memories of Mexico began to return, and he realized that's why he'd put the harmonica away. Sunset chasing the moon, always another day coming. He wondered every day why he got those symbols. But at the same time, as he pondered the years since he first ran from Mama's death, he realized how often he escaped death.

On the day he passed his 24th year, Boone sat on the wood bench in the train's engine, hands charred up from stoking coal, and pulled out his knife. The snows were light with a surprising warm spell, so he had work more often than not. He etched his symbols into the wood bench, symbols that came to have no meaning at all. He needed to move on. For now, though, and until the winter storms were behind him, he found no better place to be than as a boarder in Cheyenne, with his horse rented out to others by the day. He needed to build his purse for the long journey into Kiowa territory that awaited him.

Maybe his father was already dead. But then so much of his life would move on unanswered.

In his time riding the rails, Boone hadn't seen an Indian except from a distance. White passengers took them for shooting sport, or saw them already dead and bloody on the ground. Supposedly President Johnson's peace policy worked, the one the newly elected Grant would soon adopt -- providing better agents who didn't steal from them. Boone wondered how people trusted Grant at all.

Boone pulled out his ornate harmonica from its secure leather pouch inside his shirt and played the song he taught himself as a memorial to Bark. He learned another one for Crabby. He hadn't thought he would find her dead in her stall like that, but then, he never knew that much about her. "Ode to a mule." He sang the words to himself as he played the poem based on inspirations from a Shakespeare story of a mule. "He felt hurt so sudden he could not sit his mule, and the mule, so foul, would not sit him. The mule, a carcass, the toad and the lizard, all lap the blood as he drifted away, until the mule bit! And up into the saddle again he came."

Boone knew madness as the desire to cause death to that which he loved most. Innocent horses and unwilling Federal soldiers suffered in his killing mood all the way to Mexico after Emily and his son died. But nothing had been able to touch him, as though he lived under some sort of charmed spell, an instinct for survival from somewhere deep inside -- even when death was desired.

He had to confront and kill his father but must have the right questions in his head first. "Why did you kill my mother" could not be the first question. But what was? "Why did you give me back when I was three?" As an almost father himself, he could not figure out an answer to that one. Sam told him it was because of the death of a baby who did not have to die. Boone told Sam to shut up. He didn't need Shakespeare tales told about his own life.

As his harmonica wailed on he drifted back to Emily's death. From Brownsville he jumped into Matamoros, Mexico, where he and Lean Ear Jackson found jobs working the docks. Every day they ducked bullets as though only migrants to be shot at. He even killed a few but mostly kept to the shadows. Lots of border crossings, raiding and thieving, by Indians and anyone else who could cross without getting shot by sporadic guards meant to prevent illegal migration. Some banditos used him to rob silver shipments from the wagons and later from trains, using his innocent face and half-breed nature as cover, all the while with the gun pointed at his back. He had begged like a dog to be allowed to leave and that's when they kicked him until he couldn't move anymore and they threw the harmonica at him as his pay. It cut his head open. They never found the money he stole from them. He was thankful to have escaped with his life.

When he realized this harmonica had been stolen from someone, he was determined to find them. One day he saw a Mexican woman beg for food from the whites who traded lead for corn. They shoved her aside, time after time, until one man pushed her down and kicked her. Boone watched until she sobbed alone on the dock. He put his hand on her shoulder and she whimpered, tense with fear.

"Let me get you home."

"Need food … for my two children."

Boone never figured out how but he understood her fine. "We'll find you some food. But we must leave here. Too dangerous."

She looked up into his eyes and with a trembling hand brushed his long hair from his face. "Are you Mestizo?"

He moved her away from the approaching dock guards. She staggered, barely able to keep up. They rounded the back of a wagon and he grabbed a bag of corn meal for her family. "Keep moving. To your house. Hurry." Someone shouted behind them. He pushed the bag into her arms and pulled his guns, firing to buy them more time. "Keep going!"

Her house was a shack, barely four walls of tin in a lean-to fashion, where two children, one black and one a lighter shade, sat outside half naked. They drew listlessly in the dirt and did not react to the gunfire behind them. Boone pushed them all inside and turned again with guns out and firing, in time to take one down. The other ran off.

He darted inside the shack. "You live too close to the docks. You must leave. But first, find some water, clean, and make them some flat cakes."

"We will not leave. They will not hurt us."

Boone stared at her determined eyes, hair fallen from clips, and almost loved her. "Suit yourself." He peered outside the shack, ready to leave, when he heard her call to her children. The dangerous and illegal activity at the docks with unfair trade kept tempers high. But what did she mean by not being in danger? While other civilians had been gunned down for begging, she was not. What sort of Diablo protected her?

He realized he may have just saved a whore.

Boone looked down to see the boy had taken his harmonica from his pocket. As Boone watched, he put it to his lips and began to play.

His mother sucked in a sharp mouthful of air. She grabbed the harmonica from the boy. "Where did you get this?" She waved the harmonica at Boone's face.

"It was payment --."

"By who?"

Boone told her about being forced to rob a train. After listening, she collapsed, sobbing, the harmonica to her chest.

"My father's."

"This same one?"

"Men killed and robbed him. When I found him, he was little more than dirt in the desert. And he had been a big man, a proud man, a ..." and she used another word he didn't know, but he finally understood her father had been of high rank in the Mexican military before Maximilian brought his French government. "A terrible time to be a country."

Boone wanted to ask for it back, but instead he turned to leave.

"Noooo!" She screamed at him. "I cannot keep this. I will be killed." She held the harmonica up at him, in both palms open and upward, as though offering a sacrifice. "You are the worthy one. You must take this away, far from here." Boone took the harmonica as she sobbed and beat against his chest. "May Mother Mary and her Christ child protect you. It may be cursed and needs someone who can cleanse it again."

Boone felt the train's engine give a lurch. He shook off the memory as he tucked the harmonica away and jumped to the train's furnace. The station loomed so Boone scooped out the hot coals to slow the engine down. He threw the brakes and as usual hoped the train stopped on target. Always seemed like a crap shoot to him.

CHAPTER THIRTY-EIGHT
The Church Visit

Boone couldn't call home his room at Gayle's boarding house. Gayle chewed tobacco and nagged at him to work for her until he collapsed at night. This time she asked him for groceries from the next town, so Boone went to the livery for Impatio. Tonight the black and white jogged over and brushed his nose against Boone's neck because Boone pulled out the handful of sweet grass he found along the way.

She called the instrument sacred. He doubted the harmonica was anything more than the attachment someone else had for it. And he had no attachment to anyone's mother Mary. But this simple instrument helped him recover from grief and mourning, he reminded himself as he breathed the fresh air of this simple errand. On the way he saw the church, up on the hill, lighted by the moon and stars. Perhaps the place to cleanse the instrument, as she felt it was cursed.

How could such a thing be cursed? Bark had crawled into his lap when he first started playing. But then he put the harmonica away, until the old Indian noted it. This harmonica now felt like his symbol of life taken form, like the bright colors of dusk that hid behind the moon and came out again in the musical notes he played. Perhaps the harmonica was the arrow in his symbol. Could be, too, that the harmonica was also his curse, as it had been for the woman's father. He couldn't come up with her name, only a kind of love for her strength, and vowed to return this to her someday, as her children's legacy. He realized he might even love her and the life he left back there. Perhaps, once again, he was only running from the love he feared.

When he returned with her goods Gayle told him to help himself to stew on the stove and sat to chat with him while he ate. He asked her if she went to the church up there on the hill.

"Church? What would I want to go fooling with a church for?"

"Do you know if it's open?"

"Oh, those doors are always open, child. You can go there and give them money any time, day or night." She cackled with great venom and spit. "Will you confess your sins to God?"

"Well, I don't think I have anything worth mentioning, but I thought I would stop in and see what gets so many people believing things they cannot see."

"Yeah. Guess that's why I don't go. Want no one convincing me I can see something that ain't there. It needs to catch me during my sleep. They call them kind of people crazy, don't they?" Gayle was of Swedish descent, with big blonde ringlets that looked as aged as she did. "Would you like me to come with you?"

Boone nodded. "I would like that."

She struggled with her response. "Ah, no. You need that as personal time. 'Sides, I ain't done with my chores yet. You mind hurrying back, because I need me some more kindling for the night."

Boone stopped in the middle of a bite to look at her. After having his eyes on her for a few seconds she got up and left the room. Boone finished her stew with a piece of sourdough and chuckled as he chewed.

*

He had a full moon night. Seeing the moon rise, his habit since he became a living symbol of the sunset, was why he conjured the plan to go in the first place. He'd never paid that citadel on the top of the hill much attention but the woman's memory called him out to follow the moon's natural light on the trail up the hill.

Once he reached the top, Boone tied Impatio where the horse could nibble. He patted his chest to feel the harmonica's leather bag secured there and sat on a rock near the entrance. This Gothic architecture -- ornate, frilly, ridiculous to his mind -- showed glory to something no one could see but only feel. He almost wished he were one of those who could be so blindly led.

The building looked intimidating, almost evil in the moonlight. Boone tried to remember the last time he was in a church and decided the answer must be never.

His mother took him in that direction a few times but always changed her mind, and once she swore at the people going to church but would not tell him why. So many things he'll never know about her, because as a child he'd just accepted her.

Bill Roberts took him to church once but they stood outside while Bill told him what he believed. Then he invited Boone to come in with him. No pressure. "Come eat my body and drink my blood," he said, trying to explain the Christ mystery. Boone thought Bill had been joshing him at the time. Boone had heard of cannibalism. *That face of his the hungry cannibals would not have touched. Would not have stained with blood.* Boone hoped he had one of those faces to carry inside there, just in case. Legends get warped, sometimes. Boone was too young to know what to think and when Bill invited him, telling him about eating Christ's body, Boone had refused.

The building looked like a good place to hold a séance and contact the dead. Boone thought maybe here he could make peace with Emily, with her spirit and why she had to die and take his son with her. He ran to Mexico because Emily made him feel guilty -- that he knew they were going to die so he willingly killed them.

He looked up as the moonlight pushed at the drifting clouds. "You wanted to get away from me, Emily?" He took out the harmonica and started to play. The melody was unfamiliar, more like from a part of his soul he's not yet touched. He thought he heard Sam singing along. He realized that Sam was just another part of his inner voice, that contrary voice. But he felt comforted to believe Sam's soul was actually inside him.

All that trying for death in his madness and here he sat, still alive. Sitting here made him no more sacred or prepared for death than in the woods waiting for a deer to sacrifice itself for his dinner. For the longest time he thought he sent Emily to the bad gods because he did not go to church with her. She wanted him to know more about her God and finally just gave up. Was that why she died?

Boone walked inside the church. "For you, Emily." The doors were heavy but shut with a quiet sucking noise behind him. The air turned into what he could only call rotten flowers and then perfume. Maybe those painted ladies in Cheyenne needed a lot of God. He had to concentrate to see the top of the building through the darkness. The inside seemed as tall as the outside. Why would this God need so much space? God should be able to fit on the smallest pebble in a raging river and not get wet.

Rows of benches with backs. Soldiers could eat on the ground, while drovers sat on stools or stumps. Here they liked to lean back, maybe snooze. Must be hard to be cannibals. Boone sat in one, at first straight, and then leaned back. Uncomfortable. But maybe good if he was exhausted or worried about eating someone else's flesh and drinking their blood. He drank animal blood when he was dying of thirst. But they don't come here when they're dying of thirst. In these seats they all had to face the same way -- a ritual altar where sacrifice was made to become this Christ body. Probably just used an animal. He heard of this ceremony once that made people become one with their god by eating a real person. Was that in Mexico? They were very religious down there.

Statues of people all around him, so rich and noble. Colored glass windows. Every artifice arranged in so much order. He was glad for the moonlight to see this, all spooky and mysterious. He looked around at all the empty pews. He imagined them filled with people. People looking to their god for favors. People who needed to believe in something. Anything. He closed his eyes and found the belief that Emily died doing the one thing she'd always lived for.

Then he understood. Nodded. And left.

Back at the boarding house he saw Gayle going over her books. She spit into her brass bowl before she looked up at him. "How was church?"

"Not for people like me."

She bent back over her books. "Don't forget the kindling."

*

Boone got a break from work when a foot of snow fell in a day, then back to work when the rails were cleared. His engineer days ended for good in late March 1869, the day a band of Arapahoes attacked the train. Passengers had been shooting at buffalo, leaving them to fall and rot in the sun. The Indians tried but couldn't get

224

the rails apart quickly enough so they shot flaming arrows at the caboose and the wooden car caught fire.

The conductors panicked and told Boone to keep the engine moving, don't stop, and the flames eventually went out. They also shot at the passenger cars and wounded two, then disappeared as quickly as they had appeared.

At the Cheyenne station Boone stepped out in full engineer uniform to express his concern for the passengers.

"Look! One of them got in the engine, took over the train!"

People fled or backed away from him. He took off the hat, threw it to the ground, and walked back to town for his horse.

CHAPTER THIRTY-NINE
Rotting Meat

A late spring blizzard hit the route from Wyoming to Nebraska so Boone traveled close to the train tracks, hiding whenever a train went by so he didn't become a target. As he rode and stopped to bed wherever he could, he sometimes saw the chance to listen to council, as though a tribal member, wherever the Peace Commission was trying to get signatures for the Fort Laramie Treaty. This was to guarantee them the Black Hills and Powder River country for as long as the grass grows. Knowing white thirst for water and more, Boone figured he'd still be around when the grass stopped growing.

He heard that the rails had linked that May to unite East and West, too. He picked up another paper wherever he hit a town, usually a discarded one. Now there would be no stopping white progress. They had managed to get the rail through by separating hostile and agency Indians -- anyone was hostile who tried to interfere with the rail line properties that had been negotiated already.

This was how Grant hoped to keep the peace, by only sending military after hostiles. Right, like those Comanches, who were simply trying to live on their own land. There were many, like Black Kettle, a Cheyenne had who cried for peace before his village was slaughtered last November at Washita by Custer.

Boone also heard of an Oglala, perhaps half-breed, some say all white, who was a great warrior of the Oglala Sioux. Boone wanted to meet this Crazy Horse but was told he remained deep within his tribal lands, far from any whites -- a so-called hostile only because he wanted to live his tribal life. Boone felt they could have much in common if the rumors were true that his father was a white trader and his Indian mother committed suicide.

When Boone heard rifle shots from the train he steered Impatio into the underbrush. Those sounds were followed by a stamped buffalo herd running past him, frightened by the train that was coming. Men in buckskin with long fancy rifles sat in train car windows, shooting, laughing and puffing on lazy cigars. Buffalo dropped alongside the track like so much garbage.

As Boone watched the buffalo drop he recognized an injustice with a nagging desire from boyhood and got to work, as Sam's tribal screams to find his father soured inside him.

*

By spring 1870 Boone had a booming business selling fallen buffalo meat. He got the meat while the corpses were still warm, and to assure himself the meat was still good he ate the liver of every one he butchered. He also broke horses as he got this new business set up.

He had to keep good meat cold, though, and smoked and jerked the rest, a difficult task that first summer for a man alone. He dug a meat locker deep and close to rock for the cool, and smoked meat as fast as he could. He became pretty successful that first winter, but as spring approached his hole caved and he had to dig another. He also made a double-lined metal box and filled the outside lining with ice from the river, as long as ice could be found. The Platte River was sluggish and froze up nice in the winter.

He still needed to convince more whites to eat buffalo meat, and kept the price low enough to sway some. He hoped they would convince others who would then shoot for food, and not for fun. This was a job only to change some minds, and nothing more. *Dark working sorcerers that change the mind, soul-killing witches that deform the body…*

In the midst of butchering three cows, northern Cheyenne Indians surrounded him. He gave the familial greeting and learned one spoke English.

"You kill our buffalo?"

"No. Already find killed. Hope to convince others they are good to eat, to not waste the meat."

"You kill our buffalo to eat, but give us lousy pig." He spit on the ground. "Fat. Greasy."

"I wish to ask your help. I would give half the meat I treat to your agencies, if I could get you to give me someone to help transport it. I work this alone."

They left a boy behind -- more a man-sized boy and Boone didn't notice it at first but his eyes weren't quite right, and he knew no English. He stood silent, watching Boone, as though waiting for instructions. His shoes appeared battered and fragmented, as though he had walked a long time before the Cheyenne party latched onto him, and now found a good place to let him go. Boone walked over to the man and introduced himself.

The Indian said, "Red Feather," and pointed to his chest. "You got gum?" Red Feather turned and stared at Boone's hip. "Gum?"

"Oh, gun! No, I never carry, well, except for the rifle on my horse." Boone hung up his pistols after leaving the railroad but held tight to his knife -- his mother's knife, for that need to confront his father. "Why you need a gun?" He asked over his shoulder to Red Feather, to get the lad to follow him. "Where is your home?"

"Home?" Red Feather indicated sleep. "Here." He pointed at the ground.

"Well, come on in then, and we'll see what you can do."

And sure enough, Red Feather attached himself to Boone like a red hawk to a mouse and Boone didn't mind. He never had a real brother, except for that brief time knowing Stu, and decided Red Feather was just the business partner he needed, strong and compliant. He first set about cooking them both a small piece of meat because Red Feather tried to grab a hunk reserved for someone else.

After they ate Boone led him outside and told him to brush Impatio down. When they walked past the cage, Squawk got their attention. A month past, Boone found an injured baby owl and nursed it back to health. He tried to free it but the ornery owl kept returning to the cage.

Red Feather leaned over the cage, his eyes wide.

"This is Squawk. I'll let --."

But Red Feather lashed out at Boone with a fist, knocking Boone to the ground. Boone jumped back to his feet and wrapped his arms around the boy before he could swing again.

"What is it?"

Red Feather threw Boone off and paced around the yard, flailing his arms. "Not squaw! Not squaw!"

Boone watched the boy's frantic moves like the owl flapping sporadically when he found it. The owl hadn't been long out of its nest when it must have hit a tree and injured its wing. This boy, fascinated by the owl, seemed broken, too. "Squawk, his name is Squawk." Finally worn out and shaken, Red Feather sat down by the owl's cage.

"Me Squawk, too."

Boone laughed. "You sure did!" He sat down next to Red Feather and put a hand on his shoulder. "Would you like to stay with me? Work with me? You'd have to do as I say." He used the best Cheyenne words he knew.

"Home. No squaw."

Boone had little more in mind than giving him a home, but as the days passed realized his motives were selfish. Red Feather turned out to be a valuable asset in the business, helping with the butchering. He showed Boone how to use other parts of the buffalo. Having him in charge of the shop while Boone made deliveries gave him great piece of mind.

One particular family he took a liking to. A widow woman, Angela, had two small boys. Her husband, a cavalry captain, died in a fight with some Apache, but she didn't hold that against Boone. She always had coffee for him when he delivered her order, the same thing every week, when meat was available. Boone always lingered at Angela's house a few extra minutes. He spent time with her boys, ages 5 and 6, because they had so much energy and hers dwindled. He couldn't guess how old she was.

Boone learned their names were Peter and Nick, which so completely startled him that he backed up and fell over their dog, a mangy animal that never got that near him again. They were both dark-haired, with German gypsy blood. Angela told him they were both blonde at birth.

He taught them a game he remembered as a child. With some trial and effort he rigged up some rough but passable equipment. He found two good sticks thick enough and long enough for two young boys to grow with at least for a few seasons, and made rope netting attached to a thin metal hoop. He found the ball at the local mercantile. The boys were quick and eager learners and Angela enjoyed watching.

On this particular visit he planned to spend a few minutes helping them with the game before excusing himself to go back to the store, where he left Red Feather with another bull to carve. "All right, usually we play this with more boys, so we're going to adapt this just a little bit so the two of you can play together. You want to throw the ball over each other's head and try to get it into your basket. Never use your hands! The ball has to stay in the hoop when it isn't in the air." He set up a basket on each end of the playing field and told them whose was whose. He didn't expect that six-year-old Pete would have the advantage because despite being older, he wasn't any taller. "If you get the ball into your basket, you get a point. Got it?"

He stood back and watched as they tried to throw, getting nowhere close to their baskets or catching each other's toss. But they laughed and ran around the playing field and tried to fake each other out. They soon turned their ball playing into a new game that Boone didn't recognize.

He turned to Angela. "As long as they're --."

But Angela had disappeared. Near where she had been sitting stood Red Feather. Against Boone's wishes, he had followed Boone here. That meant he left the bull to rot. "Red Feather. Job to do!"

Red Feather was learning a little better English, too. "Job done. Not much good meat." He pointed at the boys, as though hoping to play with them.

"Ah, I'll have to ask her." He rapped on Angela's door.

With hesitation she peeked out at him, and saw Red Feather still standing in the yard.

"Angela, it's all right. He's harmless. I'll vouch for him. He works with me."

"But Boone, he looks so strange. You know I'm a'feared of Indians."

"Not me, though."

"No, you're different."

"So is he. He's wearing white clothes now. He doesn't carry a knife. Don't judge him by his slow mind. He won't hurt you."

"But his hands are so big. And his one eye looked at me funny."

Boone understood. Women feared being raped out here, where they were outnumbered ten to one. That Angela hadn't remarried yet she put down to stubbornness. "Just stay inside, with your rifle ready, if it makes you feel safe. Just let him deliver to you once a week and play with your boys. I'll stay here so we can watch them together."

Nothing more came of the issue and Red Feather came to love his weekly delivery there.

Red Feather had other episodes, too, what Boone came to call "fits." The boy wasn't going to realize a long life, he feared, and was happy to give him a home as long as he needed one. *For quiet days, fair issue and long life, with such love as tis now.* Boone's Shakespeare thoughts come out only in spurts these days. He still had his book, but his readings tend to send his thoughts soaring to earlier times. He would then engage in inner thoughts, mind soaring, eyes closed, as Red Feather sang by the fire.

He watched Red Feather give Squawk a flying lesson one day, on the day he knew his people would never return for him. The owl belonged to Red Feather now and no longer could survive in the wild, but he saw no problem with letting Red Feather keep it.

As he twined new rope Red Feather suddenly put the bird back in the cage and ran to the edge of the smokehouse. "Bad!"

Boone thought the lad had picked up on Boone's thoughts which had drifted back to killing his father. But no, this was more, as the lad scribbled in the dirt. He drew several buffalo but on each one he drew a circle over the buffalo's back. Then he scratched the drawing out and with his stick pointed at Boone.

231

"Go!" Red Feather jumped up and ran into the barn. He came back out with the saber that Boone found after his days in Mexico and tried to shove it into Boone's hand.

"What's wrong, Red Feather? Are soldiers coming? They won't hurt us. We've sold them buffalo before."

"These are not soldiers," Red Feather said in a clear and unusual burst of words. "These are cow-boys."

Boone turned to face his metal-lined meat shed. It was nearing the end of 1870, and cattlemen wanted to drive him out. He supposed he could pack up what he had and go where the cattle business doesn't reach. Selling buffalo had gotten harder, too, because people started hunting it on their own and cattle on the hoof dropped in price. He hated quitting with the chill of winter coming on, though. But Red Feather was right. With the attitude toward buffalo meat changing, as he'd wanted, he needed to move on.

"Will you go with me, Red Feather?" Boone figured to sell his enterprise to that old butcher who'd been asking. At this time he could get top dollar. "Come on, let's get busy."

When the cowboys arrived, they found an old man setting up a butcher shop for buying cattle. He shot at one of the cowboys for unjustly accusing him of wrongdoing.

Boone sent Red Feather ahead and stayed long enough to make sure the old man wasn't harmed. But Red Feather hadn't taken the route Boone sent him on. Disappeared. Maybe he went back to his people. He could have been slaughtered and robbed by cowboys but Boone did not want to know. He preferred to think that his old friend, who earned the wagon and goods he had taken, had found his way back home.

CHAPTER FORTY
The Kidnapped

Boone patted Impatio, his underweight black and white pinto, as he looked back at the long trail behind him. The trail from western Nebraska into Oklahoma took him through Kansas, mostly low plains, so when he hit the buttes his eyes were closed and he nearly fell off the horse by the sudden downhill turn. The lay of the land always amazed him, where he could be in the top of the mountains and see nothing but flat land, lulling him into complacency.

Winter hit hard and this trail didn't have the fodder he expected. Some of the time they had to make their own road through deep snow. Often they were tormented by a deep threat of storm in the shape of clouds overhead. But he kept moving through it all, hoping to find the right Kiowa village before reaching Indian Territory, which could be wicked with outlaws and despondency.

He followed one blind lead after another, finding tribes and rested for a spell with their common hospitality, before being sent off in yet another direction. He sometimes felt his father followed, laughing at him.

Why do you feel he laughs? asked Sam. "Because I delay so long." *Why do you delay so long?* "I am afraid of the truth." *What truth?*

"That my mother didn't just die. She killed herself." *There is a lot of truth to fear. But once conquered, truth makes you whole.* "I will never be whole." *Not if you cannot conquer fear. By east, north, west and south, I spread my conquering might.*

Boone laughed aloud. Now Sam was quoting the Bard.

Once Boone crossed into Indian Territory tribal leaders recognized Kae-Gon's name and looked at his son with some suspicion. No one could, or would, say where he was.

233

Heavier than usual snows that winter curtailed much activity, and more to come, as Boone struggled to find food and shelter and turned another year older. How fast the time could go! He only wished he realized that sooner. Everyone he met suffered as he did and few had anything to spare. The snows seemed to follow him as he headed south, and along the way he heard of many Kiowa who fled into the warmer lands of Mexico.

Most of the time he begged for food from already food-poor tribes on or near reservations. The government made any excuse for the lack of annuities, especially now, with the treaty executed, the transcontinental railroad done, and little care what happened to them. Kiowa were wanderers, as many tribes were, always searching out new food sources, from new buffalo herds to wild onions.

But most roamed Indian Territory and received their annuity goods at Fort Sill, and that's where he headed. He hoped to be accepted as an interpreter there and could break horses while he waited to see the man from the campfire, the man he came to accept was his father.

Another ranch ahead. Their misery drove them forward in hope. The ranch buildings seemed deserted. Boone pulled Impatio up and it pranced but Boone didn't alight. As he got close he saw an old pair of boots, still muddy, at the front door.

"Name's Boone Tyler," he called out. "Need a little food and rest. Can work for it."

A boy of about 10 came around the corner of the house and stopped short when he saw Boone. "Injun!" he shrieked. "Injun!" He jumped up on the porch on the other side, ran into the house and slammed the door tight.

Before Boone could blink the door flew open and a man stood on the stoop with a rifle pointed square at Boone's chest. "What do you want here?"

"I come to work for you. In exchange for food. If you're in need of your field cleared or your barn cleaned. I work hard. I break horses, too."

"You'll have to ask the old man." The man with the rifle indicated the barn with a motion of the barrel. Boone alighted. The rifle lowered with him as the man maintained his threatening stance. "I'll be right here, so don't try nothing."

Boone approached the barn with the caution of a stranger. He hesitated outside the door when he heard mumblings. The old man sat alone and looked ill-tended, dirty and ragged. Boone rapped on the wood frame before he stepped in, horse in tow. "Mister?"

The old mister fell to his knees in the hay and muttered about loose joints and stirrups. "Gotta be some way, some way."

"Mind if my horse has some hay?" The old man waved and went back to digging.

"I hear you're looking for a hired hand." He let Impatio go to sniff out the fresher hay.

The old man with skeletal features looked up. The eyes were blank, face drawn tight and his mouth wore a bitter, turned-down expression. "A guest! Ah yes. Well, welcome, welcome. Say, have you come for the boy?"

"The boy?" Boone glanced back at the house. "No, I'm here to work for you."

"Ah, work, yes, work. Boards loose. Up there." A shaky hand pointed to the hay loft. "Gonna get me a bride, yessir. That's what's needed. Too many days alone, you know."

"Yes. I'll … need tools."

But the old man slumped on his stool and appeared to nod off.

"Don't get up. I'll find something." Boone poked his head back outside to ask the son or grandson, but those two had disappeared.

He climbed up into the hay loft. The ladder steps were firm but he found two loose boards in the loft flooring and some of the hay had gone bad. He spent the rest of the afternoon salvaging what could be salvaged and tossed the rest out the window. The old man seemed to have frozen, maybe died, in that same odd position.

When Boone came back in from working outside, hammering loose boards, old Samuels had fallen and, groggy, tried to get up. "Let me help you, sir."

"Help me?" The man held his back and groaned. "Give me a new body maybe?"

"Into the house."

"Ha! Not with the likes of them. Thieves is what they are. Get them out. Out! Owwww!"

"Just lean on me."

"Hey, you Injun? Or half-breed?"

"My mother was white."

"Bless her. You tell her that for me."

"Yessir."

"Polite, too. She done taught you manners."

If this old man's mind was sharp, then those two inside were just what he said they were. "Can we go inside?"

The old man sensed his hesitation. "Hey! You afraid? House. Where we stay warm. Like your teepee. Yeah. Come on."

"But that man --."

"If he shoots you, I'll make sure … to bury you proper." Samuels cackled. "Once an Indian, always an Indian. Owwww!" He gripped Boone, squeezing, and as they walked to the house, the porch door opened.

Boone saw the face of the boy staring at them. They heard the booming voice from the dark room behind him. "We got no food, Samuels! And you know why!"

Samuels slumped down on the porch rail as Boone let go. "I keep giving our food away."

Boone sat next to him. "It's good to give to those who have less than you. But you gotta keep some for yourself."

Samuels laughed. "I don't give it to people who need it. I give it to them that threaten me." His bony hand grabbed Boone's arm. "You can help me. You can kill them."

"Who do you want me to kill? The boy or the man?" At the moment he thought he could kill both, and then realized another meaning of his symbols. Blood, arrow and hide. He had to read it backward, the opposite of what he wanted it to say. Symbols of death for his father.

The front door opened and the boy called Richie stepped out. "Pa says you can have some stew. Not much left. Nothing after, neither."

Richie led them to two half-empty bowls of suspect meat and puny potatoes, with a scattering of onion. They were each allowed two swallows of milk. For a time all that could be heard was clinking silver and the heavy sniffles of Mr. Samuels. The stew was bland and there was no salt on the table. Boone didn't care. He hadn't eaten all day and had to concentrate to eat slow. The father and son had disappeared, leaving them alone.

Boone was nearly done eating when he wondered what poison tasted like.

"How long you fixing to stay, Injun?"

Boone almost responded with *I'm not staying Indian.* "My name's Boone Tyler. I don't live with Indians."

Samuels only grunted.

"If it's all right, I would like to bunk in the barn tonight. I'll do more clean up behind the barn. All I need in the morning is a wash and a way to fix some hominy I got with me, enough for all of us. Then I'll be gone."

"Not good enough." The father came around the table. "We'll take your hominy, but then the old man, he needs a bath."

Boone blinked. "I'm sorry?"

"I'll warn you, though. He fights like a son of the devil. Makes you want to drown him. And then you go." The man headed outside. "You better hope you didn't lead anywhere here, neither."

Boone looked over at Mr. Samuels. He was a skinny old coot. How hard could bathing him be? And he did have some kind of bad odor coming off him.

The father dove back in the house just as a glint or flash of sun through the window caught Boone's eye. He grabbed Samuels' arm and pulled him to the floor as bullets peppered the house.

"Come out of there, Richard Harrington! Come out or we'll blow the place down."

Richard the elder and the son he called Richie took positions at the windows with weapons of their own. They fired off a few shots before joining Boone and Samuels under the table. "Friends of yours?"

Richard pointed his gun at Boone's nose. "You're one smart bastard, ain't ya? Now you're gonna get out there and tell them we're not here."

"How do I do that when you fired at them?"

Samuels backed out from under the table and used a chair to get to his feet. "I'll go out. This is my home. You ain't using this Injun. He done nothing to you. I did. I give hospitality to someone who don't deserve it and then never leaves."

When Samuels reached the door Richard turned to shoot the old man. Boone knocked the gun away so the shot went high. Richie leaped on Boone and bit his arm. As the three fought each other off, another round of gunfire hit the house.

"All right! I'll go out." Boone stood in time to catch Samuels as he fell, shot in the back, a bullet through the door also driving a chunk of wood into the wound. He laid the man down on his side. "Feel bad?"

Samuels coughed blood. "I'm an old man. Want to protect mine … with my life." He shuddered, coughed, and died.

Boone laid the dead old man out and turned to see Richard with a gun on him again, and Richie with another, although shaky.

"Now you get out there, do as I say, or I kill this boy." Richard grabbed the kid's gun away. The kid whimpered but otherwise didn't move. Could be a trick, Boone figured, but then, what in life wasn't? *Well, if I be served such another trick, I'll have my brains ta'en out.*

Richard held the gun to the kid's head, so Boone turned with slumped shoulders to the door. He thought of calling the man's bluff, but the men outside could be law and easier to deal with. He felt the harmonica in his shirt pocket grow heavy against his chest as though trying to spread out to protect him.

He stepped out of the house, hands raised. "You got yourself some nervous homesteaders in there. But we don't know any Harrington."

Three men on horseback, one law, the other two probably lynching party, kept their rifles leveled at him. *Stall stall stall and think.* He felt Sam inside him take wings and fly off to look for help, a feeling he'd had before but thought nothing of. Was there something inside him that could take wings? The lawman, graying hair and a drooping mustache, prodded his horse a step closer.

"You don't fit the description of the one we want. They inside?"

Behind them came a loud rifle blast and one man was shot off his horse. Boone leaped sideways and scuttled under the porch as the two men on horseback opened fire in return. One of the men threw a lit torch inside one of the windows and caught the drapes on fire. Before long black billowing smoke swept upward on the wind.

As gunfire continued and the fire blazed, a loud yell from somewhere off in the distance sent him lingering memories of his days fighting Union soldiers, until he recognized the sound. Comanche. They saw the smoke. *And pluck the wings from painted butterflies. To fan the moonbeams from his sleeping eyes.*

Boone saw the two surviving posse ride off hard as the Comanche surrounded the house. No gunfire came from inside. Several ran inside the house while the rest used dirt and horse blankets to lessen the fire.

Within moments they pulled the man and boy, both injured, out of the house, killed them and scalped them, and rode off again. Boone waited until he was sure the fire would go out, and rode hard on that Comanche trail.

*

Pounding hooves, dust on the prairie like fog and Boone heard the yells. Comanche and Kiowa were running and soon he got swept up. Some had been at the house, but all seemed to see him as one of them. Impatio loved the run and was trained for this, and they could tell that, too. Boone gave the horse the lead, his own blood pounding with the sheer excitement, of not knowing why and yet sensing the danger, of running with them and yet remaining alone and apart. Even though they accepted food and their coming fate at Fort Sill, they still rode out on the wind of revered freedom.

Then white marauders came into view and began firing. Boone felt a bullet glance off the harmonica in his pocket as he turned the horse and dashed off into a thicket, there to hide until they'd gone on past. Staying alive sometimes meant not choosing a side.

Only between them will he find peace. The trick was to find that land to stand on.

CHAPTER FORTY-ONE
The Search

Fort Sill, Indian Territory … with spring moving him toward moving to his 28th year. Now there was no longer a road block between him and his father. Here, someone will know him.

General Phil Sheridan had this fort town built as a resource for military to stop them from raiding into Texas and Kansas. Boone first talked with Colonel Albert Gallatin Boone, with whom he found an instant affection. Boone Tyler was named after Albert's legendary grandfather, Daniel Boone. The Colonel did his best, but because of Grant's peace policy, the army was not allowed to go after any Indians who stole cattle in retaliation for the killing of buffalo. He made Boone a sub-agent and sent him to quiet the settlers nearby.

Boone knew cow towns, but this afternoon a different tension than filled the air. A crowd of people stood outside the telegraph office, the silence thick. Boone held his horse back far enough to catch an ear-full. He alighted and stood near the mercantile, and took out the harmonica to play as he listened. Another kind of emotion stirred in the air around him, making the dust in the air sparkle in the sun. His father was nearby.

A woman stepped out of the telegraph office. She was smartly dressed, not young, but wore a beggar's frown. Boone was surprised to see a woman hold this crowd's attention outside of a saloon.

"It's official. Nothing can be done." Loud protests rose in waves through the crowd. She raised her hands to silence them. "Grant will not allow any military punitive action against the Indians."

"They see us as weak!" One heavyset blustery faced fellow cried out. "My girl was pret-near scared to death when one of them savages came on her bathing in the river."

Boone's harmonica playing sharpened at that instant. He remembered hearing about a battle against Comanche and Kiowa at Adobe Wall in 1864, one that kept those at Fort Sumner on guard against them, and why they had sent him out. But he didn't know the whole of truth of what happened there until later, two years after that supposed peace agreement in '62. Easy to ask for peace when the war raged in the East. The Indians had only been responding to wagon trains of white settlers killing their buffalo. The Kiowa remembered it as the time they chased Kit Carson away. But the U.S. Army declared the engagement as a victory.

"Then I suggest she bathe at home or in town. And we no longer call them savages --."

"Bullfeathers! They always was and they always will be."

"We have had a treaty of peace with them since 1862 and they have been --."

"They break it! Every day they break it! You know what they done to us after that."

"They use that fort as a sanctuary!"

"In response to your violence!" She bathed in their stunned silence after her stormy declaration. "Leave them alone and you'll see no trouble. Many try to farm on that poor piece of land the government gave them. The rest just want to live free as they always did. They don't understand your land boundaries. Stop shooting at them."

Boone kept up his soft playing. He saw several Indians try to force their way into a nearby tavern and were thrown out again. White man's disease. Anger rose up. "You want them to starve? You kill their buffalo and leave it to rot. Kill only what you can eat. We are learning this."

The whole of the crowd turned to look at Boone.

Several began to shout at him, things like "kill their food, kill them" but the woman held up a hand. "Enough now. Stranger, identify yourself. Are you Comanche?"

"You can't exterminate the tribes so you kill their food and make them depend on the government. The Indians will take what's due them for this deliberate destruction."

The man who approached Boone smelled like days of uncleanliness. But his shoulders were squared back and his eyes held the look of a lawman. "Give me that." He held his hand out for the harmonica.

Boone hesitated. Mr. Bad Smell grabbed it from his hands and studied the silver scroll-etched harmonica.

"Awful fancy for a half-breed, ain't it?"

"It was a gift." Boone reached to take it back, but the man shrugged him off.

"Looks like real silver."

"Plays fine." Boone snatched the harmonica back. He walked over to his horse and feigned tucking the harmonica in his saddlebag, slipping it instead into his leather pouch around his neck inside his shirt, as the crowd continued to argue with the woman.

Boone focused on the woman as he moved toward the crowd. She gave Boone a sense of hope sorely needed in his life, that there could be another like Emily out there.

"Regardless of how you feel, this is the way it is. There is no area anywhere else available for them --."

"We was told every effort would be made to keep them away from us!"

"And unless verifiable incidents occur, the government is reluctant to take further --."

"You mean, until someone is kilt!"

"We ain't gonna wait for it!"

"I have been elected justice of the peace here!" Her voice hinted at her rage that grew with impatience. "If one of you takes matters into your own hands you will find yourself in jail."

"You're only a woman, regardless of how you got that title. Where I'm from a woman stays home where she belongs." The blustery-faced man waved a fist at her. "Now you close them pretty blue eyes of yours and let us do what we gotta."

"How do we know she even telegraphed the government?"

The crowd began to merge as one angry voice.

"They'll listen if we all wire…."

"They'll listen to us in numbers…."

"We'll get some action if we all demand it…."

The crowd converged on the telegraph office, pushing the woman aside. They bulged the walls as they all demanded a wire be sent with their names. While the tail end of the crowd stood outside, several turned again to point at Boone.

Boone jumped on Impatio and rode out in the direction of the closest Kiowa tribe. His father's people were threatened by this crowd's anger. But Boone wanted to get to Kae-gon first.

*

As he rode the windy sky-blue day his anger found an intensity that surprised him. He didn't believe that he had any false notions about the whites. The killing that went on among his parents' people continued with a mutual dislike by both sides. He didn't harbor any grand notion that he could mend the dislike. Not anymore. Confront his father, and on to Chicago to live in a real white man's world.

Boone nudged Impatio into an exhilarating gallop. Riding hard through the wind combined the best of the two worlds, the horse's and the earth's. *I'm not here, Boone. I'm wherever you go.* His mother never let him go, reminding him of a sacred vow he made over her grave. He could not remember his mother's face. He did not want to forget Emily's. His hand drifted down to the locket he carried against his bare chest under his shirt, and an unwanted memory of Mexico returned.

The cattle drive north from Paquime, Mexico hit a band of rustlers and Boone barely escaped with his life, only because he sensed them coming and ran before he was noticed, leaving the cattle to be slaughtered. He ran north, away from the ruins of his life in Mexico, until he found himself crouched over a familiar plot of dirt. He dug with a knife, rocks that had covered the dirt tossed aside, surrounded by new growth of weeds. There was a larger, longer rock pile next to this small one, which he ignored as best he could, casting an occasional a tear-filled eye that way.

He concentrated on the feel of the dirty grit under his nails, the sound of metal striking rock. Gently he smoothed with a trembling hand the dirt from around a small hairy mound. As he brushed red tufts of hair came loose. He held the tip of one finger against his boy's skull.

"Your spirit is not here. You have moved on to a beautiful new world, better than this."

He clutched a snatch of loose hair tight and wiped the tears from his face with the back of his dirty clenched hand. He fell backward in sudden agony and ripped some hair free in his fingers. With his elbows he pushed the dirt back over the baby's body. He flopped over on his back and used his legs and feet to finish pushing dirt and rocks into place.

That hair was neatly tucked into the locket he wore with the small drawing he'd made of Emily a few days before she died. Lordy, that woman did not like to sit still. He remembered the last time they made love and felt blissfully happy in the memory.

Though exhausted and covered with dirt of their graves, he felt fully purged, as though he had crawled inside the grave with his son but got permission to crawl back out again.

CHAPTER FORTY-TWO
The Kiowa Challenge

When Boone found the river he alighted and led Impatio into the water. He had the sudden urge to lose himself underwater, so he let loose Impatio's rope, stripped off and saddled his clothes and submerged, swimming with the freedom of a fish before emerging again. On the other side of the river, horse's rope in hand, Boone smelled the smoke of the village. He redressed in clean clothes from his saddlebag before following the smell.

Partway through the thicket Impatio stopped and tossed his head. He'd spotted some fodder he decided to have. Boone tied the horse to brush and investigated the greenery around him. He stepped toward a bush loaded with berries and picked one. He held a berry to his mouth to test it with his tongue.

"HO!"

Boone turned. A young Kiowa boy with a large leather pouch stared at him, shock deep in his eyes. He pointed at the berry and spit and finished with words Boone didn't understand.

"I wasn't going to eat it."

The boy shrugged and picked some of these berries for his bag, along with various leaves.

"What do you want them for?" When Boone spoke in clear Kiowa the boy didn't seem surprised.

"Traps. And sickness," the boy answered.

"What do you trap?"

"What is sent for food to eat. Where do you come from? You are not Kiowa."

"I am but ... I was raised by my white mother."

The boy nodded and continued with his work.

"You live near the fort where white food feeds you. Why traps?"

"White food?" The boy spat again. "White food makes us sick. Or there is never enough. They want us to starve and die."

Boone had spent his entire life threaded to the white world, but more and more he found lies. There were so many whys that Boone felt he'd done nothing since age 12 but run in circles.

"They teach us white ways in school but I don't always listen. I am Kiowa and want Kiowa ways. Do you prefer the white world?"

Boone looked down at his shoes, soft buckskin with hard soles, the only part of his clothing not of white origin. "I prefer middle world."

The boy's eyes revealed no further emotion as he nodded. "Come. My father can help."

*

His father was the tribe's blind shaman who seemed to see Boone clearly. While waiting to be spoken to, Boone looked around at he entered the home village of his father. He saw a wooden army wagon wheel propped up against one of the lodges that belonged to the one they called chief. A skinny big wheel from an army ambulance. Boone had heard tales of this gift to the Kiowa. A couple of the spokes were broken and Boone imagined the state of the rest of the army wagon disintegrated into the ground, given to the friendly To-hau-sen after the wood had begun to rot.

The boy addressed his father by sitting at his feet. "We have a guest who is a stranger. A stranger who is a friend. Can he stay?"

The shaman concentrated on the air around Boone. "He can stay." He patted the ground. "My eyes do not take in light from the sky but that does not mean I cannot see."

"Papa sees more than all."

"You have a purpose in your quest."

Boone sat. "As do all people."

The old Shaman gave Boone a wide-mouthed grin. "You are sensitive. And yet you do not use your gifts. You must let me teach you." His eyes blinked rapidly. "Or I will have you teach me."

Boone was puzzled by this sudden change in the man's demeanor. "I am honored." He took a deep breath, pulling in courage despite the curious people around him. "But I seek a man who knows my blood because he gave it to me."

"You seek the man who created you. You are correct not to call him father, if you have never seen his face nor learned his wisdom."

"I have seen his face. I know that I must learn his wisdom as a man." Boone took a breath. "I must learn the reason he killed my mother."

A woman behind them shrieked. "You are the one!"

Boone's heart thumped erratically. All those years of hatred led to this moment. With courage disintegrating in his veins, he turned to the woman. "You know me? You know him?"

"My husband tells stories of a boy he lost to his white woman."

Boone sighed the air out of his chest and tried to remain calm. "If his name is Kae-gon will he see me now?"

She shook her head. "He is off on elk trail. Will return soon with ... or long without." His stepmother, Abwana, was small and thin, with a wide honest face and arms that fluttered as she gestured with good attempts at English.

"Did he ... have other children as well?"

She turned into the crowd of people and opened her arms. "Kae-gon children come," and three children ran into her embrace. Two girls, perhaps a year apart and under 12, and a boy, nearly grown. Boone looked like his brother. Abwana was not much older than he, so the boy was from another mother, too -- also perhaps white.

Abwana led him to the fire where she motioned for him to sit. Her daughters with shy giggles brought him some smoked meat, still warm. As he savored the smoky sweet taste, other women and children sat around him. Most of the men left but several watched behind them. They reminded Boone of army guards who stood around the officers to protect them.

They talked, one at a time, and Boone got the idea they treated him to a story, a children's story with descriptive gesturing, and children laughed, oohed and shrieked at the right moments. Boone understood enough to know this as one of their legends of the ancient past. He let his imagination wander into the story of how coyote and rabbit tricked each other and the people into leaving their underworld havens to see the sun again.

Before the stories were finished, they heard horses. All the people stood, and Boone stood next to the men, as white men with rifles rode into their village.

Boone recognized two of them from the town. He stayed back as the men went to the strangers' horses. The blind shaman reached out to the closest horse and stroked its nose, as though he had not felt a horse in a while. He spoke Kiowa to the strangers. His stepmother came to Boone's side as one of the whites pulled a gun. The elder leaders held their ground.

"Your weapons ... not welcome here." Kitaeyi translated for his father.

"You think we ride into your camp unarmed, old man? After what your people do to harmless pioneers on the trail?"

Shaman gestured after Kitaeyi whispered to him. "Perhaps some of our Comanche and Kiowa brothers shoot after being shot at but we --."

"Yeah, you people are all the same, savage scalpers, the lot of you. My name is Randolph Phillips and I represent the U.S. Government. Where's your bucks?"

"Our men hunt stray buffalo, where buffalo run, men run. Bring food home to people."

"Your people hunt elk skins for trade, not stray buffalo. You know that's forbidden. So is leaving the reservation for deer. White man's deer. Your people don't need food. We feed you now. If you weren't so lazy, your crops would feed you."

The boy struggled with all the words. "I have no food. White men take it."

Phillips jumped off his horse and strode up to Shaman, his hand in the air in a threatening gesture. "Don't smart talk me. Now which way did your bucks head?"

Boone stepped forward. "These people have been forced onto a poor piece of land against their will. It's not good for farming and still your government underfeeds them. What right have you now to tell them what they need or don't need?"

Phillips looked official enough in his plain civilian clothes, but he seemed like a turtle to Boone, happy enough to stick his neck out when he could bite. He turned to Boone, startled by the clear use of English and Boone knew him as the man who tried to take his harmonica. "I don't talk to no squaw man." He turned to face the blind old Indian in front of the fire. "If your bucks are caught hunting off the reservation they'll be shot as the savages they are."

Boone clamped a hand on Phillips' shoulder and forced him to turn. He slammed his fist into Phillips and knocked him backward to the ground, stunned into silence. The other whites alighted and started toward him.

"Hey, you punch like a white! Who are you?" As Phillips got to his feet the other three came up behind Boone.

"He's that loudmouth from the town meeting the other day," said one as he and another grabbed him and held him tight. The beatings were fast and brutal, even as the people screamed and cried, and some fled. He heard his mother's voice telling him to live in the white world, stay away from your father's people, mixed with Sam's *kill the whites, kill them all.*

A rifle fired. As the four men turned to face a new threat Boone slipped to the ground. Kitaeyi had taken one of the soldier's rifles and aimed at the men around the fallen Boone.

"Hey, look at the kid trying to act like a buck."

"He'll never get old enough."

But the other Kiowa men had their knives out and moved to threaten the two whites who advanced on Kitaeyi. Boone could not get up. He could die here let that silence Sam's voice. Kitaeyi pulled the trigger again and one dropped to his knees, shot through the arm. As the white soldiers backed away, several women ran to Boone with water.

"If I wanted you dead you would be. Go." The boy stood firm and unwavering.

"This isn't done yet. Don't think you've won." They rode off.

Abwana ran after them. "His mama was one of you! His mama was white!"

Boone thought, as he slipped into blessed darkness, that those soldiers looked like General Tyler.

CHAPTER FORTY-THREE
The Father & the Son

Boone groaned, dreams uneasy and pain vivid. His red-headed son rode hard chasing buffalo and with rifle out shot randomly into the herd. Tall and red-headed with a toothy grin, his son held a bloody strip of buffalo fur in one hand and an Indian scalp in the other. Boone reached for his son but instead found a medal in his hand. "Dead buffalo on one side, discouraged Indian on the other," his son cackled. "No law to protect what's theirs."

Boone awoke with a sharp spasm in his gut and rolled to his side. He wanted to run from the dream but his body ached.

"Easy, son. Do not move." His stepmother soothed his face with her cool wet hand. "You are brave. Your father will ask that you join the tribe."

Boone blinked at Abwana through swollen eyes. "It's not … I can't…." He forced his eyes open to stare at the grass and brush roof of the wickiup. *If she knew…*

But Sam responded, *Maybe she does.*

"When your father comes, you will talk. Rest now."

They let you get beat up enough to keep you here. Everything had been taken from him -- his mother, his wife, and his freedom to choose.

Abwana left him alone, without any attempt to understand his need.

Boone threw off the deerskin. His face felt twice its normal size, skin over his ribs busted open in several places and crusted over with blood, and his gut won't be ready for solids for days. He jerked himself into a sitting position, but his vision blackened and he sank back down into oblivion.

*

"How long has he been bad like this?"

"Three days now. I think he is trying to force himself to die."

Mouth sealed with thirst, Boone felt Abwana's cool touch on his face and the presence of a man next to her. She forced his mouth open and let water trickle in until he responded by choking. "Ah … more."

Abwana sat Boone up and gave him a cup, allowing him to drink. The man moved behind Boone, out of his vision.

"Do you feel good now?"

"Better. Not good. But better than bad."

"My son," the man behind him said.

Boone braced himself. This moment defined his life but he was in no position to kill, or even to run. He had only one choice now. To listen.

"I am sad you are hurt, my son." Kae-gon, the scar-faced Indian with the slumped shoulders and graying hair, moved into Boone's vision, into his life, as though a dream. The man from the campfire, from the hunting party, he taught Boone how to sleep protected, maybe protected him all his life. Through a fog of unreality caused by the tear-filled eyes of a boy, Boone looked upon the man who murdered his mother.

Isn't he beautiful? Sam said. *You look like him.*

Boone tried to stand but made it only to sitting with effort. "You wanted to take me from my mother. Then she died. Why didn't you take me then?"

"She should have come with us. I wished for this. When she died, I felt your blame. And I felt you would find your way to me on your own. You learned to be Kiowa along the way."

"I could have died out there."

"Your strength comes from many times not dying. I watched you grow but stayed far enough away so you may decide on your own which half of your heart speaks loudest."

"I will speak to you with my whole heart." Boone patted the locket on his chest and pulled it out. When he opened the locket the tuft of red hair spilled into his open palm. Eyes blinded by tears he grabbed his father's hand and placed the hair in his palm. "Meet your grandson, Peter Nicholas."

Kae-gon touched the hair with the tip of a finger. "My grandson? You scalp? Why did you not bring him? I must meet him, his mother too. They will be welcome here, as you are."

"Oh, you say you followed me all this time? But you don't know what happened to them?"

"I followed always with my heart, not always with my horse."

"That was you that night, teaching me to sleep in a circle."

Kae-Gon thought about this. "I too have had such a dream. Perhaps that one night our dreams connected. You have vivid dreams, dreams of symbols, of your future?" Boone stared at Emily's face in the locket. "Can I meet them, son?"

"No!" Boone tried to moderate his anger. "They are dead. She died after his birth. He died being delivered."

"You lost mother and son?"

"I stayed with a woman who was too good for me. At the risk of her health she bore me a son. Both were taken from me."

"Perhaps the reason is this day."

Boone struggled to his feet and waved off all offers of help. He brought his eyes up to meet his father's. Though his father was now shorter, both were struck by their similarity to each other. "I am not here because they died. I am here because they lived. I am here because Mama lived." He pulled his knife from his pile of belongings and stood with the knife shaking between them. "I have lived and died many times since then. But I made a vow on my mother's grave. I must kill you."

Boone grabbed a handful of his own hair and made a clean cut with the knife. He clutched his hair tight in his fist, the knife making his other hand ache. He jerked his father's hand close and mixed his hair with his son's. "You did not stay with the woman who was too good for you, and I lived. I stayed with the woman who was too good for me, and she and my son died. Where is the justice?"

"Is your justice in my death? Take it."

"Louie told me to ask you. What happened that day that she died?"

"Ah. Louie." Kae-gon sat and waited until Boone sat across from him. "You wish for this world to be fair. You walk your white path, or you walk a path between them and us. But why not try this path?"

"You have killed --."

"Not unjustly," Kae-gon said. "We ask for peace, but never get peace. You want justice? Once our Kuato tried to escape a battle with Sioux, but we were told that men stand and fight or the hereafter will not welcome them. They were all destroyed. We now know that the great sky father welcomes all, even those who do not fight." He mingled the hairs in the palm of his hand and fisted them. "Your mama and I were not meant for happiness. Lin-One kept you from me, but not so far that I could not find you. Her love for me, as mine for her, was not strong enough for us to leave our families. I hoped to make her understand that you belonged with me to become a man. She would not listen."

"So you killed her."

Kae-gon stared down at the hair in his hand. "I tried to stop her."

Boone felt the air sucked from his lungs. He sank back down to his deerskin mat. "You lie now to save your life," he whispered. "She would not kill herself."

"Do you wish to know the truth of that day, son? Can you bear the pain?"

Boone looked at his father, his eyes large and wet, and nodded. Kae-gon took the knife that hung limp in Boone's hand and sliced off a lock of his hair. He mixed this with the hair in his other hand, blending until it seemed all three were of the same head.

"By the hair of three generations I speak the truth. I did not kill Lin-One. I came to tell her again I had the right to be your father. This time she said I have that right. She was wrong to keep you from me. She said she will continue to be wrong to keep you safe. I tell her she cannot keep me away. I ask her to come, too." He looked down at the hair in his hand. "She ran for her knife. Before I can stop her --."

"No. Don't say it." Boone's protest escaped as a small sigh as he stood and squared his shoulders. If Kae-gon did not kill her, then this had to be the truth. She simply would not live to see Boone as a Kiowa.

Kae-gon's eyes closed tight. "The knife was sharp and she drove it hard. I do not know how."

"I do." Boone often found her weeping over the ending of Romeo and Juliet, a storybook ending that became an obsession. "Because she was crazy."

Kae-Gon nodded. Abwana wrapped her arms around her husband from behind, encouraging him to finish. "My people do not know this need to kill the self. I did not take you for fear you will do the same, as though sickness comes in a white heart."

"She is dead because of you."

"I loved your mother but she had weak spirit. She is dead because of fear. And because …" he tapped his head. "She was bad up here."

Boone put his fists over his eyes and sobbed, feeling 12 years old again. "I know. Oh, I know."

"You face life bravely. This is why I sometimes found you, to see your mind. It is good and strong. You and I are meant for this day."

Abwana stood before Boone, brushing at his tears. "You stood with your father's people against whites. You came with hate for your father but stood with his people. Your courage traveled far with you, and now comes out from behind darkness into light again."

Startled, Boone looked at her. His symbols. With trembling hand he squatted and drew them into the dirt. Light coming out from darkness. "She wanted me … to stay a white man. Because your world is doomed."

"Perhaps. But it is not bad to die. If you die true to you. You are Kiowa. From the day of your birth. You are brave because of how you have lived." Kae-gon took Boone's hand and pressed the hairs into his palm. With a grimace, Boone closed his hand around them. "I am honored to have you carry me with your son. Take us wherever your future travels take you."

Boone looked at the three different shades of hair mingled. "I promised Mama I would kill you. But if she was crazy, there is no promise to keep." Boone picked up his knife.

"I accept whatever choice you make." Kae-gon stood with eyes closed, hands behind him, chest bared to Boone.

His mother killed herself to make Boone run, to keep him from the Indian world. Did that make her wrong? *He sent me hither, stranger as I am, To tell this story, that you might excuse His broken promise.* Boone screamed and drove the knife into the lodge post, grabbed his belongings and ran.

About a mile from the reservation he let Impatio slow up. Since his mama died he envisioned meeting his father so many times, always with the same end -- his father's bloody carcass on the ground, with him holding the scalp.

He ran again, but with different visions, new sounds and relinquished truths. His mama killed herself. Time to leave his father in peace. But for today, he belonged nowhere.

*

Sheriff Kane shook his head. "If you want me to stop Randolph Phillips and his boys you might be too late. Saw 'em ride out of town over an hour ago."

Boone had ridden days away before getting a bad feeling and rode back to town. He wanted to talk to the woman but couldn't find her. "Toward the Kiowa?"

"Yup."

"Why didn't you stop 'em?"

"Boy, they're federally appointed Indian police. They have the right to keep the Indians where they belong. Can't have Indians traipsing over white land, now can we?" The sheriff grabbed Boone's arm as he started to leave. "You have to choose which world is yours, son."

Boone tore out of the sheriff's office. His mama kept him with her but she didn't have to die. His father was right to want his son to learn his ways. *Where death and danger dog the heels of worth, he is too good and fair for death and me. Whom I myself embrace to set him free.* Though his ribs ached and his stomach was sore he leaped on his horse and kicked it hard.

As Impatio ran Boone leaned over the saddle to ease the pain.

He sensed that he was too late when he rode into the village. Even after his beating he could be calmed by their songs and the sounds of children playing. Now total silence greeted him. He rode past a row of lodges to where he first attacked the Indian Police, thinking them white bullies with limited government authority.

As he reached his father's lodge, Abwana stepped out with her two girls clinging to her waist. "Whites come in to arrest…" She started to sob.

Boone alighted and ran to hold them close. "Why are they so hard on your people? What have you ever done to them?"

"We cooperate. Many Kiowa still run wild, resist. They believe we are all guilty. Your father still believes we can be friends with whites. He is wrong." She glanced back at the lodge. "One rifle and one spear could not help against their gunfire."

Boone looked inside the lodge. Four Indians were stretched out on deerskin, lovingly tended in death. Boone looked close into their faces. All young, all dead too soon. His father wasn't one of them. Boone mourned these good people.

Abwana put a hand on his shoulder. "They take him. Kae-gon."

"Where? Where did they take him?"

"To prison or death. Matters little." A sob escaped again as she led her children back outside the lodge to tend the fire.

Boone looked to Sam for guidance. Mama saw two paths to walk in life but Boone had hoped for a third, of working for the whites while protecting the Indians. But had that third path ever existed, or had he been walking a dream world?

Boone put an arm around Abwana. "I'll rescue him. I'll find out where they took him and bring him back."

"Please stay with us." She sobbed against his chest. "He is already lost. He has been many years already."

"No!" Boone jerked his arm away from her.

"You must know the truth about your father."

"What truth? That he would kill his own people rather than kill any whites?"

Abwana turned and sat on the ground, knees up to her chest to bury her face.

Boone sat next to her. "If I can't rescue him, I will try to come back. I will try."

She looked up at him, with a smile creasing her sadness. "Yes, you must try to rescue him. Only he can tell you the rest of his story."

CHAPTER FORTY-FOUR
The Rescue

Boone rode off to the prison at Fort Sill but Kae-Gon wasn't there. They told him Fort Griffin in Texas, on the southern road, but also that he was probably dead by now. He rode on hard. Odd how life could turn on him, after so long wanting to kill his father, now hoping to save him. He needed to convince someone there that he was an Indian agent. Problem was, he was bare-headed again. Hard to keep a hat on, and without one he was just another Indian, even without the longer hair. So Boone sought out the stagecoach road into Texas. Hats blew off in the dusty trail and were left behind, free for the taking.

One those shortcuts, when the ride was slow and mindful of rocky paths, he pulled the harmonica out and played his Bark song, which soothed the horse and corralled the impatience inside him. Music also tended to heighten his senses and lead him to solutions -- quick, fierce and gay. How to rescue his father. He could not ride without a plan. He played the tune that had been inside him since he was a child. How to live on the wrong road for so long and still find the right one. His song changed to the one he had written for Emily.

Boone knew why they arrested his father, rather than killing him. Kae-gon surrendered to stop the killing. But living corralled by whites meant watching your family drown, a breath at a time. Maybe Kae-gon still believed that whites and Indians could live together, as Lynelle once hoped. But she lost that hope. Could he find it now, like a hat, floating in the dusty breeze? Whites and Indians both wanted to live their own way, one with land free and open, the other with corrals and fences.

Boone closed his eyes and gave his horse the rein. Land. Lots of land out here. Sharing should be easy. Lots of land. But farming? Not for Kiowa. Why farm? Enough wild food and plants. Not anymore. Boone felt his mind travel up into the clouds, felt the moisture on his brow, the water running down his face. Moist. Wet. Farming. No rain. Not enough water. Water. Lots of land, but not enough water.

Leaving Mexico, arriving with bursts of sanity, the first thing he wanted. Water.

Plenty of open land out west. But they both needed water. The whites wanted more and more land but only prime land -- with water. The Navahoes got their land back but were they given the water? No, they were told they lived on government land. Not their land. Fighting for land always took place around water. The rail lines followed the rivers, set up stations near water.

Boone saw a hat in the trail, tucked his harmonica away, and leaped off his horse. Looked brand new and it fit, too. Boone looked around, uneasy, as though the hat were a trap, then tucked it deep over his eyes.

He rode back into the trees and as he entered the shade and breathed deep of the cedar he remembered back to being 12 and on the run ... oh, the ideas that ran through his head! His mama told him the story about Columbus discovering America but also the story about how people like his father greeted him. Boone had asked her, then what did he discover? A land where people lived? He was amazed to think his mama's people came from some other great place far across the ocean. When he asked her why they didn't go back, Mama only laughed. "Go back again and be new beaten home? Send some other messenger!" She didn't always make sense, but then sometimes Shakespeare didn't, either.

Boone needed to sleep for the night, and so did Impatio, but his mount's stride was steady and he didn't feel tired either. He didn't know how to rescue his father. He shuddered at the thought of Mama crying in her grave if he decided to join his father's tribe. But maybe she killed herself for this reason. Like Abwana said, he came from behind the darkness into the light again, a better meaning of his symbols than the violent one he last conjured.

He didn't tell his father that he had gone crazy once. On a cattle drive with some Mexican vaqueros, they laughed at him for not talking or singing. One watched Boone stare off into space and fingered the harmonica in his pocket. "You suffer because your family was killed? Wife and many little babies, all brutally butchered? You are in grief, this much I can tell, senor. I can see the signs. Your eyes, they are always red. Your hands, they shake. You have murderous rage about your mouth. Perhaps you wish to die, too, no?"

Boone wiped a grimy hand over his mouth but did not answer.

The philosophical Mexican continued. "You got to understand the sadness when we lose family. Everyone dies when it is their turn, mi amigo. When it is their time. They do not die too soon, or too late. And whether you feel guilty for what you did or did not do makes no difference. So you have to put this in your head. And you have to start thinking. Can we say, oh, we don't have to look for water, because if it is our time to die we will die? No, that is not how life works. We have to find water. We have to save ourselves, if we can. And if we cannot, then we die. That means it was our time. But if we can save ourselves, then it was not our time to die. So we must find water. You people up in the new America now, you think, oh, we gotta have all this land, we gotta have all this land. We're going to populate this place with all of our people. Well, you're foolish. You're crazy! Land without water is no good! But you, senor, sit there and not help yourself find water. You sit there and die. That is crazy." He stood and gave Boone's leg a kick. "Like with a lame horse." He put an imaginary gun to Boone's head and pretended to shoot him. He blew his finger, stuck his hand into his pocket and walked off.

Boone then heard Emily in his head. *It wasn't my time. No one's time is when they're young. But we aren't always given a choice.* No, that was him. She would never say that. Emily accepted her choices, always.

He should have died many times but something always saved him. That something was called *Not-My-Time*. But because the blind shaman had been startled looking at him, Boone began to wonder if there wasn't something more in him -- something with wings.

When he saw a gathering of horses in a kind of seclusion ahead and the unmistakable face paint of the Comanche, he pulled up short, Impatio gasping in disgust. What now? Off to raid some poor white settlement? Boone felt sorry for the tribes losing their freedom, but why blame the settlers who could lose theirs as well? He thought about riding on without stopping or getting involved. But they were crouched over someone on the ground writhing in pain.

He remembered a couple of filthy Indian children -- they couldn't tell which tribe -- who showed up on his Mama's doorstep. He wasn't yet 10 and they were younger and half starved. With her fear of his father Mama could have turned them away. Boone thought she might at first. When she took them down to the river to clean them Boone thought she might drown them. He saw her drown an injured sparrow once. Mama didn't like to see anything suffer. Because she died, it had been her time to die? He shook off the thought as he approached the strangers.

One who crouched over the sick man looked up. Boone held up his hands. "Friend. You need help?" The fellow stood and strode toward him, appearing both fierce and familiar.

"Brother. I am Quanah and welcome your help." Quanah held out a hand for a white man's greeting.

When Boone's mother had those two children cleaned up, Boone saw they were half-breed, like him. As they ate, they heard the sad story of how these children were rejected by both parents. Lynelle told them to stop talking, and after they had eaten, Lynelle took them away. She never told Boone where.

Boone alighted. "I am happy to help, brother."

Quanah was a Comanche but also half-breed, with a European nose, and when Boone looked closely, saw gray eyes. He was about Boone's height, and more muscular. "We have a man with a sickness we do not understand."

"I'll hope to help." Boone got close enough to smell the man's death and saw the fluid coming out of both ends, without control. "Cholera. He will not survive."

Quanah backed away and motioned to the other two to put the man out of his misery. He turned to Boone. "You are half-breed like me."

"Yeah. I never liked the term."

"I was born with the Comanche. But I was an orphan when I was 12. Big battle killed my father and they took my mother and sister away. Because my mother was white."

Boone nodded. "I was orphaned same age, but different. My mother was white, too, but she never accepted my father's life. She would not allow me to be raised by my father."

"So your mother chose the white side, and mine the Indian. They treated me cruelly when I was no longer son of a chief. But that made me grow strong. I think your mother made you grow strong too, or you would not be here now, talking to me."

Quanah turned back to the dead man and joined in the mourning ceremony with the other two. They gathered rocks and covered him as best they could.

Boone did not take part in their ceremony because he did not know the man, but respected and observed. He mounted up but Quanah motioned him to stay. Perhaps his presence was needed as the one who condemned the poor fellow to death, but Boone had seen the disease often enough, and even had a minor case once. After the burial the men used bushes and dirt to cleanse their hands.

Quanah waved Boone over. "You are son of Kae-gon."

"You know me?"

"He is in Fort Griffin. They plan to hang him. In public. He will not tell the names of those of his people that they want, so they will kill him."

"I know. I'm going to free him."

"You have white man's law to do this?"

Boone shrugged. "Is there any white law that will help him?"

Quanah studied him, and Boone stared at the feathers pinned in his hair. "I have chosen my side. Why do you delay?"

Boone leaped into his saddle. "I have chosen to stay between. Middle ground."

"Where is this middle ground?"

"It is the place where Indians and whites are friends."

264

"Oh, somewhere in the sky, perhaps! You should call it middle sky! You live in a lonely place." Quanah leaped back on his horse. He laughed, not a particularly pleasant sound. "You want your father free? Then you must follow us."

Boone agreed to sneak into the prison while they caused a distraction. Boone had to slip through a slit for a window and nearly got stuck until he concentrated on feeling slippery as a greased wheel. One guard saw him but Boone used his moment of shock to grab his gun and knock him out. He had hoped not to spill blood but, as he crept up to the guard at Kae-gon's gate with his knife drawn, remembered being mistreated by Union soldiers and slit his throat. He grabbed the keys and nodded at his father.

Kae-gon had been watching. "You are one of us now."

Boone grabbed a couple of guns and led them back out the window, pushing his father first. Boone ran to Impatio, expecting Kae-gon to follow. His father, after the jump to the ground, got up slowly but followed, and needed Boone's help to get up behind him on the horse, weakened from his ordeal.

As they rode they heard other riders behind them and gunfire followed.

"Hang on!"

He concentrated hard, seeking the wings in his mind and made a sudden decision to veer left as the bullets took out some of the trees on the right.

Into the river they dove, swimming freely the two men and the horse, and coming up to ride out the other side. Riding hard, the horse's hooves barely touching the ground, riding with the wind.

"Keep going," Kae-gon whispered behind him as his arms loosened their once steady grip around his waist. "Do not stop."

CHAPTER FORTY-FIVE
The Death Rattle

They had gone far enough to lose those behind them, or the soldiers had given up, because the gunfire had stopped. Boone realized Kae-gon's arms had loosened. He grabbed his father's hand to keep him from falling and pulled his horse to a stop. Quanah caught up to him and the two of them eased Kae-gon off the horse.

"Shot in the back," Quanah said. He nodded behind him. "Those guards are no longer a threat."

Boone leaned over his father. "You're gonna be all right, Pa. Please. You can't die." He turned to Quanah. "Can you stay and help? We need a fire." He held his father's hands and felt the old man grow cold.

"Better to die a free man," Quanah said, and set to work on the fire.

Boone eased Kae-gon on his side. "I'm gonna try to get the bullet out."

"No, son." Kae-gon's voice was strong. "It is my time. You are a brave Kiowa."

Boone eased Kae-gon's leather jacket up in the back. "Is there a land where my mother and my father can live together?"

"How do you live with a fire that burns out of control?"

Boone eased the blood stained jacket off his father and poked at the wound as Quanah got the fire going. "I can get the bullet out. Hold still."

"I have more to tell you."

"I know you do." Quanah handed Boone a knife heated in the fire. He took a deep breath. "Give Kae-gon a stick."

Kae-gon made no sound as Boone worked, and finally held up the bullet. "Didn't go in too deep. The leather slowed it down. I think it is not your time to die."

Boone fed his father water and Kae-gon found he could sit up. "The wound is not bad?"

"You will live long enough to tell me many tall tales."

"Oh shucks." Kae-gon chuckled. "I thank my son for not killing me, and also for not letting me die."

"We'll stay here the night and we can all rest and eat. Quanah, stay."

But Quanah was already mounted. He waved at Boone and they rode. "We will meet again!" he called to his new friend.

Boone improvised a bandage and helped Kae-gon get comfortable.

"You want more tales."

"You have a terrible tale, and I must hear it."

"I would share it, too, if I were dying."

"I could still arrange that." They chuckled together.

"All right. You must know everything, and then see how well you can live. Your mother … attacked me that day. Determined to kill me. Chase me off. I stand … defend myself. We fought over that knife. But I swear to you, she was the one to point the blade at herself. She used our anger, together, to drive it into her chest. I did not want her death."

Boone held his breath. "You *did* kill her?"

"I did not come just for you when you were 12. I came for both of you. But she fought me so hard, I grew angry. But that knife into her heart … she drove it there. At the time, I believed I killed her, and could not take you because of that. But I know the truth now, too. I could not have killed her. I loved her always. As I love you."

Boone closed his eyes. Lynelle ended up hating Kae-gon and his people. He grabbed his father's shoulders and pulled him close for the hug he never expected but wanted now, and his father hugged him back.

"There is one more thing. Your twin brother."

"Mama said he died."

"Are you strong enough for this? I told her I wanted one of you. I was there when you were born and told her she must give me one. Your twin brother did not die on birth."

Boone hesitated. "You … asked to keep him? What was his name?"

"Your name. Daniel Boone. His name …." He lifted his fist in the air and shook it. William …" He shook his fist in the air again. "What your mother read."

"William … Shakespeare?"

"Your mother … would not let me have either of you. He was the weaker. Now do you understand? You are alive because of something inside you, and not because of her love. She allowed you to live, but not him. She could not give him to me. Would not give him an Indian name. She said … just in case."

Boone collapsed, sobbing, into his father's arms.

Sam flew off into the wind. *Fly, run, hue and cry, villain! I am undone!*

Kae-gon held his son tight against ensuing madness.

CHAPTER FORTY-SIX
To Be, Or Not

Northern Texas, and Emily's parents' old homestead, wasn't far. There were two paths, a fork in the road, and Boone felt unable to stay on any but the third path made of clouds and fog in a flowing river.

Boone knew how to find the house and felt living there for a time could help him sink into the instincts of the future. He and his father had more talking to do, but he needed to be free right now. There was one thing left he needed to do.

He found the old homestead, the buildings in good condition. Someone already lived here.

"Boone!" He leaped off his horse, hearing Emily's voice in his head. He had no delusions that she'd be here, that the past had all been one long nightmare and now she waited for him with their brood of five children.

"Boone."

Boone turned to the door of the house. That wasn't Emily.

"Stu!" He ran for the porch. "It's so good to --."

But Stu raised his rifle up. "Not another step. Tell me where my sister is." A woman stepped out next to him, with a small child in tow.

"She died, Stu. I'm so sorry. No one hurts over it more than me." He put a hand out.

"How did she die? When?" Stu had no more emotion than asking about Sunday meal.

"She wanted a baby. I tried to stop her. I found a plant that would prevent her from bearing children. But she wouldn't take it. She died as she lived, and the baby ... he died, too. I can show you the grave. Down in southern ... Texas." He stepped forward.

Stu fired a shot at Boone's feet. "The next one will lodge in your skull. I only accepted you because of Emily. I don't accept you now." The child now in his mother's arms began to cry, so she took her inside.

"We both loved her. And you … you've done well here."

"Leave. Before I kill you."

Boone leaped on his horse. "I'm sorry, Stu."

"Sorry for what?"

"For saving your life." Boone rode off hard, knowing the pain he left behind with words he could never take back, even if he wanted to.

*

He followed the southern trail that took him to the place where Emily died. He paid no attention to his surroundings but focused on the route until he found their old lives, a shack nearly gone, and the two mounds of rocks overgrown with weeds.

After clearing the weeds off their graves and tidying them up as best he could, Boone sat back, singing mournfully. He played his harmonica when his voice gave out, soaking both with the last of his tears. At one point during his harmonica tune a raccoon came up and snatched a piece of biscuit from his saddlebag.

Not Sam. William Shakespeare Tyler. Daniel Boone Tyler. Boone mourned a world so torn apart by greed and hate. He pitied all the ways men learned not to get along. Women did not seem to suffer from the jealousies and spite Boone saw in men. "My little Peter Nicholas, perhaps I have spared you a suffering time. May your next chance be a brighter world."

Boone picked up a hefty sized stick and found three more. With these and pieces of rope he made two crosses, one big and one little, to mark their graves. He took out his harmonica again, sat, and played.

##

The greatest grace lending grace,
Ere twice the horses of the sun shall bring
Their fiery torcher his diurnal ring;
Ere twice in murk and occidental damp

Moist Hesperus hath quenched his sleep lamp;

Or four-and-twenty times the pilot's glass

Hath told the thievish minutes how they pass;

What is inform from you sound parts shall fly,

Health shall live free, and sickness freely die.

(From Shakespeare's "All's Well That Ends Well")

For Further Reading:

Halfbreed: the Remarkable Story of George Bent Caught between the Worlds of the Indian and the White Man by David Fridtjof Halaas and Andrew E. Masich

Empire of the Southern Moon: Quanaw Parker and the Rise and Fall of the Comanches, by S.C. Gwynne.

Civil War & Bloody Peace: Following Orders (by author)

The Collected Plays of William Shakespeare (free to download to Kindle.)

My People the Sioux, by Luther Standing Bear

Made in the USA
Monee, IL
07 January 2022